Also by E. J. Rand

SAY GOODBYE
Winner of the David G. Sasher. Sr. Best Thriller Award
Finalist, 2008 Next Generation Indie Book Awards

PERFECT COVER

Coming soon
DARK SEA

HIGHER CALLING

A RELUCTANT SLEUTH MYSTERY

E. J. RAND

Published by
Deadly Ink Press
PO Box 6235, Parsippany, NJ 07054
www.deadlyink.com

ISBN: 9780978744250

First Edition

With special thanks-for many different reasons-to Debby Buchanan, Elisa Chalem, Rebecca Kandel, Dan Karlan, Elizabeth Larson, Allan Lazar, Susan Moshiashwili, Michael Potter, Ellen Rand, Jeremy Salter, Barry Sheinkopf, Ray Turkin, Eileen Watkins, Joanne Weck, and Jordan Wouk.

CHAPTER 1
Tuesday, December 11
6:03 P.M.

"CHICKEN," Ira growled and slammed a shoulder into Mahdy Dawud, knocking him back into a snowdrift. Holding his flat-bottomed sled in front of him like a shield, the bully trudged toward the road.

Mahdy stayed down until Ira lumbered out of punching range. Quivering in anger and shame, he pushed up, used a gloved hand to lift his Classic Flyer back into a standing position, and brushed snow off his thick, hooded coat.

Vernon, following Ira, paused, and Mahdy heard the singsong shout: "Mahdy's gonna cry-y."

He would *not*, despite the burning in his stomach.

His parents had forbidden him to ride his sled in the streets, especially down their hill, and across Fremont Drive—cars sped along that stretch. He had promised he wouldn't.

The three sixth-graders, neighbors and nominal friends, had been given permission to play in Terhune Park if they stuck together and returned to their homes by 6:30. But Ira wanted to start in front of their houses, slide down Chenowith Street and right across Fremont.

Ira planted his feet and raised the sled. Vernon sprinted toward the bully, kicking snow with every stride. Without a sound, Ira jumped forward onto the sled and vanished into the flakes.

"Ha!" Vernon turned back for an instant, directing the slur at Mahdy, and then he disappeared downhill.

I'm not chicken, Mahdy told himself. He listened closely and

7

heard nothing but wind. They must be in the park, laughing at him. He bit his lip and decided. He found himself standing in the road, shivering, heart thumping. He wouldn't jump. He set down the sled, lay on top and pushed off slowly. But the steep pitch and powder covering icy ruts, soon had him barreling down Chenowith. Ever faster he flew, with snowflakes slapping at his face and the sled racing toward Fremont Drive and the park.

Big trees and white drifts drew closer; he'd done it, he shouted for joy—but then he saw headlights. Panicking, he yanked the runners, flipping the sled out from under him, hurling him down Chenowith and onto Fremont.

Tchaikovsky's *1812 Overture* boomed from the radio as Gary Kemmerman turned his car onto Fremont. The storm surrounded him, but he had more than whipped snow on his mind. A recent session in the dentist's chair, eyes closed, mind wandering, had brought it all back.

Seven months before, he'd almost gotten his wife killed. Since then, Becca had been pushing him to give up his unofficial involvement with the police. He didn't want to. No point rehashing it. Better he concentrate on the repaired tooth—that awkward, warm sensation.

A gust of wind from the park to his right shoved the car sideways; hunched in his heavy coat, he gripped the wheel tighter and downshifted to avoid a skid. The engine whined, the vehicle jolted, and the plastic bag on the passenger seat slid forward. Concentrating on the road, he reached out and nudged back the card for their nine-month anniversary.

He should have stayed home, but the tooth had been bothering him for days and he'd wanted to get the card. He liked driving in rotten weather—it emptied northern New Jersey roads.

As the car rolled across the bottom of Juliana Street, a low drift slapped the front bumper. The wind must have banked snow on every street. He squinted, searching for the drift at the foot of Chenowith, blinking as water rolled down into his eyes.

When he left the dentist, before he raised the padded hood on his parka and pulled it tight, snowflakes had blown into his gray hair. He rubbed at his eyes with a sleeve, blinked again and saw a car moving toward him on the street, ranks of falling flakes backlit by its headlights. He thought to inch closer to the curb, but the other car signaled right.

Apparently, the driver intended to go up the hill on Chenowith. Gary wished him luck and slowed further to be sure the driver could navigate the turn without sliding back.

He saw the object only as it bounded down the hill, onto the street, and tumbled toward the other car's front wheels. The impact rocked the car and it skidded to a stop with the dark shape beneath it.

The driver opened his door and started out, but then hesitated. Gary stopped, too. By the time he turned off the music and climbed out onto the road, so had the other driver.

Following the man around the front of the old red car, he wished he'd worn boots. Snow had coated the license plate, but the Subaru logo glinted in the headlights. The car had lost its front hubcap. Gusting wind blew sideways; the fellow wore no coat or hat. For a moment, the beams framed him, glancing around as if he expected company. Short, with dark, curly hair and a thin nose, the man had to be freezing.

He blocked Gary's view of whatever he'd hit. The wind whipped his speech away. Gary heard it only because of how close they stood. "Ya Allah!"

Gary moved around him and saw a pair of legs. "My God!"

He glanced back. The other man stood motionless. Was he in shock? "Wasn't your fault," Gary called out as he stepped forward, dropped to his knees beside the still legs, and leaned onto his hands, ignoring the twinge in his back. Beneath the vehicle, he saw a young boy with his mouth frozen open and his head bent at an unforgiving angle. He looked like a wounded angel, his face as white as the snow.

Gary glanced over his shoulder again. The other driver looked down at him. "I'll call for help," he said, pushing up stiffly onto his knees and reaching for his phone. "Ambulance'll be here soon. Wait in my car—you'll be warmer."

The man didn't react. Maybe he hadn't heard. He kept his hands behind him and didn't move. Gary's cold fingers reached in and both wallet and phone came out of the coat pocket. The wallet tumbled to the ground at his knees, and he left it. In the moment before he flipped open the phone, the man's unusual belt caught his eye—thin brown leather with silver worked into the strap, the buckle, and especially the end, which hung down, weighted by silver edges joined to form an uneven point.

He turned away from the wind and dialed 911.

He didn't see the gun butt coming at his head.

Light pulsed through his eyelids. Something poked him, and he woke. He'd never been so cold. He couldn't stop shivering.

A light shone into his eyes. "You see this?" someone asked.

"Yeah," he groaned at the invisible man behind the beam.

Blinded by the glare, he closed his eyes and gasped for breath. Snowflakes blew into his mouth. The man spread something over him. His head felt like a spike had been driven into it. He lay on his back, arms pressed against his sides.

The light went away. He tried to focus, but his vision retained the blinding glow even when he closed his eyes.

"Stay still," the stranger said. "Know your name?"

"Kemmerman, yeah, I know." He tried to turn and couldn't. Something around his neck kept him from moving his head. "My head hurts. What's goin' on?"

"It's a neck brace—don't fight it. You nauseous?"

"No. I'm *freezing*."

When he shifted, his back screamed. He blinked. A stranger stood above him. The flashlight pointed sideways. The man spoke to someone out of sight. In the wind, Gary concentrated to hear.

"Hit him hard—probably once, no blood—tore the coat. Hood and hair cushioned it. They'll check for fracture and observe. My guess, he'll just have a hell of a lump. Good we got to him quick in this cold."

When the other man bent close, Gary recognized Vincent Alegretti, his police lieutenant friend. "You'll be fine, buddy. We'll get you inside where it's warm. I'll bring Becca."

Vincent sounded strange. "What's with the voice?" Gary asked. The words trembled. He couldn't control his shaking.

"Bad cold."

"Gotta put him in the rig," said the man with the flashlight. Vincent backed away.

A second EMT appeared, bright lights reflecting off the yellow stripes on his turnout coat. They rolled Gary sideways, slipped something hard beneath him, and used it to lift him. He swayed, but his sore head stayed level. They set him down above ground on a firm bed, and covered him again.

He might have resisted, but it surprised him when they strapped him down. They rolled him feet first. Vincent came into view and he saw the ambulance, strobes bouncing off regiments of falling flakes.

He squinted up at the lieutenant. "What is this?"

Vincent hovered above, moving along with him. "Do you know what happened?"

"What?"

The lieutenant's voice growled. "You know why you got out of your car and dialed 911?"

Had he done that? The EMTs halted and he saw one of the men open the ambulance doors.

Vincent bent and tapped Gary's chest to get his attention. "A motorist called it in." He turned away and had to cough before going on. "You're a few blocks from our homes. We found your phone and wallet on the ground. Need to keep them, for now."

"Why?" Vincent vanished when the EMTs slid Gary headfirst into the back of the ambulance. At once the wind and snowflakes stopped, except for a howling at the open door by his feet. He gazed up at a white ceiling and heard the engine rumble.

"Hold on," the lieutenant called, from outside. Gary watched him clamber in and sit to his left. "We got a dead boy, a broken sled, your car, and you with a welt on your head. That mean anything to you?"

Gary squeezed his eyes and tried to remember. Getting the filling, heading home in the storm, wanting to write his message in the card and give it to Becca—he recalled that. It wasn't the dentist's Novocaine masking the rest.

He opened his eyes, met the lieutenant's fixed stare, and said, "No."

CHAPTER 2
Wednesday, December 12
9:28 A.M.

GARY watched his wife dig into her last bite of pancakes, and the motion brought it all back. He'd called for help, offered his car, and the son of a bitch who'd run over the kid clubbed him and left him to die in the storm. The kitchen radio played "Stairway to Heaven." He didn't hear it. Behind his open eyes rolled a video of the action on the street, from turning onto Fremont Drive to blackout.

He pushed the breakfast plate away, gripped his mug with both hands, and gulped coffee. Becca, in her sleep shirt, sat beside him at the wooden kitchen table. She lowered her fork and turned to him. They hadn't switched on lights because the morning sun peeked on and off from behind scudding clouds.

"The Dawud boy's death is tragic," she said. "I can't imagine how his parents must feel—or I'd feel, we'd feel, if that happened to Melanie."

"You told her about last night?"

"Of course I did." She tilted her head. "You know how she feels about you. Mel wanted to come help, but I thanked her and said you'd be fine."

"She's an angel. She'll make a great shrink. I wouldn't miss her graduation. January 19th, right?"

Becca nodded and glanced at the bandage on his head. "No, you wouldn't—not willingly."

He ignored the tone. "I want to visit the boy's parents, so I can—"

"Well, you'd better not do that yet." She waved for emphasis. "I want you to heal first. Besides, till you remember what happened,

13

you can't answer their questions. You'd only upset them."

He couldn't deal with it and said nothing.

She clasped her hands together. "I still don't understand why someone needed to hit a retired guy on a quiet suburban street."

"It wasn't so quiet out there last night," he said, but she waited. "The driver must have had a serious reason to be gone when the police arrived. That's all. I just—"

"You're gonna tell me you were in the wrong place at the wrong time? Again?"

Twice before, he'd been shot helping the lieutenant. Becca had been drawn in to the cases and injured. He looked at her—red hair messy, green eyes flashing, the woman he'd married nine months before—and knew it'd been worth it. They'd met because of his first case.

"Give me a break," he said. "There's a difference between a concerned citizen and an amateur sleuth."

It took a moment before her eyes calmed and she sighed. "Well, it's a good sign that you're eating, sweetie. How's your bump feeling?"

"It only hurts when I laugh."

After the EMTs brought him to Ridgetop Hospital, he'd wanted to come home. But because he'd lost consciousness, he had to stay overnight. The lieutenant had tried to question him, and Becca had fussed until he'd fallen asleep. Then she'd gone home.

In the morning, as early as he could—before he had to eat hospital food—he checked himself out and arranged a ride home.

"Honey, is your *vision* clear? No blurring? God knows what you'd do without books."

"My eyes are fine."

"And what you'd do without your adventures—or whatever you call them." The edge had returned to her voice. "You know, you need a partner, someone to watch your back."

He glanced out the window as the sun vanished. The storm had dumped eleven inches, and flurries continued.

"And a happy anniversary to you, too," she said into the silence. "You were in a hospital bed—how'd you manage to get a card for me?"

"From the car. I asked Vinnie to bring it."

"You went to buy it in the storm?"

He nodded.

She looked at her plate. "I'll never marry again—if anything happens to you."

"What brought that on?" The moment he'd said it, he regretted asking.

"There is no point in my dredging it up."

He saw the slight shake of her head, and imagined her alone, him alone. "I'll clear the dishes."

She reached out and tapped at his shoulder. "You rest, sweetie. I'll do it." As she stood and stacked, she asked, "Are you starting to remember what happened out there in the snow?"

"Thanks for the pancakes. I'm glad you're off today."

She tilted her head. "Is that another veiled plea for me to give up nursing?"

It didn't sound like she expected an answer. They had enough money, and he wanted her to retire, too. But he wouldn't push. He took a swallow and watched her round the kitchen island. She set plates and utensils into the sink, and turned off the radio in the middle of a Doors song. Dish washing had become one of his jobs since they married. Use the dishwasher, she'd said, but he wanted to be helpful.

"It's a plea we might consider other things today," he said.

She returned with a smile that told him she knew what he'd meant. "Bump and all, huh? Oh, boy, you're healing fast." She pointed at his cup. "While I'm up, would you like more?"

He shook his head.

She caught his eye. "Your memory's coming back, isn't it?"

It wasn't easy keeping things from her. He flattened hands on the table and leaned into the chair. "I need to speak to Vinnie."

The words brought her smile. "Oh, sweetie, that's another good sign."

"It's just a bump."

She tilted her head again. "Please tell me. What *did* happen?"

"I didn't hit anyone. But I need to let Vinnie know what I remember. And Mahdy Dawud's parents."

She frowned. "Can't a visit to the Dawuds wait till tomorrow?"

"What if *you* were his mother?"

Her shoulders slumped.

"Probably best if Vinnie speaks with them first. Then I can express sorrow rather than dwell on details."

"*We* can do that," she said. "I'm going to come with you."

Whatever the reason, he appreciated the gesture.

She leaned closer and her eyes pinned him. "Now, *tell* me."

He reviewed it for her, using the opportunity to check his memory. "It was an accident and a crime," he finished. "The guy couldn't have missed the kid. But then he conked me and left the scene."

She reached out and patted his arm. "You didn't deserve to get hit." She sighed. "I am so relieved you weren't hurt worse."

He took her hand. "You know, we all have to make choices." Without looking down, he played with her fingers. "I stopped and called for help. You would've, too. Even doing the right thing can have consequences."

"How could you know the other guy was a loon," she said, and sat back, drawing her hand away. "Why would he take your driver's license?"

"My wallet lay on the ground. Open it and the license is on top."

"Even so."

"I have to file a police report and get a new one."

She scrunched her mouth. "Not today."

He resisted the urge to reach out for her. "Maybe you'll drive me Saturday? I can't legally get behind the wheel till I replace it."

She tapped his right hand. "I meant, why would he find the wallet and leave everything behind except your license?" She tilted his mug, found it empty.

"Identity theft?"

Becca shook her head, grasped both mugs, and spoke over her shoulder as she headed for the sink. "I don't think so. He left your credit cards and the veteran's ID you always carry around. The driver's license shows him what you look like and tells him where we live."

He watched her, tall and curvy, as she ran water into the cups and plates. She didn't miss much. He thought about what she'd said but, studying her, his focus changed. "I'll get him back. I'll tell Vinnie what he and his car look like." Observing her as she returned, he wondered if surviving the attack had made him feel so alive.

"Why don't you come along to the Alegrettis' with me?" she asked. "I have to deliver peanut butter and cereal I bought for Angela before the storm. I'm sure we can coax Vincent home to talk to you." The shirt bounced as she dropped into her seat. "You won't be out for long. I certainly wouldn't want to chill your bump."

"We'll be back soon, right?" He couldn't help it—he reached out.

She smiled and pushed his hand away. "Okay. But after." Then she must have thought of something—her expression darkened. "Gary, you're just going to tell Vincent what happened, right? You're not getting involved, right?" She squeezed his arm.

"Right," he said.

Half an hour later, hand in mittened hand, they moved along the plowed street. Last night's stiffness had gone from his cranky back; he moved with ease. She'd insisted he wear the heavy coat, hood up, to protect the wound. He'd locked her left arm against him— otherwise, she'd slip and fall on the ice, though she always laughed about it.

"This is more exercise than the doctor ordered," he said. The simple act of making small talk pleased him.

"I'd like us to get back to the gym. When do you think you'll be ready?" she asked.

Seven months before, exercise had been prescribed for his gunshot wounds and she'd become an Enforcer. Most mornings, they jogged—but not in cold and snow.

"Springtime," he said.

She laughed at him. "Are you trying to get me fat?"

"Where? Might be interesting." She frowned, and he changed the subject. "Can I hold that?" He pointed to the shopping bag she carried.

"I'm fine. See?" She took little prancing steps, almost slipped, and giggled. She had on a long blue coat, and a green wool cap pulled down low. The hair that escaped glistened when the sun popped out.

"You bought Angela *peanut butter*?" he asked. "She gives Vinnie peanut butter sandwiches in his *lunch* pail?"

"Silly." She chuckled. "Angela takes a spoonful in the afternoon—a pick-me-up." She freed her hand for a moment and used the mitten to wipe blowing hair out of her eyes. "Be careful not to catch his cold. Angela says it's wicked."

"Funny if we showed up in surgical masks."

"That would be—you should've mentioned it before we left. I have a few at home. I'd have brought one for Angela, too."

"Well, no more excitement—had enough last night for the week," he said.

"...For the whole next year."

The street narrowed where two cars, one on either side of the road, had become snow mounds, covered by the storm and the plows. When he heard a vehicle climbing the hill behind them, he found a cleared driveway and guided Becca to the right, up onto it, and off the road. In tandem, they moved along the shoveled sidewalk. The path narrowed as they reached the buried vehicle. Still gripping her, he let her walk ahead.

"Whoops!" she said, almost slipping.

He chuckled. Except for the bump and his missing license, life had returned to normal. Even walking in the snow with her warmed him. He'd put last night's ordeal out of mind. They'd taken a few small steps when she lost her footing for real, and this time tumbled in slow motion toward a mattress of snow. Falling backward, she clutched his arm and heaved up the bag in an effort at balance. They were both laughing as she dragged him down.

Shots rang out, blasting from the road, slugs whizzing above them, and he fell on top of her. The bag exploded.

Snow mixed with bits of glass from shattering car windows sprayed toward them. He covered her face with an arm, lay flat, and kept her from moving.

CHAPTER 3
11:13 A.M., Wednesday

GAZING upward from the corner of Forty-Ninth Street and Rockefeller Plaza, Sean Dwyer turned slowly through a complete circle, eyes on the surrounding office buildings. He imagined shattered windows raining onto the crowds.

When he lowered his eyes, he spotted a policeman standing like an island in the sea of humanity. He grinned. Was the officer searching for terrorists? Dwyer stopped in front of the man, caught his attention, and pointed to the tree. "Sure ain't she a beauty?"

They stood a city block from the eighty-eight-foot-tall Norway spruce, lights blazing through the dank morning as several hundred people flowed past it in all directions. The lights had been turned on two weeks earlier.

"Too crowded," the officer said, and glanced at the pad and pen in the left hand of the large blonde man.

"I'm Dwyer, with the Belfast Telegraph. Want to see credentials?" He reached toward a coat pocket. When the policeman shook his head, Dwyer motioned at the crowd. "Almost 600,000 people live in Greater Belfast, and I do think I see more bodies than that right here."

The officer smiled. "We average a quarter million a day. More now, with Christmas coming and everyone shopping."

"Did you know," the ruddy man replied, "that when the tree comes down, a chunk of its trunk is donated to the U.S. Equestrian team in New Jersey? They use it as an obstacle jump. Imagine."

"No I didn't," the cop said. "You must do homework." He nodded. "Have a good day." The officer stepped away in his thick black boots.

Dwyer ambled off and threaded through the crowd, grinning,

giving way, enjoying the experience. His shoes were wet, his feet as cold as his hands, but he didn't mind. He identified groups of tourists, teens from the suburbs, serious shoppers, and working people annoyed by the crowds, just trying to get from one place to another. He smiled at them all.

He approached the line of charter buses parked nose-to-tail along the street, which ran beside the Lower Plaza and the tree. Vehicles were barred from Rockefeller Plaza, the north/south cross street cutting through the complex, but either Forty-Ninth or Fiftieth Streets would be close enough. Tall buildings surrounded the buses, except for the Lower Plaza cutout, where ice-skaters could look up at the tree.

Most of the vehicles were empty. He saw plates from Massachusetts, Vermont, Virginia, Ohio, and North Carolina. On the sidewalk across the street from the Lower Plaza, he joined the shuffle toward the tree. His favorites were the red globes. So many ornaments and lights. In a way, it'd be a shame.

At the entry to 30 Rockefeller Center, which houses the headquarters and broadcast studios of NBC Universal, he sidestepped out of the flow. Gazing over the top of a bus at the tree, just like other tourists, he leaned back against the tan stone, slid the pad and pen into a breast pocket but left his hands exposed, and waited.

A short, dark haired man appeared beside him as if the crowd had spit him out. The dark man hesitated, unsure which direction to take. Dwyer nodded toward the tree and said, to no one in particular, "It's a thing of beauty."

"To string all those lights, how long must the wires be?" asked the dark man.

"Oh, I believe there are five miles of electric cord up there."

Dwyer found Abdel Siddiq different from the photo he'd seen: thinner, darker, bushier hair, ears pinned back. They moved along together in the direction Dwyer had come from.

"Is your sister-in-law doing well?" Siddiq asked.

"She is, and the three kids. Thank you for asking." Dwyer smiled and nodded, though he knew the remark had been meant to remind him of his dead brother. The Arab's features gave him a perpetual frown.

"You enjoy teasing their policemen?" Siddiq said it with a smile.

So he'd been watching. Dwyer had been told he did that. "They're my brothers. So many Irish cops. We get on famously. Famously." They found another spot from which they could see the tree between buses, and they leaned against the building, each eyeing the passing crowd.

"Did you know," asked Siddiq, "that one of the buildings beyond that plaza is called the British Empire?"

"Oh, yes. Yes, I do know that."

"And off to your left is the International Building, where British intelligence—MI6, another of your favorites—once made its home."

Dwyer opened his mouth without speaking; he suspected the needling had caused him to flare up, not the British. "There are so many people," he said. "This Christmas tree is the biggest, brightest, and most famous of them all. Television can bring the whole world here in seconds."

Siddiq shifted sideways, drew a pack of cigarettes out of his coat and bent close, offering one to the other man. "Will it work?"

Dwyer pulled a cigarette from the pack, but when Siddiq offered a light, he declined. He closed his fingers around the paper cylinder, crushing it in his powerful hand, and smiled at something that had nothing to do with the squashed mess he let fall onto the sidewalk. He took a half step so he faced the building, inches from the other man.

"Anchor thick steel plates to the left side of all three baggage compartments, and leave the right-side doors unlocked. Tape plastique to the plates—M112 blocks'd be beautiful—and work in steel scrap or ball bearings. Fill the gas tank. The blast will take the other buses with it. With the surrounding buildings reflecting, it'll feel like an atom bomb. Glass will fall in curtains for blocks. We might kill hundreds, devastate the area—remind them of the World Trade Towers."

Siddiq looked as if he'd just been given a recipe for baking bread. "You will arrange for the bus and the shrapnel," he said.

Dwyer nodded. Siddiq's role would be the explosives—and the suicide bomber.

"How soon can you have them?" Siddiq asked.

Dwyer smiled at a matronly face in the crowd and turned back to hide his words. He couldn't keep the smile on his face. "Before Christmas, for sure. There'll be even larger crowds on Wednesday and Saturday afternoons. I'll let you know when. If there's any problem from your end—"

"Don't worry."

Dwyer considered how he'd spend the rest of the day. Not sitting in Finn's small apartment, for sure. "Ah, the merriment, the revelers. When can you provide what we need?"

"Whenever you ask."

Did Siddiq already have the explosives? Dwyer would never know. He checked off steps in his head, and thought of something. Before he spoke, he came up with a different way to express it.

"And the driver for the final block? Those people are your specialty."

He almost flinched when he saw Siddiq's smile. For all those he'd seen commit murder in the name of justice, rights, or revenge— including him—he knew that those who claim to work in God's service were the most dangerous of all.

"The boy who will drive will be ready," Siddiq said. "We finished video for Al Jazeera. It will have great impact, for he is an American. The boy would not make a bus driver—his head is empty—but he can push a pedal, steer for a block" —just for an instant, he offered the smile— "and push a button."

Dwyer leaned against the building, gazed at the tree, and took a deep breath. "A block is all we'll need, Siddiq."

Glancing at a blonde girl who smiled at him as she strolled past, Dwyer missed the dark man's frown at the use of a name. "There must be no leaks," the Arab hissed.

Dwyer nodded, his eyes following the girl through the crowd until the dark man drove a sharp heel down onto Dwyer's right shoe. Dwyer's head swiveled, he almost shoved Siddiq to the ground, but he guessed the hand in the dark man's coat pocket must hold a gun.

Siddiq lifted the foot. "No one," he whispered into Dwyer's staring eyes. "Leave no one alive who knows of us."

Dwyer flattened his palms against the rough, cold stone of the building. A leak meant they'd both be tracked forever. Their families—his brother's children—would become someone's vengeance. The Americans wouldn't do it; they'd call in a favor from the Orange Volunteers. "Trust me," he said.

Siddiq bumped his shoe against Dwyer's. It got the ruddy man's full attention. "I do not trust," the Arab said. "Leave *no* one."

Damn the gun. Dwyer coiled, certain his bland expression would not reveal his intent. If the shoe came down, he'd break Siddiq's nose. The resistance groups played by different rules, and for a moment he considered what might happen when the dark man didn't need him any longer.

Then Siddiq's foot moved away and his hand came out of the pocket. The small man scanned the crowd before looking back. "I am not wrong."

Dwyer turned again toward the tree. His goals and Siddiq's might be the same, but their styles were not. The few left in Dwyer's camp were calloused. They could live, laugh, love—and still kill. Siddiq's kind festered. He looked down at him and said, "In truth, you are right."

Siddiq stepped away from the building and rubbed at an eye, the arm hiding his mouth. "Allah must be smiling on us. I've already killed one of them, a boy, and maybe two others."

Dwyer watched the small man slip into the flow of people and vanish. He himself moved off in the opposite direction. He quickened his pace. Perhaps he could catch up with the blonde girl. Though here in New York, there were so many lovely women.

CHAPTER 4
11:14 A.M., Wednesday

THE two women were sitting on the Alegrettis' living room couch—Becca, still stunned, a thick afghan folded over her shoulders, beside Angela. Mugs of tea rested on the coffee table before them. They whispered, heads close, and every now and then Gary caught his wife's worried glance.

Vincent had insisted that no one would shoot at them in there. Despite the assurance, Angela had asked him to close the blinds. Then she'd turned on two lamps.

The crime scene unit had spent an hour in the cold, processing the street. They'd found four slugs, two stopped by the car. Wide circles had been blown out of the shattered side windows in front. A technician had stepped in to give the lieutenant the crushed, peanut butter-smeared Honey Bunches of Oats cereal box from the shopping bag, but Vincent suggested CSU keep it. They did not need Becca's blue coat, which had a small tear from the slug that had missed her arm and blown apart the peanut butter jar.

Gary had been in turmoil since the shots almost hit her. It had to be the past catching up and he didn't like it. He slowed his plunge into emptiness by forcing his thoughts back into the room and glancing at his wife. Finding her so late in his life had been a miracle. He closed his eyes. The only sound came from the manned unit that idled in front.

"I don't believe this," the lieutenant said for perhaps the fourth time since he'd switched off the digital recorder. Angela had brought him tea with honey, but his voice sounded gravelly.

"The key has to be in something I told you," Gary said, and couldn't help glancing at Becca again. He knew *he'd* been the target and was furious with himself. He saw her left hand grasp the afghan, drawing it tighter and adding to his upset. "The car. Go for the red Subaru," he told the lieutenant, though he knew it had already been called in.

Vincent shook his head. "You're sure of what you saw?" Before he could finish, he had to turn away and sneeze into his hand. He breathed through his mouth. "Dawud kid's death—an accident?"

"Totally. He came flying down the hill. The Subaru couldn't avoid him. The car wasn't speeding or weaving. Its turn signal flashed, it was slowing. I feel terrible for the kid's parents, but don't blame that driver."

"Maybe, but what happened to you last night and this morning—*they* sure weren't accidents."

Gary nodded. "Hitting the kid and meeting me were not in that man's plans."

"I had someone check on the boy's parents." Vincent's expression revealed his distaste. "They've been with relatives all day. Tough for any parents, but maybe worse for the Dawuds. I'm told Muslims prefer large families, and the boy is—was—an only child." He had to clear his throat. "They let him play outside with two other kids who have nothing of value to add. Big surprise, if they were sleighing down Chenowith. They claim they split—"

The lieutenant's cell phone rang for the third time since Gary told his story. Vincent put it to his ear. "Yeah?" With all eyes on him, he listened. The women were sitting behind him and Angela leaned forward as if expecting news. When he said, "Thanks," tucked the phone away and bent toward Gary without looking at them, they gave up and continued whispering.

"We got everyone looking for old red Subarus," the lieutenant said. "But without a license, that car's most likely a dead end. May be painted black by now. We couldn't pull tire tracks from your shooter. The slugs are from a military pistol made in several countries."

"A military weapon?"

"Russian. Popular in the Middle East."

"The man looked like he might have come from there. And what he said—"

"Please." Vincent reached out and patted Gary's knee. "I wanna

26

get him, too. Remember, you were out in a storm, shocked by a death, then hit in the head."

Gary looked away. He didn't like being a victim. "The car started up the hill, into the neighborhood."

"Gary, as difficult as it is for you, I'm asking you to back off. I have a bad feeling about this one. We'll send it upward. Trust me."

"Don't you believe me?"

Vincent shifted in the chair. "If you were me, you'd believe that car was heading to Route 4—it's all of three blocks from where we found you. The shooter could be anywhere by now." He coughed again.

That surgical mask would have been good, Gary thought.

"You know what worries me?" the lieutenant asked.

Gary nodded—Becca had hit upon it earlier. "Guy must've thought he'd finished me, or if not, that I'd freeze in the storm. He took my license so if I survived he'd know where to find me. That what you mean?"

Vincent leaned back, shook his head, and crossed his arms. "Part of it. The motorist who called us—he waited till we got there, you know that, he wanted to help but didn't know what to do—well, he said the car drove off in a hurry. Said it pulled away soon as he turned onto the street. He didn't get a good look, 'cept it fishtailed, too much accelerator, and went straight—so no, it didn't turn up the hill."

Vincent dropped his arms, leaned closer, and lowered his voice so the women couldn't hear. "Just between us, by stumbling on the scene right away the guy may have saved you."

Gary nodded. "You get prints off my wallet?"

"Smudges."

When the lieutenant hesitated, Gary asked, "What else?"

Vincent blew out air. "I don't like it when a friend's in danger."

"Tell me what's worrying you so I'll know what to watch out for."

The lieutenant looked at him. "I know you too well," he said, but nodded. "For him—or them—to be right on you this morning means they staked you out. Had to be waiting. We asked neighbors, but no one saw a thing. You said he had no coat. Could've been in the car, but I think he would've thrown it on. More likely, he was going somewhere he knew people and didn't need a coat."

"Meaning if *he* doesn't come back to finish me," Gary said in a murmur, "there could be others?"

The lieutenant nodded.

"Why am I so important to them?"

Vincent bit his lip. "Like I said, we'll report it upward."

"There must be something I can do."

"You stay *out* of it." The lieutenant's brows came together. "You were a crisis consultant, not a cop, and this may be more than garden variety crime."

Before Gary could reply, Angela called out, "Guys," and they both turned. She rose and put a hand onto Becca's shoulder. A lamp highlighted Angela's white knitted sweater, showing lines of green reindeer pulling red sleighs. "I'd like Becca and Gary to stay with us. At least for a while. Someone *shot* at them." She glanced down at Becca, mute and wrapped, and then back. "It would be safer."

Like old times, Gary thought, when Becca and Melanie bunked there while he tried to get to the bottom of a friend's death. Staying down the block hadn't protected her then, and he doubted it would now.

"Thanks, Angela, but we've been through a lot and we'd be more comfortable at home." Becca's expression told him that she agreed. The whispering must have been Angela calming her down and trying to persuade her to stay.

But Vincent insisted that if the Kemmermans were going home, then for a few days, until this got sorted out, a unit would be posted in front of their house and a police officer would drive Becca to work. Angela would return the favor, he said. She could do their food shopping.

"You're grounded," the lieutenant told Gary.

"Don't be cranky, honey," Angela said to her husband, but she smiled at Becca, happy to help.

Vincent wouldn't let it go. "Gary, stay inside for a few days." He looked like he wanted to say something else when he heaved a breath, cleared his throat, and Gary knew he'd changed the subject because of the women. "Give your hard head time to heal."

It didn't sound appropriate, having to stay inside, and Gary meant to complain, but a glance at his wife stopped him. Anyway, he knew what he had to do, and he didn't need anyone's permission.

CHAPTER 5
1:58 P.M., Wednesday

ALREADY in her nurse's uniform, Becca jabbed a finger at Gary. "I'll only be gone for four hours," she said. "I want to find you here when I get back."

The remote lay on his lap and a re-run of a college football game that had taken place six years earlier flickered on the muted television. It didn't interest him, though he pretended otherwise.

"If you get hungry, you have lasagna to nuke—you like that," she said. "Be sure the bottom of the plate is hot, or it'll still be cold in the middle. And salad's already made. I cut it into pieces for you, tossed it with ginger dressing, even added—ugh—olives."

"French toast, lasagna, olives—maybe I should get slugged more often? Or are you tying to get me fat?"

She waved instead of pointing. "You don't have to do anything but read, watch TV, and heal, sweetie." She tilted her head. "I want you here—and healthy."

Upset when they returned from the Alegretti's hours before, without a word they'd undressed and slipped into bed. The quilt had come up over their heads, Becca had cried, and for the longest time they'd held one another close, silent at first, then speaking in whispers. After awhile, they'd made love tenderly, with relief and gratitude.

"Your police chariot awaits outside, but I'll take a kiss first," he said.

The clock showed 1:59 P.M. and he sat on the lounge in the TV room, feet up, covered by a blanket, head back against a pillow. She'd left a stack table beside him and when he declined her offer of an apple, she'd set a glass of ice water on it, a napkin, the cordless phone, and the latest thriller he'd checked out of the library before the storm.

"We're due at the Dawuds' at 7:30," she said. "I don't want you going out until we leave together."

"Where am I going? Of course I'll be here."

She frowned. "You're calm and content until something happens to interfere with our lives. Then *bam!* I don't know when you're happiest—with me, or with that."

He almost said she'd been involved with him in "that," when it counted. "Please." He reached up but she leaned back and peered at him.

"So you'll be home?"

"Probably sleeping, but you have permission to wake me. I'll give you the latest bump report." He made kissy lips, and when she bent close, he captured her with his arms and pulled her down.

"Sweetie, cut it out!" She braced against the wall beside the lounge and pushed up to escape. They were both laughing by the time she left for the hospital.

The check-call he knew she'd make came forty-two minutes later. He yawned while they spoke, and said he'd head up for a nap. He felt tired and he did go upstairs, but only to turn on the answering machine. Ten minutes later, he switched off the motion-detector light by the side door and slipped into his heavy coat, put on a watch cap, fastened the hood over it, and pulled on gloves. When he stepped out of the recessed doorway, he went through two back yards and onto the adjoining street.

Minutes later, breath steaming, he tramped along Fremont Drive and reached the bottom of Chenowith Street. The snow cover had hardened in the chill and crunched underfoot. Norman Rockwell could have painted the scene: snow-covered tree limbs, roofs, and lawns, smoke curling from chimneys in ineffable stillness.

Whatever the police had done at the spot of the accident, the intersection almost a day later looked just like any other. His memory preserved the only connection, here, to Mahdy Dawud's death. And to the attack on *me*, he realized as he glanced up the hill. His head throbbed—he hadn't taken the Tylenol, didn't like taking pills—so he steered his thoughts elsewhere.

The suspect car had fled the scene straight along Fremont. But Gary recalled the turn signal. He figured the Subaru's driver, faced with a second witness approaching, had gone straight so he wouldn't have to risk climbing the slippery hill from a standing start, or leaving clues to his destination. Someone desperate enough to attack him, clever enough to steal photo ID, and serious enough to stake out his house and shoot at him, might think that way.

Fremont Drive defined the bottom of Chenowith and the street rose up to Taylor Road, which crossed it in front of the Jefferson Elementary School. Houses were set back on both sides of the football-field-long street. He started up the sidewalk. With a thirty degree—or greater—pitch to the road, navigating the tricky slope required care. It wound around slightly to the right as he climbed. If the boy had been riding a sled downhill, he must have been going faster than the car that had hit him.

The houses were colonials and Tudors with pitched roofs, overhangs, brick and stucco walls, and arched doorways. The homes were well maintained. He'd climbed two-thirds of the way up the street, wondering where to look, when a woman came down a driveway to his right, toward a gray Volvo parked at the curb. When he glanced at the house, he saw an older woman through a second-floor window. She appeared to be comfortable and there by choice, possibly sitting.

He waved at the woman in the window. She waved back.

"Excuse me," he said to the approaching person. She had keys in her hand, wore a heavy black wool coat, and her sandy hair looked like the perm had let go this morning.

"Yes?"

"May I speak briefly with the woman in the window?"

She leaned away and frowned. "Why?"

Her tone had an edge and he hoped she wouldn't pull out a whistle or pepper spray. "Well, an old red Subaru dinged my car yesterday, and it headed up the hill." He nodded toward the window. "Maybe she's seen it."

Unexpectedly, the straggly-haired woman laughed and shook her head. "Six degrees of connection. A few days ago, Mom told me about this old red car that looked so awful without hubcaps. I don't

31

know if it's a Subaru—or the one you're looking for—but she said it turned left on Taylor." She pointed uphill. "That's it. There are only three homes to the left. The school's on the other side and the street ends at Route 4."

"Thank you," he said, hiding his excitement. He nodded, they parted, and he continued uphill on foot. He heard her car engine balk and then catch. She waved at him as she rolled by. She turned right. He turned left.

Taylor Road dead-ended at a fence, with a barrier across the street and Route 4 beyond in a ravine. The first two of its three homes had turrets, slate roofs, and black metal fittings that could have adorned a castle. Their garages had solid doors and the well-appointed structures looked as if only Mercedes or Land Rovers would be allowed in.

The last house, Number 1058, appeared smaller, older, and in blatant disrepair. Its storm door had space for three glass sections: two were missing. Gray paint was peeling off the house. Several roof tiles had been blown away, and one of the aluminum leaders, forced out of its gutter, leaned sideways on a bent strap.

But its detached two-car garage, set back along the left side of the house as he faced it, had a line of four square glass panes across the top of each of its two closed doors. He hesitated on the sidewalk. Blinds were drawn tightly in every facing window. Several of the slats had broken, offering peepholes from within. If the shooters saw him, he'd be an easy target. If they got him inside, no one would know where he'd gone. The woman he'd spoken to wouldn't come to his rescue.

But if he didn't look, he'd have accomplished nothing. He marched up the cracked asphalt driveway.

The rows of garage door windows were above his eyes, even on tiptoe. He glanced around and found a pile of bricks stacked along the house side of the garage. As quickly as he could, he moved three of them to the front, and set them one atop the other. Leaning with both hands against the door, he pushed up onto the pile. The door rocked back a fraction and the bricks quivered, but he managed to keep his footing. He moved his face close to a grimy pane and used his hands to block reflected light so he could see into the dark garage.

The slot in front of him revealed nothing except a cracked and oil-stained concrete floor. But across the garage to his left, parked face in, rested an old, red Subaru with two missing hubcaps.

When he hopped off, the stack toppled. The clanking noise caused him to glance at the house. He saw motion at a blind—or light play from a cloud crossing the low sun? He rushed down the driveway, reaching for his phone.

He imagined the small man who'd slugged him braced behind a window, holding a powerful weapon, sighting at his back. The call rang through. He stepped onto the sidewalk, turned away from the highway and pictured the cross hairs steady between his shoulder blades. The shooter's finger tightened on the trigger.

"Alegretti."

The lieutenant's rough voice sounded like a gun burst and Gary jumped, sure he'd wind up face down, bleeding onto the concrete. For an instant he couldn't speak; he heaved a breath and moved faster. As he crossed the top of Chenowith, he began to talk.

When he got home, he activated the motion-detector light, turned off the phone machine, undressed, and slipped into bed. His hands and feet were cold, though not like last night. He set the electric blanket on "2" but even with the warmth, and curling into a comfortable position in the early twilight, his heart kept pounding. So he got dressed and went downstairs.

He switched on the front lights. Becca would be home in less than two hours. He wandered into the kitchen but decided to save the lasagna and salad for her arrival. He'd eaten alone too many times. To tide him over, he snacked on pieces of dried pineapple. Then it came to him that the lieutenant might arrive before his wife. No matter how useful his discovery of the car, he expected that Alegretti would be less than pleased.

Given the circumstances, though, he'd do it again. Finding the car should be the end of it. In a few hours, they'd pay their condolences to the Dawuds and move on with their lives. The loss, the emptiness he'd felt inside from imagining Becca shot, gone—he'd seal away and bury very deep.

He returned to the TV room, switched on a lamp, and found the remote. Then he slipped back onto the lounge, covered himself, and adjusted the pillow. He turned on one or another football game and muted the television so he could think. It surprised him when Becca appeared in his head, as she'd leaned above him hours before. He knew what it meant.

At times the loneliness welled up, the little kid grasping for parents who'd never return, finding a cold aunt, bottling everything inside. Though it still tore at him fifty-one years later, he could recall his mother's face, her kind, probing eyes and long, dark hair. A memory bubbled up. She'd enjoyed touching him, fingers in his hair, a hand on his shoulder, infusing him with pride and love—

"Not now," he heard. He'd said it out loud and had to blink, his eyes were brimming. He breathed deeply and knew why he wanted to hug Becca, keep her from vanishing, too. He glanced around and focused on a wooden statue they'd brought back from their honeymoon. The danger they'd just been through—that's what he should concentrate on. He tried to imagine 1058 Taylor Road. If the shooter, or shooters, operated from that house, what would the police find?

But his thoughts wandered. Becca would be home soon, courtesy of the police. She'd find him just where she'd left him. He hoped when the lieutenant chewed him out, she wouldn't be there—and she wouldn't find out what he'd done.

Something about that gnawed at him.

CHAPTER 6
2:05 P.M., Wednesday, New York time
8:05 P.M., Wednesday, Amsterdam time

WHILE he waited, an image of people blown apart, bloody and staggering, slipped into Pierre Caubere's mind. He knew it had to do with footage he'd seen on television. But, before, others had been the cause.

He pushed the thought away. The cold rain falling on his close-cropped gray hair, hitting his glasses and trickling into his collar, must have brought it on; he'd left his umbrella in the truck. He masked his irritation and instead imagined a woman in a yellow bikini beside him on a beach. It was a tall order, standing in a downpour on a jet-way of the vast Amsterdam Schiphol Airport. He'd almost succeeded when the cargo handler interrupted.

"Can it get wet?" he asked, referring to the large shrink-wrapped crate resting on a pallet inside the lift-ramp of the refrigerator truck that Caubere had driven in. The handler wore a reflective yellow slicker and a clear plastic cover over his uniform hat. He tapped at the carton.

Caubere glanced at the Nippon Cargo freighter parked across the tarmac and relaxed. He knew the carton's manifest—shipper, cubic content, value, destination, security-tracking code—was in perfect order.

"Wet is okay," he said to the man. "But not warm or crushed."

Anyone opening the box would find exotic flowers—real attention-grabbers—packed carefully, cushioned by foam partitions. En route, in the warehouse at JFK International, and on the delivery truck, the box's contents would be kept close to freezing—perfect for cut flowers but too cold for sniffing dogs.

35

He imagined the money he had coming from both sides—first for preparing the shipment, and then even more for providing information about it. The Americans paid well. He'd only give basic data. He didn't want either side to turn on him. This time he'd vacation somewhere warm and sunny, without all the damned rain.

Caubere allowed airport sounds to wash over him. The four-story, glass-sided building spread out behind him, the tubular aircraft in front, glistening sides reflecting white, red and yellow lights in the rain, were interchangeable among so many others. For a moment he smelled jet fuel, blown close and whipped away by wind and rain.

What happened next to the cargo would be Siddiq's job, not his. He knew the man's name. He'd been told that the guy, short and vicious, should only be dealt with by phone—if he ever met the man, he wouldn't live to do so again.

The handler intruded into Caubere's thoughts, speaking loudly so he'd be heard over the throttled whine of an aircraft rolling past. "You are *gellukig*" —he frowned— "lucky it is slow so I do this for you. You should not be here."

"Well, my boss works at the flower auction down the road—he's a regular, handled the paperwork, you can check, his name and the company's are on the paper. But he got sick and needed a fill in. Got me a smart card, so I don't get locked up."

The man in the yellow slicker nodded as he fired up the orange-painted forklift. He climbed on and leaned closer to Caubere. "I hope your *werkgever* gets well "

Caubere smiled and removed his glasses to wipe them as the handler worked the fork into the pallet. The crate rose above the lift. "It would be on a rainy night," Caubere said. "I think his problem's a girl. Or maybe it's not a problem."

The cargo man nodded as if he understood and wiped moisture from his chin. "You should not be here."

"I know. Sorry. A last minute order—expensive flowers, they get delivered or they're worthless. I thought of the women they'll make happy in New York, figured it's almost Christmas, what the hell, I can get wet." Rain dripped from his brows and soaked through his tan trench coat.

"*Verlof,*" the handler said, and added, "Better leave."

"My boss insisted I see the carton get on the plane. He'll ask."

The handler nodded. "Then go." The roar of the forklift drowned out whatever he said next.

Caubere watched the carton jounce along the taxiway to the aircraft. He turned to slam the truck's rear doors. The handler lowered the box onto a loading ramp and backed his machine away. Carefully managing the slick surfaces of the loader he clambered to the ground and flipped a lever that sent the rain-splattered container rolling into the 747's open hatch. It spun forward in the plane, out of sight.

The cargo man looked around, saw him and waved, perhaps in irritation, expecting him gone. Caubere waved back, got in the truck, and pulled away. He followed the curve of the large cargo building around toward the airport exit ramp.

He wouldn't feel responsible for the explosives. He might as well be wearing a FedEx uniform. The ones who'd provided it, and the ones who would use it—they'd be guilty. He saw the security booth ahead, drew out his ID card and went back to dreaming of a beach.

CHAPTER 7
5:42 P.M., Wednesday

IN the honeymoon photo on the mantle, Gary and Becca were smiling on a beach in Bermuda, arms around one another. The memories it evoked always delighted him. Gazing at it now, he realized his wife would be home in twenty minutes.

He stepped into the kitchen, lifted the cordless phone, and leaned against the island as he dialed the lieutenant's private line. Had the police found the car? If so, did the man who'd shot at them live in that house? Had he been caught? Was Vincent questioning him?

When the call rang through to message, he punched off and dialed the station direct. Alegretti might be anywhere in the building.

"Police," said the man who answered.

"Lieutenant Alegretti there?"

"Who's calling?"

"Gary Kemmerman."

"Minute—yeah, hold on."

Impatient, he shifted his feet. Could be his curiosity would get him yelled at louder. But even if it irritated the man, he had to ask.

"Distler."

The stranger's voice had an edge. Gary recalled Vincent mentioning the name—a sergeant he worked with. Vincent must be with him. "Lieutenant Alegretti, please."

"Who wants him?"

"Gary Kemmerman." The line grew silent. Distler must have put a hand over the phone.

"He's not here," Distler said.

"Then why'd I get transferred to you?"

"You home, Mr. Kemmerman?"

Gary didn't answer. What was going on? Was Vincent on the way to him? Would the lieutenant come marching through his front door any minute?

Distler spoke into the silence. "He wants you to stay away from that car."

Gary turned and leaned elbows onto the countertop. "So I did find it—"

"You hear me?"

"Yeah, but that's tough to do." After he spoke, he realized he'd thrown gasoline on the fire.

The sergeant's voice grew cold. "Why?"

"Well, we're paying a condolence call at the Dawuds this evening. They live right around the corner from that house." He noticed it had grown dark outside.

"If you don't get any closer, it'll be fine," Distler grumbled.

"What'd I find?"

"He said you'd have lots of questions. Said if he can, he'll tell you himself."

Gary turned away from the window. The wall clock showed ten of six. "When's he due back?"

"Just hold on—how 'bout I deliver the rest of the lieutenant's message?"

Gary'd been squeezing the small phone. He changed hands.

"Alegretti knew you'd be making the condolence call," Distler said. Gary guessed Becca must have told Angela, who'd relayed it. "He says you're not to mention the other driver, the car, the shots, or the house. Got it?"

"But they're connected."

"Doesn't matter—it ain't optional."

The ominous tone pissed Gary off. "Is Vincent too busy to ask me himself?"

"Matter of fact, he is."

Gary imagined Distler caught between him and the lieutenant's instructions. Asking his friend about it was one thing; having Distler call Vincent and complain about him seemed quite another. Maybe the police had the house staked out, waiting for the shooter or his crew to return.

"Tell him okay. I'll keep it under wraps. What's this about? Come on, I took risks for you guys." He heard Distler breathing.

"Alegretti said I could tell you this—it's not the car, it's the house. We're done."

CHAPTER 8
7:30 P.M., Wednesday

THE Dawud's small house hid its secrets behind white vinyl siding trimmed with brown edging, gutters, and leaders. The flagstone walkway had been shoveled, probably broom-cleaned, and it glimmered in blues and pinks between knee-high mounds of snow.

In silence, Gary holding Becca's hand, they traveled along the walk, up three stone steps and to the solid front door. The temperature and wind had moderated but he found it one of the longest, coldest journeys he'd ever made. How do you express regrets to the parents of an only child who'd been taken at age eleven?

What did families do in Africa and the Middle East, where so many young people were snuffed out by poverty and oppression? The statistics boiled down to grieving mothers and fathers who could not understand. He'd seen it over and again in the media. The dead eyes of the living said it all. The word "accident" would not diminish the heartache here. Every toy, every cry of a child, every "normal" family activity—

The door swung open as his hand reached for the bell. Before they could speak, the lanky man who blocked entry nodded to them. "Are you the Kemmermans?"

Gary picked up an accent much like the guy's who'd slugged him. The man wore a white gown that reached from a Nehru collar down to his shoes. The sleeves were long and wide, and the shoulder and neckline embroidered. Could he be a cleric?

"Yes," Becca said.

"Then welcome. Come in, please. Zahid and Leena Dawud are expecting you."

The man stepped aside. They entered the vestibule. Becca moved forward, but Gary waited while the man closed the front door. Then

43

he extended his hand. "I'm Gary."

For a moment, the lanky man stared back, and his fiery, distraught eyes reached for Gary's soul. Pain and much more, some consuming purpose, lurked behind the glare. The connection became so strong that it startled him when he felt his hand taken.

"I'm Haroun Rashid, the Dawud's imam—their prayer leader," the lanky man said. "Come, let us go in."

Why did he feel like Little Red Riding Hood being asked into grandma's house? But before he could deal with it, Rashid turned away.

He followed the man through a glass-paned door that stood open at the inside access to the small vestibule. They stepped into a silent living room. Becca, who'd arranged the condolence call, had told Gary that they'd be the first visitors, because the Dawuds wanted to hear how their son had died.

Three lamps were on. Yellow shades diffused the glow and muted shadows. Crocheted doilies had been placed beneath lamps, framed photos, and candy dishes, to protect three dark, Mediterranean-style side tables. A single large couch and four comfortable chairs were grouped in a rough horseshoe.

Despite their obvious pain, the Dawuds asked Gary to recall every detail. But when he came to the part where he'd seen the man who ran over their son, as he'd promised, he lied. Rather than decline comment he said that he'd been looking under the car and hadn't gotten a good look at the other driver before he was knocked out. He expected the glance from Becca but hadn't anticipated the relieved, almost appreciative look from Rashid. He finished to a strained silence.

"We are sorry...you were hurt," said Zahid. Eyes on the carpet, the man absently wrung his hands.

That stalled the conversation. Leena Dawud moaned into the stillness. "I have...what do I do with...Mahdy's essay for English class?"

She and her husband had talked about their son, the words sprinkled with pauses while they fought for composure. Leena, a stout woman with short, dark hair, wearing a black headscarf and layers of black clothing from her neck to her shoes, sat on the couch a few feet from her husband.

She gasped and raised her right hand, clutching several yellow sheets of paper. The hand shook and the paper rustled with a life of its own. The thought of what she held must have overwhelmed her. Her face fell apart and she began to sob. Her shoulders shook, body rocked back and forth, and the fists she made crinkled homework that no longer had purpose.

Whether for religious reasons or because the Kemmermans were there, neither her husband nor Rashid moved to comfort Leena Dawud. Becca did. She pushed from her chair and, with a strangled sound, knelt before the woman. For an instant Leena drew back—but with tears streaming down her cheeks she moaned and accepted the embrace. The two women hugged and cried.

Gary glanced at Zahid, who had closed his eyes. He gave the Dawuds credit for not castigating the boy for riding his sled in the street. Some kids climb trees, fall out and break an arm. Others—

"She is a mother, too," Rashid said to Gary, nodding toward Becca.

He took it as a question and turned to the cleric. "Yes. We have a daughter."

Sitting in the chair beside him, Rashid nodded again, as if he approved of what Becca had done. He bent close, used a hand to cloak his mouth, and whispered so low Gary barely heard it. "We must speak in private."

What was this? The man must want something from him that had to do with the driver who hit the boy. How was Rashid tied into it? The man waited, inches away, and Gary wanted to help. It took him a moment to figure out why he couldn't. He imagined Becca's eyes when he walked off without her. His little white lies, plans made and actions he'd taken alone had begun to form a crust—around him, maybe between them.

She wanted in. He wanted to keep her safe. He wanted so many things. "I'll only get involved together with my wife," he said.

Rashid fired a disapproving look but Gary knew he wouldn't budge. He spoke again when Rashid hesitated. "She and I work together." He said it softly and it sounded good. "You'll benefit from that."

They glanced at the women. The crying had stopped. Between

gasps they were whispering, heads close.

"I need to speak privately with the Kemmermans for just a few minutes," the imam said out loud to Zahid. The words startled the man. He breathed deeply, paused as if considering what he'd heard, and nodded. "May we use the basement room?" Rashid went on.

The women were watching. When Zahid nodded again and the imam rose, Gary followed suit and helped Becca up. She'd found tissues. She offered one to Leena and used another to dab at her eyes.

Rashid led them into the kitchen, through a doorway and onto a landing. He switched on lights, closed the landing door behind them, and motioned for them to follow him down the stairs.

The basement must have been Mahdy's playroom. They found an easel with chalk, games piled neatly, and drawings taped to the paneled walls. Paddles lay on each side of a ping-pong table, one trapping a ball. Bench seating had been built above cabinets along the far wall.

"You want something from us," Gary said. "And the Dawuds don't know about it."

"Yes," from the imam.

Whatever their religion, Gary noted, clerics were often blessed with a wide-eyed earnestness, as if the world were a continual wonder. "Becca," he said, "Haroun Rashid is the Dawuds' prayer leader. He asked me for a private meeting and I told him we worked together. I don't know if he's comfortable with—"

"There are difficult choices here," Rashid said, "but it will be fine. We must adapt to what Allah gives us." He turned to Becca and added, with gravitas, "Thank you for providing comfort."

Gary saw the praise had embarrassed her. "What can we—"

Becca touched his arm. "There's so much about Islam we don't understand," she said to Rashid. "Gary says you're a prayer leader. Does that mean you're the congregation's imam?"

The question thawed Rashid, who nodded. "Yes. And much as a cleric in any religion, I speak to many people and hear many things."

"What is it you want from us?" she asked.

"Providence put your husband at the scene of the accident, so a higher power may have selected him for the role. And…I also have a friend on the police department."

"Do you mean Lieutenant Alegretti?" she asked.

Rashid smiled. "No, but the man talks to the lieutenant."

"It's more than that," Gary said. They both looked at him. "You must know something that you—and maybe your friend—don't want to tell the police."

Rashid's face tightened. He gazed upward, as if seeking guidance. Then he breathed deeply. "We are loyal Muslims and loyal American citizens—just like Christians and Jews. Most of us admire what America offers. We are one of so many groups who have benefited. But at times—I suspect for every group—there are lines that are difficult to cross."

"You know him," Gary said. "The man who killed the boy and hit me. He must be Muslim."

The imam glanced from one to the other. "Zahid cannot know. It would—he blames himself for what happened to his son. The boy wanted to be like the other children."

Becca reached out to him, palm open, and did not touch him, but he looked at her, eyes glowing, as if she had. "Of course," she said. "We won't tell them."

Looking at Becca but speaking to Gary, the imam went on. "Despite what you said before, you *did* see the man who hit the child. You described him in detail."

"...That's right," Gary said.

"We would like you to identify him for us. We need to be sure. And we ask you to do this without telling the Dawuds or bringing in the police."

"But the man's committed serious crimes."

Rashid clasped his hands as if in prayer. "Until we know it is him, this man has done nothing wrong."

"We may *have* to call in the police," Gary said, wondering why Rashid's eyes were still on Becca.

"We'll do as you ask," she said, answering for them both.

Her hand had dropped but Gary saw that the imam and Becca were locked in that connection he'd felt in the vestibule.

CHAPTER 9
7:59 P.M., Wednesday

Gary gripped Becca's hand in his and slipped them both into her coat pocket as they turned right off the Dawud's walkway. They started up the hill, moving slowly, affected by the visit. Their breath steamed.

"How awful," she said.

He didn't reply. Glinting from the few street lamps, the snow cover was tinged pink from low clouds that reflected the glow from New York City to the east. The temperature was falling and a fresh breeze ruffled their hair.

They walked in silence. Others had arrived to express sympathy, and they'd been able to slip out with murmured goodbyes, a choked thank-you from Leena, and a knowing nod from Rashid.

"Least I don't feel in danger anymore when we're outside," Becca said, as they turned right at the corner, off Chenowith and onto Taylor Road. "Think we are?"

He knew if they turned back three houses, he could show her the vipers' nest he'd uncovered hours before. Were police lurking? Had the man who'd hit him, the one he'd been asked to identify, been taken? If so, Rashid hadn't been informed. It took effort to keep facing forward.

"Probably not from what happened this morning," he said. "But tomorrow morning might drop us back in the thick of it." They'd arranged for Rashid to bring the policeman friend he'd mentioned to their house just after eight A.M.

She watched where she put her feet and spoke without looking at him. "What do you think that man has to add?"

"My guess, he's the one knows the suspect. It's good he's a cop. I won't agree to anything dangerous."

"Because of me?"

49

"Haven't you always asked me to be careful?"

"Haven't you always done just what you wanted anyway?"

Her retort had come without a pause. He wondered why. "So they'd better have a plan."

"A plan?" she asked a few steps later.

He considered how to put it. "If I find the man who slugged me and shot at us, it wouldn't be good if he saw me." When she didn't respond, he added, "You were quick to leave the police out. We're dealing with serious crimes—we may need help."

"I understand," she said. "You can bend the rules and go to Vincent in confidence. But if we're dealing with Muslims and murder, can't we go to the FBI?"

"You're fudging the meaning of 'police?'"

"I sure meant to."

"Good thinking."

Hearing that, she turned toward him with a grin. They stopped, and she clutched at his forearm as she wobbled on a slick spot. "Did you mean what you said in there?"

He nodded. "It's taken me awhile, but when we got together, didn't we sign on as full partners?"

"I insisted," she said, and the grin faded. "Oh, God, after another condolence call, wasn't it?"

Ten months earlier, they'd shared a first kiss outside a murdered man's house. He'd tried to keep his involvement in the investigation a secret, but Becca had demanded honesty and a full partnership in everything or she'd walk out of his life. Neither of them had known the killer had been watching from behind a tree, and that tender kiss would be what saved her. He'd understood, many times since, that the kiss had saved him, too.

"You were right to insist," he said. His cheeks, ears, and nose were stinging from the cold.

Her frown turned into a smile and they continued on. He tried to keep her hand in his but in places the shoveled path narrowed beside large trees. "Darn," he said as he fell behind.

"Sweetie, I have to learn to walk by myself—it's time, don't you think?" Moving like a duck, giggling as she shifted weight onto each planted leg, she laid a foot down where the path widened.

He watched: learning stability on snow, another metaphor for life. He followed along. She'd had a child, fled an abusive marriage, made it on her own as a single mom in a different part of the country, managed to raise an incredible daughter. When did the challenge end?

They reached a cleared section, and without trying to recapture her hand he said, "Have I lost a job? You look proud of yourself."

"Silly." She turned, leaned up, and kissed him.

He hugged her and kissed back.

"You get to keep that job," she said. She slipped her hand into his again and they stood facing one another. "You surprised me before."

"When I said we worked together?"

The breeze caught her hair and blew it across her face; she waited the moment. "Yes."

"Told you I wouldn't get involved without your okay." He knew that didn't cover it. They started forward.

"But you went out this afternoon after you said you wouldn't." She spared him embarrassment by going on, "I forgave you when I learned what you'd done, all in a short walk."

"From Angela?"

"She says Vincent's steaming. I wasn't going to bring up your tour of the neighborhood because I knew how much you needed to do it. But if you can't leave well enough alone, I want to be with you. You must have known that."

He gazed at her. The breeze lifted flakes from a tree and sprinkled them across her hair. "I felt sneaky," he said. "Couldn't say yes anymore without you."

Still concentrating on her feet, she gave his hand a serious squeeze. "You'll kiss me again like that when we get home?"

"Becca." He couldn't help his serious tone, and it stopped her. She turned. "What?"

"You always warn me to be careful. If we're partners in this—"

She put her free hand up to his lips. "Shush. We'll both be careful, and we'll do the best we can. It's like you said this morning. We'll make sound choices and hope they work out."

"I don't want you in danger. I—"

She took his face in both hands. "I don't want to lose you either." She scrunched her mouth, searching for words. "You won't be happy, feet up, reading books. I'd rather be with you than waiting home with a candle in the window." She chuckled; he wondered why. "It might be safer. You almost got me killed twice when I *wasn't* your sleuthing partner."

She turned away, took a step, and he followed along, taking her hand. "I can't lose you," he murmured. He hadn't meant to say it.

She didn't slow, just turned to him. He saw on her face what he imagined she found on his. When she spoke, he knew she'd changed the subject.

"Maybe you should write about your cases—or whatever you'd call them. They'd make great novels. No one would believe it. And you need a hobby" —she laughed at another thought— "you're *mostly* retired and you have time."

He considered it. It made him think of her time. "If you're in this with me, will you be able to get free of the hospital—I mean when you might have to?"

They crossed a half block in silence. "I'll do the best I can," she said without turning.

A few steps later, a sloped, icy spot got her. Her right foot slipped out and again she fell back onto a lawn piled high with snow, pulling him down on top of her. This time neither laughed. They tensed, recalling gunshots. But they felt only the breeze, cold snow, and their closeness.

He looked down and saw her smiling up at him, long hair framing her face against the snow. She radiated happiness.

"Oops," she said.

CHAPTER 10
10:45 P.M., Wednesday

It made Sean Dwyer happy, being in Connolly's Pub with ale on the table and noisy jabber all around. The place smelled of burgers, onions, and beer.

Dwyer and Ryan Scully were sitting in a booth separated from others in the row by five-foot wooden dividers. To Dwyer's left, a wide aisle ran between them and the long bar. Behind the bar, a mirrored wall contained three rows of glass shelves laden with bottles. A variety of green shamrocks and leprechauns hung from the shelves or were taped to the mirror.

The rickety stools in front were set close together and occupied by noisy patrons. Did they give a damn for the symbols of a time long past? he wondered. Before he could turn away, the dark-haired bargirl appeared with their drinks. Dwyer looked up and found her appealing. He saw something bruised in her young face, something behind the idling eyes that attracted him.

"Here's your refill," she said to him, loud enough to be heard over the chatter. "Yours, too." She meant Scully, though her eyes never left Dwyer.

When she bent low above the table and pushed the chilled mugs toward the men, her long hair hung down and her blouse fell open. She smiled, only at Dwyer, as both men stared at her breasts. She surprised them when she shook her torso, setting them swaying so the men had to glance up at her smiling face.

"You interested, Irish?" Her voice had a little-girl quality, an innocence that her words, and her eyes, belied.

"What's your name?" Dwyer asked.

She straightened, and the view disappeared. "Lynn Turner."

"What time you get off?" He saw she had quite a figure. New York girls put shy Colleens to shame. Granted another life, here's

53

where he'd want to spend it.

"I'm on overtime," she purred. "Tell me when, give me ten minutes."

He read promise in her smile and glanced at his watch. "Half hour?"

She nodded. No smile, he noticed, now that it'd been arranged. "What's your name?" she asked.

"Sean."

"Meet you out front. Don't disappoint."

He watched her move off and found potential in the sway. She took chances. He'd pay, gladly, but he bet she wouldn't ask. The good ones never did. The thought of her with him at Finn's safe house made him pleased that he'd taken the man's apartment. He hadn't wanted to, but now—

"Never happens to me," Scully said.

"You got a look."

"Whets the appetite."

"Find your own."

"She found you." Scully sounded tired, not upset.

Dwyer looked at him across the lacquered wooden table. The overweight man's gray hair had thinned. Drinking lines ridged his nose, and his dark eyes looked rheumy. The gray coat had been stained with something that cleaning couldn't remove, and the frayed collar spoke of use.

He'd been a firebrand. He had the credentials. Now he ran a metal shop, a legitimate family business, making little things for smaller companies and individuals. Dwyer hoisted the icy mug. "Luck to finding your own."

They clanked and drank. Scully wiped his mouth with a napkin and got to it. "They told me you'd arrive, but that's all. I thought we were moving toward peace with the bastards."

Dwyer almost had to read his lips, what with the noise level. "Oh, we are, we are."

Scully looked confused.

"But maybe we arrange a final fling. Something we can remember and that won't come back to haunt us."

The old man glanced at his mug and gazed back. "How can I

help?"

Dwyer put his left elbow onto the table, bent forward and used his hand to cloak his mouth. "Need a bus. Can do?"

Scully followed suit, used his right elbow and leaned closer. He rubbed his right cheek with the stein to hide his words. "What kind?"

"Tourist job. Luxury. Out of state plates: Massachusetts, Ohio, Virginia. Luggage compartments empty but the gas tank full. Not hot." He knew that Scully remembered everything. That had always been his trademark.

"When you need it?"

"Quick—next few days. I'll pick it up." He'd bet the pickup would be somewhere remote and deserted. That would be perfect.

"How much you giving for it?" Scully asked.

In passing, a young man almost touched Dwyer's shoulder; the man stumbled slowly, tapping the edges of the dividers for support as he headed toward the restrooms in back. Though it had become noisier, Dwyer waited until he'd gone. "You tell me."

"Fifty grand."

"Don't want to buy the bus company."

Scully took a deep breath. Dwyer saw his frown, read the concern in his eyes, and realized the importance of the old man's role. "You got demands," Scully said.

"How's thirty? At pickup." It wouldn't matter anyway. He expected to kill him; he knew Siddiq had been right about leaving witnesses.

"I've been at this for awhile," Scully said. "Are you interested in what we do? The service that's worth fifty and cheap at that?"

Dwyer suppressed irritation and nodded.

"I'll be brief. It's me and my four sons. We do it in-house. Visit the target to ID the usual buses—what they'd expect. Steal the same type of bus and repaint it if we must. Travel out of state to pick up plates and try to get 'em from a vehicle that's been in a serious accident. What you get fits your scene and the cops can't make the vehicle or plates. That's a lot to do for quick."

He sounded more weary than proud. "Y'need perfect, not cheap. Don't want you compromised 'cause of me. Never happened before, never will."

Dwyer understood the value of the clean license plates, and smiled. "Fine. I'll call you every day. Noon okay?"

"Where should the bus fit in?" Scully asked.

That, Dwyer would not reveal. Before the pause could grow uncomfortable, laughter burst from the bar and both men swiveled. The crowd had grown. People stood two and three deep. Dwyer had no idea what had caused the fuss.

When they turned back, he had realized it would be easier telling Scully a lie than playing evasive games. Big out-of-town buses went everywhere.

"The New York Stock Exchange," he whispered. "Doesn't even have to be open. Maybe we show our humane side and take down the symbol of bloody capitalism without wasting a single child."

Scully nodded. "Make the calls at five P.M. We can do the exchange after dark."

"Suits. And Ryan—"

"Don't say it, Sean, we go back too far. You know I wouldn't screw you or the cause. Got a good woman at home and the kids to watch out for."

"Your boys in on this?" Dwyer saw he'd struck a nerve.

Scully frowned and pursed his lips. "Only the little crimes, helping people." He shook his left hand toward Dwyer in nervous emphasis. "You can work with them on that, but no causes or killing." The hand dropped and lay where it had fallen. "What I brought across the sea is my own," Scully said. "The boys, they're—"

"American?" Dwyer asked. That's what happened most times, a generation in pain replaced by kids with something else until they, too, learned the hard way.

After a pause, Scully pulled the hand back into his lap, and nodded. "What you'd do, too."

For a moment, Dwyer considered that murdering their father might do to Scully's kids what the Protestants, English, and their American backers had done to him. How different was he, after all, from Siddiq? Then he put it aside, straightened, and hoisted the mug again. He wanted to look at his watch. He should have told the girl fifteen minutes. "To old times."

They clanked and took a few swallows. "They send you in, something good's gonna happen," Scully said.

Laughter erupted from the bar, this time more intense. They didn't turn. Eleven o'clock, Dwyer thought, and people were still pouring in. Oh, but he wished he could he find another city like this. He wanted to be outside in the bracing chill, waiting for her.

Scully looked at him and offered a tired smile. "Something good beside the tits, I mean."

Dwyer laughed.

"Last year," the old man said, "some guy in the U.K. got life for coming over and taking photos of the stock exchange. Just for photos and making plans."

Dwyer took another gulp. Good, cold ale, but he didn't give a damn for it now. "Like you said, some guys have all the luck."

"They won't even know it's us—probably blame it on the Arabs," Scully added, looking down at the stein, shifting it in his beefy hands.

Had Scully's remark been a wild guess, or had the man been turned? Dwyer looked and found that his companion's watery eyes registered bleary, not probing. Just the same—

"Nothing for you to worry about," he said, "nothing at all." He finished the ale, dropped a bill on the table, and rose.

CHAPTER 11
Thursday, December 13
8:25 A.M.

AFTER handing Gary a steaming mug and setting her tea on the coffee table, Becca sat in the chair beside him, facing their guests. She'd already served them. She leaned forward. "If you won't tell us what's going on, we might as well just drink our coffee and complain about the weather."

She missed her husband's glance.

Imam Rashid and the policeman he'd mentioned the night before—whom he'd introduced as Talal Siddiq, but who'd asked to be called Tony—were sitting on the large couch in the Kemmerman living room. Tony wore a dark suit and tie, Rashid the long white *dishadasha.* Both men looked uncomfortable. The morning sun hid behind the neighboring house, and the room appeared unnaturally still and dark to Gary—a perfect complement to their halting conversation.

Rashid glanced at Tony. The policeman remained mute. "But you are drinking tea," he said to Becca.

The joke fell flat and Rashid glanced around helplessly. Gary doubted anything could make Tony laugh. The man looked tense. Had Rashid forced him to come? Better not to ask Lieutenant Alegretti about him—this had to be linked to the Subaru driver and might get his guest into trouble. He wondered whether Tony knew that he'd found the car and the house.

Gary asked Rashid, "Who do you want me to ID?"

Tony nodded. The imam said, "First, Talal and I need your promise to keep what we discuss in confidence." He steepled his hands. "No one else must learn from either of you. If this becomes a matter for the police, well, Talal is one of them."

"Fine," Becca said.

59

Gary wished she wouldn't be so quick on the trigger. Catching that man *was* a matter for law enforcement. Gary wasn't prepared to hand out a free pass to anyone who'd shot at her.

Tony leaned forward, hands on his thighs, and weighed in. "You must come to the funeral."

"Mahdy Dawud's?" Becca asked.

The imam answered, though he kept his eyes on Gary. "The boy's funeral will be held at 3:30 this afternoon at Makbarat As-Salaam Funeral Park in Piscataway. We believe the man we want you to look at will be there."

Gary turned to Tony. "How do you know that?"

The policeman looked ill at ease and did not answer.

"Wouldn't be good if that man saw me, would it?" Gary said.

"Why do you ask these questions?" Tony growled. The lines chiseled on his face conveyed resentment even in repose. He appeared older than Rashid, balding, heavier without being taller. Something about him reminded Gary of the man he'd seen in the snow. Probably the mind's stereotyping.

Gary licked his lips. "I need to know what we're walking into. He slugged me for a reason. Can you explain?"

The policeman's mouth set into a thin line.

Rashid spoke. "We only need you to tell us if—"

"He *shot* at us," Gary snapped, leaning toward Tony, eyes locking on the man. "He could have killed us."

News of the shooting surprised neither man. Almost against his will, it seemed, Tony's eyes were drawn to Becca and back, but he remained mute. A first shaft of sunlight slanted into the room and cut through his sparse hair.

Suspect must be the cop's friend, Gary figured. If he could identify the man, it would turn him into a felon. Then the cop would have to act.

"We cannot cross the line," Rashid said. "Not yet. Maybe not ever."

Gary found that frightening.

Becca spoke up. "Justice must be blind to race, religion—"

"But it isn't!" Tony hissed, startling her.

"Please," Rashid said. "We are not enemies here."

Gary breathed in. He'd prefer not to be their enemies anywhere. "How do you know the man?" he asked the cop, who crossed his shiny black shoes and fidgeted.

"It will stay among us," Rashid said, but let Tony make the decision.

The cop rubbed his lips. "We lived in the same town. We were schoolmates, growing up."

"In what country?" Gary asked.

"Syria. My family came here. His went elsewhere."

But the cop wouldn't meet his eyes. Gary knew he'd withheld something important. "And he looked you up when he got here—"

"Better we don't go into this," Rashid said. "The details will not affect the outcome."

Not so, Gary knew, but he moved on. "How can you guarantee our safety?"

"Haven't we learned there are no guarantees?" Becca said flatly.

Gary blinked and saw her serious expression. What had he done, making her a partner?

Tony leaned forward. "Wear a long, dark coat, a hat with a brim, and a muffler around your face," he said, in his deep, serious voice. "We'll arrive early—though separately—and I will show you where to stand. When I see the man coming, I'll leave our group and walk to him. The two of us will move toward the mourners. If you're sure he's the one, rub at an eye."

Gary nodded. That would allow the policeman to take action as he stood beside the man, apart from the others. Would he try to apprehend him? The suspect had to be carrying a weapon. The secrecy these two men had insisted upon might mean they weren't sure what they'd do.

"How far is the cemetery?" Becca asked.

"An hour's drive," Tony said. "But you cannot come."

Her mouth dropped open.

"Why not?" Gary asked.

The policeman looked to the imam, who answered while facing Becca. "Only men can accompany the body to the gravesite. I am sorry."

"I'll drive Gary, park a distance away and wait in the car," she said, without a question mark.

"Becca," said Gary, "you don't have to—"

She shook her head. "You're not getting out of my sight. Do your thing and come right back to the car. We don't want to be shot at any more. Will that be acceptable, Rashid?"

"Not wise," Tony said.

The imam turned from Becca to the policeman and then back.

"The man who hit Gary also stole his license," she said. "He can't drive."

Rashid sighed. "If you remain in the car it will work."

Gary knew better than to protest when she glanced at him. He shrugged. "Guess I'll need a suit and tie."

"It would be appropriate," the imam said.

"Anything else I need to know?"

Tony answered. "Follow my example. You do not have to join in the prayers. Rashid will be busy leading us."

"What will you do when—if—Gary rubs his eye?" Becca asked.

Their guests exchanged a look. "We don't know," Rashid said.

"If he ran down the boy, hit my husband, and then shot at us, he sounds like a... ."

Thank heaven she'd left out "terrorist," Gary thought. He glanced toward his wife and reminded himself he'd only agreed to identify the person. He'd rub an eye, or not, and then they'd be done. He wanted her nowhere near people who killed as a career.

"Allah will show us the way," Rashid said. But his eyes were closed, as if it might happen only in heaven.

CHAPTER 12
9:05 A.M., Thursday

Dwyer sensed the light and felt he'd woken in heaven. He'd begun to stretch under the quilt when a hard snap against his left arm startled him. He reached for the gun beneath the pillow.

"It's not there," she said.

Coiled, he blinked and looked at her. Lynn Turner stood naked, the wet bath towel in her right hand, his gray pistol in the other. She wasn't aiming. The gun dangled from a finger in the trigger guard as if she had no use for it. The business end faced the wall.

"Didn't want you shootin' before you looked," she said. "I'm showered and starvin'."

He relaxed and leaned up on an elbow. "Gun doesn't bother you?"

She looked back without a smile, holding her ground and the weapon. "Feels odd."

"Made special—plastic and ceramic. Gets by metal detectors."

"Are the bullets plastic, too?" She peered at the weapon as if she could see into the clip.

"Ah, I'd be revealing trade secrets." He studied her face and found nothing but curiosity.

She laughed at him. "I know how to use it. For sure it would bother if it pointed my way."

The night flashed through his mind, the sex, her tenderness once he'd cracked through. She'd found the gun. Had she been afraid he'd use it on her? He lay there astonished at how well she'd dealt with it. He knew he should dump her. He didn't need entanglement, especially during an operation.

Behind her, he saw the chair on which she'd piled her clothes. Frayed pink panties lay on top. He wondered if she had much of a wardrobe or her own place. In the light of day the colleens faded, but

63

this girl's body would make a sack look good.

"You due at work—got somewhere to be?"

She folded her right arm, covering all but her left breast with the green towel. "Not if you're providin' breakfast. Eggs and bacon would be nice, and rolls. I love hot rolls in the mornin'—" the excitement in her voice collapsed— "but I never get 'em. Or I'll be on my way."

"Put that thing down and get in here." He folded the quilt back.

"Not till you feed me."

"Aarrr!" he growled, without moving.

He saw the hand holding the pistol splay at the unexpected sound. She'd have it on him fast. Had she been trained? There's more to her than the body, he thought, considering his options.

When she got the jest, she chuckled and let go of the towel. Very gently—it impressed him—she laid the automatic on the night table, muzzle facing away. The mattress rocked as her knees hit the bed. She pulled the cover off him and looked down. "Sean, I like holdin' you, but that's it till after food. I'm really hungry, so pack in the gear."

"Food's your fee?" He saw her tense, sparks in her eyes. She must believe he'd called her a whore. "Ah, we gotta joke about the world or it'll bite us."

She looked at him hard and then smiled. "You're a funny one." She dropped on top and he hugged her as her curves nestled. Her face burrowed against his neck. Grady Finn's apartment was one of so many rooms throughout the world, all of them transient. But it was suddenly glowing.

"What makes you so wild?" he asked, speaking through her hair.

"Never thought about it." She lifted her head, looked at him from inches above and frowned. "Never charged in my life either, not even for food."

His laugh shook them both. "Well, don't start charging, but tell me what I asked."

"Why bother?"

He shifted, brought her down beside him, to his left, and locked eyes. "Why not?" If she'd been trained, had she been sent to get him? The night spoke against it—and he realized she'd had him, could've blown him away while he slept, and gone home.

"You're not lookin' at my tits," she said.

"Your eyes are shining."

"You give me breakfast money, I'll throw it back at you and we'll nod to each other in passing at Connolly's."

"You think that's what we'll come to?"

"Sure I do. I picked you up; we had our night. Breakfast together would be good—" she averted her eyes, as if she'd revealed too much— "but I don't care."

He had to know what had found him the night before—and what he'd found that morning. "What's made you so wild, then?"

She pouted. "Not worth goin' over that crap."

"Could be."

"You a gun-totin' shrink?" She grinned at the thought. "Naah. Had fun last night. Time for me to go, now."

But she didn't move. Ah, he recognized something in her. "Tell me," he insisted.

"Before or after we eat? You tryin' to ruin my appetite?"

"Tell me and I'll take you out. Buy you some clothes, too, or whatever you like."

"You a rich one?"

He pursed his lips. "I got money."

"Money, a plastic gun, I don't know about your future."

"You think much about yours?" She had no comeback. "Get you lunch if you want," he said. "Not because you're good in bed—"

"'Cause you like me, right? Oh, I heard that one before."

"Bet you have. Maybe I'm different. Tell me."

She looked at him oddly, turned onto her back, locked hands behind her head and spoke at the ceiling. He could have the body any day; he listened.

"The usual. Sweet family, lived in Armagh. Dad taken away. My mum walked to the post with our bills—blew up in her face. Foster care for me at thirteen. Old enough to show, not to know. A rapist and his accommodatin' wife—English, Irish, Protestant, Catholic, who cared—till I ran off."

She'd told it flat but he found it alive in her, rearing and biting. "Sex your weapon of choice?"

She smiled without turning her head. "For sure. Worked on you. Yours is the gun." Her arms came down, and the hands clasped over her belly.

He saw she had no tan lines, probably never lay on a beach. Ivory skin that touched back.

"You're the one's crazy," she said into the silence, and looked up past the ceiling. "I'm only beat up."

He bit his lip, wanting to protect her, to make love until she responded and forgot. *Until he forgot.* "Bet you were brilliant in school," he said.

She turned, confusion in her eyes. "No one's told me that since Mum. When I went, I passed. Why'd you say it?"

"You're quick and clever."

Her expression made a joke of it. "Come on, you're raggin' me."

He knew that she'd have to decide whether to stay. He didn't want to frighten her off. "I'm not, but believe what you will."

She pushed up onto her right elbow and brought her head level with his. Her loose hair swayed, and the confusion in her eyes turned into something else, probing him. That close, he liked the soft cheeks, the strong brow. Green flecks in the searching eyes.

"You talkin' the truth, now?" she asked.

"Yeah." For moments, he couldn't read her. Then the expression changed again.

"Dinner, too?"

"Anywhere but Connolly's."

She laughed.

He had her. "How do you feel about the ones killed your family, did this to you?"

That surprised her. She looked back at him, pools in her eyes letting slip what he needed to know. Then she leaned even closer. "Who did it to you?"

It shocked him into silence. She'd distilled him. Her eyes were on him, twinkling. She knew what she'd done.

"When you're ready," she said, "tell me. I do wanna know." As she watched him, she giggled without realizing it. "If you won't look at my tits, a girl's gotta do somethin'."

"How old are you?" He couldn't hold in the question, amazed at what he'd found—and then knew she'd have to take it wrong.

The frown came back, quickly tempered by the start of a smile. "Won't get you in trouble."

"Ah," and his arms reached for her, "but you will."

E.J. RAND

CHAPTER 13
9:32 A.M., Thursday

"You wanna know if you're in trouble?" growled Lieutenant Alegretti. "I'm the least of your troubles."

Gary heard the lingering cold in his voice. "Steaming," as Becca put it, hardly covered the man's irritation. But none of it excused what the lieutenant had just done.

Alegretti closed the door to his small office and as he turned, Gary snapped, "That's the *second* time you had me locked in the back of a police car. Lucky I'd been dressed—your guy wouldn't have let me put on shoes. Hell of a way to treat a friend."

It surprised him when that didn't rile Vincent. The lieutenant wore an old gray suit and a guarded expression. What was going on? He pointed to a chair and Gary sat, wondering what the man's troops had found in that house.

Alegretti paused by the closed door as if listening. Gary glanced around: windowless, brightened by fluorescent lighting that gave everything a buttery sheen. The three vacation photos of Vincent and Angela were still there, but the succulent plant had been moved from the right side of the ugly desk onto one of the two grey metal file cabinets. Its fat green leaves were drooping.

When Vincent turned toward him, Gary said, "Though I *am* in your debt. You didn't tell Becca I went out yesterday—Angela did." He thought Vincent might smile at that, but no—he reached the chair, looked uncomfortable, didn't sit.

Gary couldn't help it. "What'd you find in that house?"

The lieutenant took the kind of breath reserved for people who are drowning. "You sure get into shit." He cleared his throat and dropped into the chair. "Listen—and you never heard this." He leaned forward and spoke low and fast. "You found a stolen car, a house rented by mail. They must've been packing to go when they shot at you." He had to swallow. Their faces were close. Gary wasn't concerned about catching the cold. Vincent went on. "They couldn't know you'd find the place for us."

He frowned in a way Gary had never seen before. "We found timers, traces of military plastic explosive." He looked like he didn't believe any of it. "This is fucking suburbia. What else did they cart away? They must have a second vehicle and shot at you from that. Maybe, 'cause of you, they thought we'd make the red Subaru if they used it."

Gary sat speechless. The lieutenant twisted his lips, put his left fist in his right hand and almost whispered. "Told you I'd bounce it up. Two men are coming to interview you."

Explosives, weapons, Gary could understand Vincent's upset about that. But it seemed the lieutenant was more concerned about the two men. Who? *Why?* He knew nothing else. The police had been given every detail he could recall. He leaned toward Vincent. "Who are they?"

The lieutenant squirmed. "*Far* outta my hands. The ones who'll talk to you, you'll know."

"*Tell* me."

Vincent waved a hand as if he wanted all of it to go away. "I can't. I'll have to leave when they get here." Gary picked up on his distress. "Be careful," the lieutenant said. "You and Becca may not have options."

Becca? She hadn't been involved except for being shot at. She'd seen nothing. What was he supposed to be careful about? He hadn't volunteered for anything, and suddenly, he wanted no part of it for either of them.

"How 'bout you drop me back home?"

Ignoring the question, Vincent rose. "Here, let me show you—"

The office door swung open. They both turned as a man in a black suit with a linebacker's physique stepped through. He had a laptop computer with a matte black finish. Along with his short, sandy hair, white shirt, and thin, dark tie, his suit had the lump in the right place. A pair of sunglasses were sticking out of his breast pocket. He'd been cut from the mold.

"What'd you tell him?" he barked in a nasty voice.

Vincent had to swallow. Gary reacted to the attack. "What business is it of yours?"

The intruder ignored him and trapped the lieutenant's eyes. "Your crony at reception tried to warn you. Can't be any other reason."

The lieutenant pushed shut the drawer he'd opened, and straightened. "I told him you'd be kicking me out of my own office."

Did Vincent flush from anger or embarrassment? Probably both.

The man in black turned to Gary. "We're just following regs. This is private business." He swung the door further open and stepped aside. "Thank you for the use of the office."

Cued, Vincent heaved a breath, crossed to the doorway, and vanished without looking back.

Gary hated to see his posture as he walked out.

The man in black stepped back, leaving the door open but blocking access. Probably waiting for Number Two. Gary dug fingers into his palms and leaned forward. "I'm Gary Kemmerman. And you are?"

The man spoke without looking at him. "Jeffers Thompson."

Gary couldn't hide his festering irritation. "The guy you're waiting for CIA?"

That spun the man's head around. "Alegretti say that?"

Gary shook his head. "No. Any fool can see you're FBI. Go look in a mirror—but maybe you'll need to put on your sunglasses first. You steamroll a fine police officer for no damn reason, so I figure you're just the muscle for someone with a brain."

The man in black glared. Gary met the look but couldn't see behind the eyes. "Wait here a minute," Thompson said.

"Thanks for making it sound like a request. I won't touch the phone to call for my lawyers till I meet the other guy."

Thompson backed out and closed the door. Gary tried to slow his hammering heart. He noted the blinking phone console, the computer screen-saver with the gray cell bars sliding left to right, and wondered if Becca had eaten breakfast. He almost phoned to ask her to stay away from the windows and not open the door. If something he'd seen Tuesday night lit up the Thompsons of the world, it

71

frightened him.

Twenty minutes to be driven back and forth and maybe twenty more for Vincent to chew Gary out, Becca figured as she entered the kitchen. Would Vincent be right to dump on him? She didn't think so. She considered what Gary had done to locate the Subaru and knew she'd have tried to do the same thing. He was clever. She had a lot to learn.

Poor guy wouldn't be back until 10:15 at the earliest. Probably out of sorts. Who wouldn't be? She'd wait breakfast—it'd be brunch by then—but maybe she'd have a little something now. Eggs and milk were in the refrigerator, hot and cold cereal in the pantry. She'd already put up water for tea.

The doorbell rang.

CHAPTER 14
9:47 A.M., Thursday

THE loud noise startled Ryan Scully. His hands flew up; he backed
away from the motion above him and bumped against a car to one
side of the cavernous entry. The jangling stopped when the steel door
to the abandoned parking garage smacked down, blotting out early-
morning sunlight that had been pouring in from the Manhattan
street. For a moment, Scully and Lucas Matin were blinded, even in
the dim wash of fluorescents widely spaced along the garage ceiling.

They'd entered the building together and, before the door started
down, Matin had stepped to the right, pressed a button, and flipped
a lever. Now he pointed to the wall. "Switches for door and lights."

Scully blinked until his eyes adjusted. He'd begun sweating during the walk, and as he looked around, he unzipped his blue jacket.
The controls were set close together, shoulder high. He noted that
there were two metal front doors. The bus would fit through the
one they'd used; the other had jumped its tracks and looked as if it
hadn't worked in years.

On the floor by the wall with the controls, stripes marked spaces
for six vehicles to parallel park, but there were only three. Two sad-
looking cars were resting nose-to-tail, with a gray file cabinet standing in front of them. Beyond that, furthest from the doors, he saw a
damaged van with flat tires. Grime covered the vehicles, though the
top of the steel cabinet was clean.

"What's with the file cabinet?" Scully asked.

"For a bosses' cousin—must've decided against it."

"And what are these?" Scully waved at the vehicles.

"Junk, found 'em below, brought 'em up to dump. They cleared
the lower level. Got light, heat, and room down there to store mate-
rials before they blow the place." Matin moved back into the garage.

Scully followed.

The stale air smelled damp and chilled him, so Scully closed his jacket. Doors to the office Matin had described earlier, the bathroom, and the elevator—for people, not cars—were on the wall ahead. To the left of that wall, the space curved into a down ramp. With his weight, Scully hated walking stairs and ramps. The diet he'd promised his wife that he would follow rested on two sheets of paper in the top left hand desk drawer in his business office. Ale at Connolly's was the more powerful lure.

Both men descended the ramp, turned right past a round concrete pillar, and the larger space opened up before them. It smelled musty. A few steps into the room, gasoline odor took charge.

"Like I said, it's perfect for you." Matin swept his right arm around the lower deck of the old parking garage. They faced the empty, vault-like space and his voice echoed off bare concrete walls. Even with lights, darkness curled from the corners and lurked behind regularly spaced columns bulging from both side walls. At the back, a pool of oily liquid glistened on the floor.

Scully knew Matin wanted the payoff he'd offered. Six thousand dollars in tax-free cash meant a lot to a low-level executive charged with managing shut down properties slated for demolition. But knocking down the vacant building to make room for the next office tower might be months off. In the meantime, though the sign in front had been dimmed forever, utilities remained on. The small main-level office had a desk, a few chairs, and a lamp. He'd been told the bathroom and elevator both functioned, and he'd been shown that the roll-down door worked, if loudly. First thing, he'd try to disconnect the damn alarm. OSHA wouldn't be visiting.

"Yeah, it looks good," Scully said. The bus would fit, ride down the ramp, and rest in this subterranean space with room to spare. The boys would come in after breakfast, carrying lunch, and the front door need only be opened two, three times a day. Down here, surrounded by structural concrete, any noise they'd make would never reach the street. The building had no tenants to complain.

Scully's hands were already cold, fingers stiff; the air had a meat-locker quality. He glanced around and shuddered. Frozen, dark, silent—this is what a crypt must feel like. For an instant he imagined…he didn't want his boys getting sick because they'd spend time here. He peered up and saw two heaters against the back wall just below the ceiling.

"Need to check a few things first," he said to Matin. "Turn on the heat, flush the toilet, test the elevator. Let's warm the place up so I'll know we can work here for the next five days."

Matin hesitated. "Heat works good, but it costs money."

"Well, then," Scully said, turning away, "you walk me out, I'll thank you and go."

"No, no. I meant—okay, I show you how to fire it up." Scully saw another concern cross Matin's face. "I can't lose my *job*. You sure—?"

"Denny Fovarque told me your company's inspecting this space on the twentieth, is it?"

Matin took a deep breath and nodded. "Mr. Ambrose said. Every week or so they inspect. He don't want surprises."

"You know Denny." Scully smiled. "He and I go way back. He vouched for me, didn't he?"

Matin nodded again.

"So I know not to damage anything. We'll be gone in five days—maybe three. We're fixing a vehicle here is all." He'd never told Matin the vehicle would be a bus. "Two of us'll work here. We'll keep the door closed and clean up good before we leave. You can check the space, oh, the afternoon of the eighteenth. That work for you?"

"Okay," Matin said, nodding vigorously.

Scully imagined dollar signs floating in the man's head. "For our time here you give us privacy, right?"

The manager stiffened. "Gotta stop in to make sure—"

"You don't gotta," Scully said.

"Only be me. You can't—"

Scully pointed a hand at him, fingers extended like he held a gun. He knew the look in his eyes and the tone of his voice were different. "We'll do any damn thing we want as long as we turn it back to you clean and on time. You agree to this, you stay clear until Tuesday afternoon."

Matin stared at Scully's hand, his face a mask of confusion. No point in frightening the man off, Scully thought. He shifted the hand into a coat pocket. The manager's eyes widened for an instant before Scully pulled out a wad of bills. Matin sighed and nodded.

Scully held out the cash and reached for the keys with his other hand. But once he had them, he pulled back the money. "Heat, bathroom, elevator—then you get part of it."

Matin's expression showed concern, but he nodded.

Once again Scully peered around the gloomy chamber. A chill crawled through the soles of his shoes, climbed his spine, and told him to get out, right now.

But he couldn't. Before he left the metal shop to come here, he'd spoken to his youngest son. Two hours from now, Scully would open the door and Frank would drive in the bus. The garage needed to be warm. The boy had a cold. This month, everyone had something.

CHAPTER 15
9:51 A.M., Thursday

In his zipped-up jacket, Gary had begun to sweat. As he opened it, Alegretti's office door swung in. A small man entered and carefully, without making a sound, closed the door behind him, slipped into a facing chair, and offered a slight smile that looked more sad than smug.

Gary glanced back. This must be the CIA agent. The fellow didn't look the part. His shirt had a yellow hue, and he wore a solid brown tie too wide to be in style, though it went well with his tan-and-brown tweed sport coat. A pipe stem stuck out of a side pocket, pushing up the flap. He seemed like a befuddled grand-father, his appearance so disarming that Gary wondered if he'd ever been—or still was—the perfect killer.

He nodded. "Yes, I am with the CIA," he said. "And I apologize for—"

"Your bully-boy."

The man's eyes glimmered. "Don't tell him, but his nickname is 'Thor.' He can be nasty even to me. But I'm near mandatory retirement age, and I suspect they feel I need a keeper. I don't believe he cares for the assignment."

"He told you what went on in here and you told him to keep out, you'd handle it, that what happened?" Handle me, Gary meant.

A bemused expression beamed from the agent. "Something like that."

"So you're in charge. Why am I here?"

"Shall I deal first with your assumption or your question?"

A fussy quality, Gary thought. "Whichever."

"Then, while I hold senior rank, Special Agent Thompson—that's his real name, by the way—is in charge. Simply because within the

United States, our charter limits me to analyst functions." With a slight curl of his mouth and eyes, the grandfatherly look turned venomous.

"You're *not* an analyst?"

The agent smiled. Dimples showing, he said, "Hardly, though I haven't shot anyone in years. Soon I get my little pension, and then I can start a flower garden."

Gary breathed in. If that had been a joke, it'd failed. A threat? "I didn't kill the Dawud kid—or anyone. Why am I here?"

The agent nodded. "I can tell you that your country needs your help. I do not expect that you, or your wife, will be exposed to danger as a result. Before I can say anything else, though, you'll need to sign some documents."

"Documents?"

The agent sat back in the seat, placed both arms on the rests and crossed his ankles. "You were a naval officer for three years back in the late '60s, on destroyers. Excellent job performance, but we gather you spoke your mind—were almost charged with insubordination. Judging from the integrity you demonstrated in your business career, your skill as a crisis consultant, a certain bravery while working with the police on at least two cases, we have no qualms about trusting you."

The extent of such knowledge on short notice gave Gary pause. The "we" implied some vast government bureaucracy.

"We know why you don't care for guns and why you're protective of your wife. Of course we've interviewed Alegretti—he spoke highly of you, and since I checked on him also, I do respect the man. Thompson had his way, and you showed loyalty to a friend when you beat him back. I've rarely seen him retreat." He paused. "Don't look so surprised. Wouldn't you expect at *least* this from those charged with defending your country?"

"What's your name?" Gary asked.

The man put thumbs to his cheeks. "We don't use real names. Those I work with call me Moriarty. Should you have reason to contact me, use that."

The name fit, but Gary wouldn't explore the irony. He knew something about the Agency. "You work for the Directorate of

Operations, don't you?"

Moriarty took his arms off the rests and bent towards him with a twinkle in his eye. "Yes."

"What'd you find in that house?"

"Traces of a military weapon. Plastic explosive." Without a smile, Moriarty added, "But Alegretti has already told you that."

Gary wanted out. "I've passed along everything I know to the lieutenant. I'm sure he'll cooperate with you, if not Thompson. I'm outta here."

The agent frowned for the first time, lifted his left arm, pushed back the coat sleeve, and glanced at his watch. He lowered the arm and looked up purposefully. "I want you to understand...you've become involved in a serious national security situation. That an accident caused the involvement makes it no less serious—and you no less useful to us. Your security clearance has lapsed. We must renew it. Then we can explain—and then you must keep it secret, even from the lieutenant."

"A *security* clearance?"

Moriarty nodded. "It's so much easier abroad. We would prefer that you agree to help us without being difficult."

That froze Gary. They wanted something. He peered across at the agent.

Moriarty chuckled. "Perhaps the best way I can gain your undivided attention is to tell you that your wife is no longer at home. We have taken her somewhere where she'll be safe."

CHAPTER 16
10:05 A.M., Thursday

CRADLING the crate of flowers, the deliveryman wrestled it out onto the lift. He'd tried to pull the refrigerated truck to the curb, but double-parking on Stewart Avenue, in front of Field's Florists, was as close as he could get to the shop.

Bright sunlight cheered the chilly morning in Garden City, a village in Nassau County, New York, nine miles from JFK International Airport. Forty-eight hours after Tuesday's intense storm, dirt had speckled the snow that remained on lawns and wherever plows and shovels had piled it.

Carlos Arrington, wearing the florist's green jacket, with the logo, stood behind the truck, squeezed his bushy brows together, and peered at the shipping container. Absentmindedly, he ran a hand through his curly hair, took the form the driver handed him, and used the box as a support to sign the receipt.

"Where you want it?" the driver asked.

Just then a patrol car eased up close beside the truck. Both men turned as the unit's passenger side window slid down, a view of the scowling officer replacing reflected snow glare. Arrington pointed at the container and held up a finger.

"What'cha got?" growled the cop.

Arrington knew that the officer's presence shouldn't jangle his nerves. Double-parking had to be the policeman's concern. But he'd asked about the crate—the curly-haired man's right hand moved, and he said nothing. The trucker saved him.

"Box of flowers," the deliveryman responded, pointing to the crate. "I turn it over and I'm outta here."

"Five minutes," the cop said.

The trucker waved at the row of cars along the curb. "No way I could've—" He stopped talking as the window slid up.

The patrol car pulled away and Arrington let go of the automatic holstered under his coat. "We don't need you to cart it in —just set it on the dolly," he said to the driver.

"Sure." The man wrapped his arms around the crate and leaned back to hoist it. He lifted it easily despite gray hair and what looked like a beer belly.

"Careful," Arrington said with a laugh. "Don't piss off the fancy flowers."

The man grinned, walked it over to the padded dolly on the curb, and set it down.

"Thanks," Arrington said.

The driver straightened, slowly rotated his back with his hands on his hips, and flexed his fingers. "Hoisting isn't easy, 'specially when it's cold." He took the form Arrington held out, tore off a copy and peered at it before handing it back. "Pre-paid, huh?"

"Guess so. The boss must know why. He's off today."

The man shrugged and jammed his copies into a coat pocket. "If that cop's hassling double-parkers, he won't have time for donuts. Glad there's no more snow forecast."

"Me, too. Thanks again." Arrington stepped onto the sidewalk and reached for the dolly rope.

"These special?" the driver asked, nodding toward the box.

His interest surprised Arrington, who turned back, hoping the man who watched from inside the shop wouldn't come out. "What you mean?"

"Never delivered such a large container here before."

Arrington smiled. "Look for 'em in the window tomorrow—these are beauties." He glanced at the sky. "Sure hope it doesn't snow. Weddings, company year-end parties, sweet sixteens—these flowers are expensive suckers. Gotta sell as many as we can, and quick." He snickered. "I think the Christmas Season's gone to the boss's head."

The driver nodded, pulled down the truck's rear door, and ambled off around the vehicle. Arrington waited until it rumbled away. Leaning backward, one hand on the dolly strap and the other guiding the crate, he pulled it into the alley beside the store and around to the rear. He'd left the door open, but the man inside must have locked it. After he used the key, he tried to get the dolly up the two steps. The container almost slid off. Alone, he couldn't manage it. He bent into the dark shop and called, "Siddiq!"

Hearing his name annoyed the small man who had watched the delivery from the darkness inside. This trip, he'd taken the alias Khalid Bukhari. Since he'd been seen at the accident, he'd shaved his head and begun to wear a pair of wire-rimmed glasses. That should be sufficient. The Americans would not be expecting him. To them, Abdel Siddiq was dead.

Working to hold in his anger, he moved back through the shop to join the curly-haired man in the green jacket. "I put the 'closed' sign out front," Siddiq said. "Get on your"—he paused until Arrington looked up at him—"your *gloves*, Ma-li-k." He pronounced the name with three syllables. "And from now on, use my correct name."

He saw the agent flinch. The man always looked like he needed a shave—Siddiq knew the outwardly rugged appearance did not extend inside. The reminder would be sufficient. Malik Aziz had taken the name Carlos Arrington while he lived in the United States, and for good reason.

"Sorry." Arrington pulled out a pair of white latex gloves like the ones Siddiq already wore. "Help me with the box."

Siddiq grasped the crate as soon as Arrington put on the gloves. The two of them lifted it and, once clear of the steps, Arrington slid it across the smooth wooden floor on its shrink-wrap. Siddiq carried in the dolly, double-locked the back door, and checked that the window shades were drawn tight. They kept the lights off. Sunlight, and snow-glare filtering in through the large front window, would be enough.

"Is your trip here gonna make trouble for me?" Arrington asked as he pushed the container close to the wooden table along the side wall opposite the walk-in refrigerator. They stood in a rear area narrowed by work counters, a desk, and two brown, steel file cabinets. Binders showing floral arrangements were stacked closer to the customer floor, where glass panels offered views of the chilled flowers.

Siddiq considered the question while he used snips on the plastic banding. The ties sprang free and skittered to the floor. "Why would

I do that?"

"You show up, people die."

Siddiq couldn't keep disapproval from his tone. "Would the deaths of Americans offend you?"

Arrington took a half step back and leaned against the table. "Look, I do what I'm asked. It's dangerous, and I do it well. I'm supposed to fit in. You stir them up, make them hate Muslims, you know that's gonna make it more difficult for me."

Siddiq held Arrington's eyes and grasped a short, sharp knife from the countertop. He saw the agent shrink back. Forcing himself not to smile, he used the weapon to slice carefully through the shrink-wrap and completely around the top shell of the box.

"We win," he said, "the day America understands it is not invincible—it cannot dictate policy to our part of the world." He pointed to the open box. "Help me now."

Working together, they extracted from the crate, one at a time, the three foam trays that contained the flowers. They set the trays side by side on the long wooden table, and Siddiq peeled away the protective bubble wrap. The flowers had been packed by color: red and purple, yellow and orange, and white, some trumpet-shaped, all with graceful petals and vivid green stalks. The shop smelled of ripe greens, though the waxy blooms in the foam gave off little odor.

"You think bombs will make them understand?" Arrington asked, eyes on the flowers.

Living here turned men soft, Siddiq thought, and he would not answer. He smiled at his companion and handed him the knife, handle-first. Arrington cut the banding into sections, folded the shrink-wrap, sliced the entire corrugated square into pieces, and slipped everything into a black plastic garbage bag.

While he did that, Siddiq transferred the flowers into vases, set them in the refrigerator, and added water, using the florist's small hose. The flowers would repay the owner for the day's missed business.

Siddiq rubbed his pointed, silvery belt for luck and set about prying off the glued-on top layer of the first of the foam dividers that had journeyed around the globe.

"Your lucky charm?" Arrington asked.

Siddiq peeled back the foam, uncovering hollowed out sections. "The belt stands for my coming of age," he said, as he pulled out the first U.S. military-issue M-112 explosive block, commonly called C-4, and laid it, backing-side down, on the wooden table. It looked like white modeling clay. It yielded to the touch and smelled right. It pleased him.

"Where does it come from?" Arrington asked.

Siddiq considered before answering. "Iraq. It's a wonderful war."

Arrington spoke again as Siddiq extracted the second half-kilo block. "You have a reputation for leaving no one behind. I'll die for our beliefs—I've proven that—but not just because we've crossed paths."

Siddiq placed the second block beside the first and reached in for the next. He knew that Arrington had friends, a good reputation, and children. "You think I would kill *you?*" he asked.

Arrington didn't answer.

Without slowing his progress, Siddiq declared, "On Allah, I will not kill you. But I have someone I need you to kill for me." The way it would be set up, the Americans would put Arrington down. Siddiq knew the man would not let himself be captured alive, sent abroad, forced to betray the cause.

Arrington looked relieved. "That's part of my job."

Siddiq worked quietly until he'd set all sixteen blocks on the table. He folded bubble wrap around each and transferred them into the two bags he'd brought along. The computer bag would hang over his shoulder. He'd carry the fashionable attaché case in his left hand. Eight blocks of C-4, less than nine pounds total, went into each.

Before he finished, Arrington had cut up the foam inserts and added them into the garbage bag. "Which would you like me to carry?" he asked, nodding toward the cases.

Siddiq smiled; most of those he worked with did not care to handle explosives. "These are both mine. You tie the garbage and toss it into the dumpster."

When the waste disposal truck emptied the trash container the following morning, all traces of the shipping carton would vanish, and the flowers would soon be sold or destroyed. Nothing would be left to track.

"You have time for lunch?" Arrington asked as he slipped off the green jacket, hung it on a hook along the back wall, and pulled on his own heavier coat, a darker shade of green.

Siddiq understood how the lure of normal life—living with a woman, dining at restaurants, counting on tomorrow—could change a man. Once, all that might have changed him. This trip, though, he had a personal score to settle in addition to the bombing.

"I must be at a funeral," he said. "Drive me back to the Garden City station."

Whether because of Siddiq's rejection of lunch or mention of a funeral, those words ended the conversation. That pleased Siddiq.

Earlier, Arrington had picked him up at the same Long Island Railroad stop. Siddiq would not bring a vehicle for the agent to identify. He could have arrived in a cab, but that would have left a trail. He decided to follow his arrival procedure in reverse: ticket to the Jamaica station, then onto the silvery westbound train. He'd sit quietly as it stopped at its next station, Nassau Boulevard. But five minutes after he climbed aboard, at the second stop, Stewart Manor, he'd leave the train to reclaim the van. He'd left it on a suburban street at the curb. He knew how to spot anyone following him on foot or in a vehicle.

He'd remain invisible to Arrington—but the man would be ready when Siddiq called. Arrington would ensure Dwyer's death. The bomb blast might eliminate Arrington as well. Siddiq would be blameless in the event they needed to use the Irish again.

CHAPTER 17
10:14 A.M., Thursday

IF the CIA and FBI had mistreated Becca, Gary decided, they could stuff their demands up their asses. It turned out that she'd been taken to the Alegrettis, the step precautionary, not punitive, Moriarty explained. She'd been told her husband was being questioned and wanted to be sure of her safety until he returned. The agent promptly agreed to Gary's demand that he speak with her.

"What's going on?" she asked.

Gary saw Thompson slip back into Vincent's office. He knew mentioning the agencies would alarm her, and he still had no idea why they'd brought him here. "I wanted to check in, let you know I'm fine, and that I'll be home in—" he glanced at both men— "about an hour."

"Vincent needs to question you *again*? Has something new come up?"

"I'll clue you in when I get home." She'd insist on full disclosure later, and he would tell her everything, even if they swore him to secrecy. They knew so much about him—didn't they know that, too?

When he replaced the receiver, Moriarty said, "We didn't want to upset her. Making use of your friendship with Lieutenant Alegretti seemed a best intermediate course."

"Intermediate?"

"Depending upon what we uncover together and what we decide to do about it."

Gary turned on Thompson. "You must've arranged her move with the lieutenant—he cooperated and you still treated him like shit."

"He can take it."

"Thompson," Moriarty said softly, and the FBI man's head

twisted toward him. For a moment, Gary thought there'd be a fight. Then Thompson sat back, balanced the black computer on his knees and opened it.

No warm up needed, Gary saw.

Moriarty spoke as if the prior exchanges hadn't taken place. "We'll show you four faces on the monitor. If he's there, point to the man you remember—the one who hit you Tuesday night. Be sure, please, before you make a selection. It would be better not to decide than to choose incorrectly."

The screen reminded Gary of the lineups on crime shows. Four impersonal, similar faces looked back at him in high definition. Only one gave him chills. "Bottom left."

At Thompson's touch, the face he'd seen standing on the snowy corner filled the computer screen. It looked crueler than he remembered. The eyes in the image flashed anger, not shock. For a moment the view remained frozen; at the touch of a key it animated, became a video clip, a close-up of the face, without sound, repeated on a loop. It showed the man turning toward the viewer and speaking to someone who must have upset him. Each segment lasted a few seconds—long enough.

"It's him." Since breakfast the day before, Gary had been re-running the event in his mind, trying to make sense of it. Moriarty's expression revealed nothing, but Gary saw a glimmer in his eyes.

"Shall we try to identify the belt worn by the man who hit you?" the CIA agent asked. "You described it in considerable detail during your interview with the police."

Had his recollection of a belt brought these people? Gary wondered.

Thompson moved a hammy finger and four very similar men's belts appeared, again in boxes on a quartered screen. They were not props. Though most everything around the belts had been cropped out, each displayed the proper shade of brown leather, with silver worked in, and each appeared to have been holding up trousers when it was photographed.

"Is the belt important?" Gary asked.

"Well, it may come down to vanity," Moriarty said. "The man took it from an Israeli agent, and he's worn it ever since. He might change hairstyle or eye color, wear glasses, pin his ears back or grow a mustache, but we're betting he keeps the belt. Take a look and tell us what you recall."

The words set off alarm bells in Gary's head. He cleared his mind and blinked at the screen, examining each belt in turn. One appeared too wide. A second had the wrong buckle. The other two might be right. When he focused on the distinctive ends, he recognized it at once. He reached out and pointed at the bottom right image. Thompson touched a button and the screen faded to black.

"Most interesting," Moriarty said, eyes on Gary.

Thompson closed the computer.

"What is?" Gary asked.

The agent pulled the pipe from his pocket and rubbed at the bowl. Gary knew the building did not permit smoking. Would he light up anyway?

"The man you identified is dead," Moriarty said.

Both agents studied Gary, who frowned and considered it. "His double wasn't on Tuesday night."

Moriarty smiled at the response. "He is officially dead. Our people were shown what the bombs did to the suspected training camp. We were provided with items that contained the man's DNA, and in subsequent contact, others from his group confirmed his absence."

"If I hadn't come up with the belt, you wouldn't know he's alive, that it?" Gary asked.

Moriarty nodded.

"Who *is* this guy?"

"You don't need to know," Thompson said.

Gary swiveled toward him but held his tongue. Nothing would get this bastard talking. He turned back. "Why's he here?"

Moriarty waved the pipe. "We—"

"Personal business." Thompson barked, sounding angry, and glared at his colleague.

"You have no call—"

"Can the crap."

The CIA agent's mouth closed in an angry line. So Gary answered for him. "Came here to do Christmas shopping, huh?"

"You know nothing," Thompson shot back.

Okay. He'd done what they'd asked. No way he'd volunteer any-thing further. He considered Vincent, smoldering somewhere out-side, and Becca, dragged off under false pretenses. These people did not respect normal life any more than the man who slugged him.

He turned to Moriarty. "He's right. I know nothing and I have nothing else to offer. I'll go to the boy's funeral and be done with this. Now that I've identified your terrorist, there's no reason for him to bother my family."

Moriarty glanced longingly at the pipe. "But that man does not know we've identified him. He may still believe you're the only one who can do that." He glanced at Thompson before adding, "The man has not been kind to those who've crossed his path."

Gary knew Tony and Rashid might very well know the shooter. But he said nothing, although his silence troubled him. Moriarty brushed the pipe stem against his lips. Gary saw the small smile, but Thompson spoke first.

"Why'd you meet with Haroun Rashid and Talal Siddiq?"

Gary believed he'd disappointed Thompson because the question hadn't taken him by surprise. "Rashid met us at the Dawuds' last night when we paid a condolence call. If you've been following me, you know that. This morning he and Tony provided details so I can attend the boy's funeral—I did witness the accident. If I'd known you were interested, I'd have invited you to my home along with them. Maybe if we served you coffee you wouldn't growl at me all the time. You want, I'll give you travel directions to the cemetery."

He thought that was it until Thompson frowned. Gary waved a finger at the agent. "Why'd you ask me that?"

Moriarty answered. "We weren't following you. The man you identified, and the one you call Tony, have a connection."

No news in that. He wondered if he'd better seem surprised.

Thompson interrupted, again with a demand. "Are you going to the funeral strictly as a mourner?"

Gary didn't react. "The death has to be devastating for the Dawuds. Either of you have children?"

"No children," said Moriarty. "No wife either. Married, yes, but she died." He smiled at Gary. "I hear you know about such things." Then he turned to Thompson. "I can plant roses in my little garden, all alone."

The agent did need a keeper, Gary thought. He couldn't help asking, "Cancer?"

"Hardly," Moriarty said, his expression set in stone, the killer loose in his eyes.

"I hope I've been helpful. My wife and I will keep our heads down and take our chances."

Moriarty pointed the pipe, pinning him. "You can recognize him. We would appreciate further help."

This is getting nowhere, Gary concluded. "You have him on video. You don't need me. I'll be at the funeral this afternoon, and then I want our lives back. When I leave here, I want to pick up Becca, go home, and forget about this. I've given you what you wanted."

Moriarty lowered the pipe and nodded. "Thank you for that. We'll contact you only if we need to. You're likely right. They shouldn't bother you." He fumbled in a pocket and withdrew a card. "But if you think of anything else or need help, please call. Here's the number. You know the name."

Gary saw that the card held only a phone number.

"My card too," Thompson said. When Gary hesitated, Thompson shoved it at him.

The sly smile returned to Moriarty's face. "How long do you think it will be before you *have* to call?"

The tone chilled him. "Why would I need to?"

The agent lowered the pipe and tilted his head. "If he doesn't come to you, I suspect you'll try to go to him. Unwise, but we are all captive to our urges."

Gary didn't respond. He got up. His concern wouldn't keep him from the funeral but it would make him more careful.

Thompson closed the door behind him the moment he left Vincent's office. At Reception, Gary inquired after the lieutenant, who couldn't, however, be found. A different patrolman drove Gary back to his house. After the unit pulled away, he went up the block and around the corner to the Alegrettis. Vincent wouldn't be there. Becca and Angela were chatting. Neither had gotten wind of the events at the station.

He'd bring Becca up to date at home. On the walk back, he could feel her tension. She kept glancing around, worried that every passing car might contain a shooter. He stayed on her street side. Twice she grasped his shoulder. He explained that the police believed they were out of danger and didn't need protection, though he suspected they'd been bumped up from uniformed guardians to a whole different level.

He listened to her with half an ear while he scanned for a tail. Because he didn't spot one didn't mean they weren't being watched. By whom? he wondered.

CHAPTER 18
10:21 A.M., Thursday

THOMPSON let go of the police building's front door, breathed deeply, and cold air chilled his lungs. After the clammy station, it felt good. The door squeaked behind him as he watched Moriarty descend the few steps. He followed, salt crunching beneath his shoes. Before he could catch up, Moriarty turned on him.

"You behaved rashly," the man said.

Thompson had thought *he* was the angry one. "Not here."

Moriarty eyed the looming police station, turned and strode away. When Thompson came alongside, the small man spoke without looking at him. "Kemmerman's history is interesting—he might have been helpful."

Always the professor, Thompson thought, as snow forced its way into his shoes. "Still will be."

Without breaking stride, Moriarty re-tied the loose belt on his stylish brown coat. "You beat up on him and Alegretti only because you're angry with me."

"Son of a *bitch!*" Thompson ground his teeth and glanced around, wanting to be sure no one was watching. He picked up the pace, forcing the small man to catch up. In the morning chill, their breath steamed. "Rose garden, dead wife—you're so damn bitter that all Kemmerman wants is get away from you."

Moriarty chuckled, dimples showing. "From you, too."

They stopped between their vehicles at the back of the parking lot that served the municipal building, the library, and the police station. When they drove in, they'd pulled up side-by-side to the left of a mound of snow shoveled from the asphalt, where they couldn't be seen from police building windows.

"You set up this operation—*and* the session with Kemmerman,"

Thompson said, working to keep his voice low. "It's nonsense. Goddamn belt could be different, anyone could be wearing it. At night, in a snowstorm, a run-over kid in front of him and headlights in his eyes, an old guy IDs a dead man and his clothing. Hell, even Siddiq's local relatives—the man's a *cop*, for Christ's sake—haven't heard from him in decades." Thompson peered at Moriarity and saw that he hadn't gotten through. "Why'd you do this?"

Moriarty pulled fawn-colored leather gloves from a pocket and smoothed them in his hands as he considered the question. Eyes on the gloves, he said, "Abdel Siddiq."

Thompson glared. Moriarty had arrived in a hunter green MG that the CIA definitely had not provided. The clothes, his car, the hotels and restaurants he spoke of—his tastes had become expensive, as if he couldn't spend money fast enough. Thompson breathed in, shook his head, and released the air explosively. "I know they told you."

Moriarty smiled, the picture of civility. "As you can imagine, they made it quite clear. They said, 'Frank, we believe he killed your wife, but we'd prefer you ignore that small detail.'"

Thompson didn't care how he sounded. "You find him, report in but stay the hell away from him. That's what I heard they told you. If he's here, he's *mine*."

"I understood my CIA brethren, and I hear you." Moriarty brushed something off the front of his coat.

Thompson wondered if Moriarty had made a reflexive motion, if at some level the man had gone for his gun. He shouldn't be carrying, but Thompson bet he was. The thought sobered him.

"Look, even if he's here, which I doubt, the rest's bullshit. He lost his family, too. You of all people damn well know that—and what it means."

Moriarty shot him a venomous look but did not speak.

Thompson went on, "Siddiq's probably lonely, wants to visit what family he has left. If he's here, the crap his people tried to sell us must have been so he could get in and out without being picked up." A burst of wind blew into the neck of his coat, and he turned up the collar.

"No way he knows you've come up from DC," Thompson

94

continued. "As for the trace of C-4 in the house, what links it to him? You'd expect him to use safe houses. With those guys, the bit of plastique could have fallen out of a pocket."

Moriarty listened without moving. At least he's paying attention, Thompson thought. "My office is so stretched, they tell me if we need help we'd better have a gold-plated reason. They don't believe it either."

Moriarty's mouth pursed as if he were smoking a pipe. Thompson heard the whine of vehicles on a distant highway. When the small man spoke, he stretched the words. "You'd prefer that answer. But what happened to Kemmerman supports my theory."

"Hell of a family visit Siddiq would have if we spot him." Thompson wondered, if the man were Siddiq, had he made a mistake by shooting at Kemmerman—or by missing him? Mistakes were most unlike Siddiq.

"We *have* spotted him." Moriarty slapped the gloves into his other palm.

"*If* he's alive, he'll probably surface in Syria next month," Thompson said. "Only so much family a guy can take."

"But we'll cover the family?"

Thompson didn't need to answer.

Moriarty pursed his lips again and tilted his head before he spoke. "It must be most annoying, being pulled off a real case to baby-sit me."

"Damn right. We make new hundred dollar bills, so do Iran and North Korea. Got others tracking the networks while I'm on this crap."

Moriarty shifted his feet—his bulky calfskin shoes hadn't seemed to get wet—and nodded as if he'd reached a decision. "Let's get to the bottom of this, so you can get back to your money trail."

Thompson smelled the bait. "Long as you stay away from Siddiq."

Moriarty nodded again. "I expect that, if we spot him, we will be together. For now, I suggest that you attend this afternoon's funeral with Kemmerman. Who knows which players may show up?" He slipped his hands into the gloves and drew car keys from a pocket.

"Siddiq hates you," Thompson said. "If he sees you all bets are off, and a cemetery doesn't have much cover. Easy for you to give up that risk."

"Should he recognize Kemmerman, I might say the same."

Thompson laughed. "Siddiq's Muslim—he knows he's not supposed to shoot during a funeral."

Moriarty shook his head.

"What will you be doing while I'm touring the cemetery?" Thompson asked.

Moriarty glanced down at the car keys. "Siddiq's specialties are explosives, Syrian Government officials, Italian splinter groups, and the IRA. I'll roust what contacts I have among the Irish."

Thompson knocked snow off a shoe and found a clear spot for his foot. "Got a hunch?"

"A top Irish operative—one of the few not willing to compromise—is also said to be loose in New York. Explosives, Siddiq, and that guy in the same mix *might* be coincidental."

Thompson laughed. "Christmas shopping, Kemmerman pegged it. The IRA's scattered their top killers, trying to lower their profile."

Moriarty's hand moved as if it held the pipe. "Have you anything else for me to do? If I can't do my job, I can always get a head start on nursery catalogs for the garden."

"Christ, Moriarty. Look, okay, that's what you want to do, fine." Thompson reached into his left coat pocket and pulled out a glove. "You've always been straight with me. So tell me how that gets you—or us—closer to Siddiq."

Moriarty chuckled. "Your girlfriend is a great cook, Jeff. You're a lucky man."

"Glad you enjoyed the meal. She did, too. You're a charmer. She thought you were off duty. But for now your business is mine, and it ain't what I want, either."

The smaller man tilted his head. "If Siddiq's involved with the Irish, my guess is they'll come together at some point. I want to be waiting. With you, of course."

"Great," said Thompson. "I'll need to watch out for *you*."

"It doesn't matter who gets him."

"You think Kemmerman told the truth?"

"About the identification, yes."

Thompson pulled on his left glove and fumbled in a pocket for the other. "Clever, the way he found the car and house. He has issues with Siddiq, too."

Moriarty started to speak but closed his mouth. He tossed the keys into the air, caught them without looking down. "Maybe you'll let me shoot. I won't tell anyone."

Thompson watched Moriarity fold himself into the low-slung driver's seat, wave, and putter off. He stepped toward his agency Ford but, minutes later, standing against the car with the cold sneaking up into his trousers, he still couldn't make himself open the door.

That's when he changed his mind, turned, and trudged back toward the police station. He had to use the bathroom, but he had another reason for returning.

CHAPTER 19
1:02 P.M., Thursday

MOMENTS after he heard Becca turn off the shower, Gary hesitated before the bathroom door. He wanted to ask her a question. But before he could knock, the knob turned and the door swung inward several inches. Had she sensed his approach? Light, steam, the smell of shampoo, and the sound of the radio flowed out. He peeked in. His wife, eyes closed, body wrapped in a giant bath towel, was vigorously rubbing her wet hair with a hand towel.

The Beatle's "Yesterday" played, and it added an emotional charge. Unobserved, he watched her, aware of how affected he'd become by the simplest domestic routines. After his late wife died, he'd been certain he'd never marry again, never find that nourishing emotional connection. He saw Becca tilt her head. Eyes still closed, something made her smile. He wouldn't put it past her to be reading his thoughts.

"Good to see you," he called over the music as he pushed the door further open.

She blinked, turned, and laughed when she saw that he wore briefs, a t-shirt, and a suit jacket.

"Does it fit?" he asked.

His old black suit would have to do for the boy's funeral. They had almost an hour before heading out to the cemetery. Earlier, after they got home from the Alegrettis', he'd told her everything that'd happened at the police station. If they were partners, she had to know.

Becca frowned at the jacket but nodded. Loosened by all the motion, the bath towel opened and slipped. She grasped it, waist high.

He stepped closer. "Yum!"

99

She slapped at his hand and restored the towel. "The jacket fits." She chuckled. "You might worry about the trousers."

"You know," he said, after retreating to the doorway, "we should go places more often. I mean, we hang around when we could share dinner out or an overnight at a country inn. Antiquing. Seeing a show. Tanglewood in the summer—you said you'd like that. We could make time. What say?"

Becca smiled. "Hold that thought until after holiday season traffic. Now, out. I have to get ready."

Minutes later, as he finished tying his black walking shoes, the hair dryer noise cut off from the bathroom. Almost at once, he heard the front doorbell.

"Can you get it?" she called through the door.

"Sure."

He found Vincent waiting on the stoop, with an expression that forced Gary back to the awful session in his office.

"Come in, Vinnie."

Alegretti moved past without a word. He unzipped his jacket but left it on and dropped onto the couch. Before he could speak, he had to turn away and cough into his hand.

"Where's Becca?" the lieutenant asked.

"Cold getting any better?"

"Since this morning? Come on. Where is she?"

"Upstairs, getting ready." He sat beside the lieutenant. "It upset me before, when—"

Vincent raised a hand to stop him. "She going with you?"

Angela must have told him, Gary thought. "Yeah—I can't drive—but she's supposed to stay in the car till I get back from the service." He wondered if Vincent would find that odd, but the man ignored it.

"You tell her what they told you at the station?"

Gary frowned. "Yeah. They said I couldn't tell you, but I will if you want. I don't owe them—"

The hand moved again, and Vincent shook his head. "Thompson came back after. We're square."

Gary frowned. "Why'd he do that?"

The lieutenant cleared his throat. "Because of you."

Gary threw up his hands. "I want out. Why does everyone keep folding me back in?"

Vincent squirmed. "Listen. In case you didn't get it, the man you identified is a terrorist—a killer. Thompson said the way this guy usually works, by the end of his operations he's left no one alive who's seen him—and that includes many of his own people." He turned away and cleared his throat. "Understand?"

Gary wondered if Vincent knew why he'd been asked to the boy's funeral. "…What operations?"

"Aside from the middle east, Thompson mentioned bombings in Germany, Italy, and Spain. Gary, do you and Becca *have* to go today? Thompson said that if the guy showed at the funeral, it wouldn't be because of you, but if you were there, he'd probably spot you. We'd both rather you stay clear."

Tempting, but he had to keep his promise. "Good. Have Thompson tag along. Now that he's being kind, he can save us."

"Kind—shit, no. He doesn't want you to *interfere*." Vincent breathed deeply, gave a small snort and shook his head. "I told him I'd warn you, but that you'd go anyway. He said to tell you he'd be there."

"Should I wave at the big guy, black suit, sunglasses, wearing a red carnation?"

Vincent rubbed his hands together. "It ain't funny. He's hoping the man shows. Don't acknowledge Thompson if your paths cross. You see guns or hear shots, drop, and fast. Make sure Becca's not in the line of fire. Don't get involved."

Gary leaned back against the armrest. "Becca won't even get out of the car. I'm hoping we pay our respects, drive home, and that's the end of it. Does that work for you?"

Vincent puffed his cheeks. "That's not why Thompson believes you're going. Between us, he's using you. He'll hang you out to dry for a shot at Siddiq."

"The man's name *Siddiq*? Like Tony Siddiq?"

"Lot of people with that name. I'm told this guy's first name's Abdel."

Whatever else Vincent knew, he wasn't about to say, and Gary moved on. "You meet the CIA guy?" The lieutenant nodded. "I picked up tension between the agents. That normal? I'll bet they dumped on both of us because of whatever's bothering them. You know what's going on?"

Vincent pursed his lips, which told Gary he did know, but the man shook his head again.

"You break the rules by telling me about guns and explosives but you won't talk about turf wars?"

"They don't tell me that shit." Vincent coughed. "My guess is—ah, who knows?"

They both turned at footsteps on the stairs. Becca descended, dressed in black, hair shiny. "Hi, Vincent. I hear you're sick, so—if you don't mind—I'll keep my distance. But I'll bet you do know the answer to Gary's question."

"You overheard?"

"The brush acted as a transmitter. I didn't mean to eavesdrop, but yes."

"Sorry I cursed. Angela hates when I do that at home." He turned to Gary. "Becca's just like Angela. From home, I swear she hears what I whisper at the station."

"And she tells it all to Becca," Gary added.

She laughed.

"In case you missed it," Vincent said to her, "the guy who hit Gary is bad medicine."

"Even so, we have to pay our respects," she said. "Then we'll try to forget all of it. But thank you for the warning." She frowned at a thought. "Did you visit just to ask us to be careful?"

"You heard what I said about not getting involved?"

She smiled. "I promise not to leave the car until we're back home. Unless the services take so long that we go out to eat afterward. Who has time to cook with this going on?"

Vincent nodded, rose, and headed toward the door. But then he turned back. "Becca, you sound like it excites you. Please, this is a game you don't want to play."

Like waving a red flag at a bull, Gary thought.

CHAPTER 20
1:25 P.M., Thursday

For the first time, Ryan Scully found himself wanting out. He couldn't lose the chill that'd come over him in the garage. Frank had pulled in the bus and nursed it down to the lower level. Thank God, by then, the space heaters had blunted the dankness everywhere but inside him.

Dwyer would be pleased. Why didn't *he* feel pleased?

Sitting at the wooden desk in his small office, paperwork for which he had little patience stacked in neat piles before him, he heard the punching machine's signature "whack, whack," and convinced himself that life was good.

Two of the boys were working and the shop vibrated. His sons were learning. The business had become profitable. He'd leave them well fixed and with a trade—more than his father had done for him. Distracted, he almost didn't hear Tommy yell through the cracked-open door, "Guy for you, Dad."

He looked up to ask what it was about when, without being invited, a grandfatherly looking man in a short brown coat stepped around the boy and through the doorway.

"Are you the one I see about an order?" he asked, in a voice too soft for the noise level.

Scully nodded to Tommy. It grew quieter as the young man left, pulling the door shut.

"What order?" Scully asked. His left hand moved to the open orders pile, ready to sort. They were pretty much up to date with what they'd promised. Besides, this man looked soft. Scully didn't foresee a problem.

The man pulled the lone chair closer to the desk and sat. "There is no benefit for either of us to my beating around the bush," he said.

"I will give you one chance and then we begin killing your sons, one at a time. The boy I've just met will be first."

Scully felt his face flush. For years, he'd been the one doing what this insignificant SOB had just done to him. The man's right hand idly stroked his coat, inches from the bulge where his gun must be.

"Get out!" Scully said, though he found he couldn't raise his voice.

The man went on speaking softly, as if he hadn't heard. "I represent a government agency charged with protecting Americans and authorized to kill to do that. You are a key IRA connection in New York. I can recite a list of your involvements going back thirty-eight years, first in Ireland and then here. I know why you had to leave the Emerald Isle, and I congratulate you on creating a successful business in New York.

"But what is important now is that an Irish operative has been sent here and been given considerable money to achieve his goal. I believe he has contacted you—or will.

"If you help us, we will never reveal your name and we will reward you with the money that man has brought. If you do not help us within two weeks, or if a terrorist action takes place before then, we will kill your children first, and then you and your wife. Tragic accidents. Acts of random violence. All the deaths will be ugly and painful.

"We'll be watching—you cannot hide from us. I am one of many. If you try to send your family away, they'll die." The man in brown paused, bent close, and whispered into the stillness. "Do you hear me?"

Scully nodded.

"If you tell the IRA man that we've contacted you—and we will eventually find out if you do—all six of you will die whether or not you've helped. Am I being clear?"

Numb, Scully nodded again.

"Well, then." The agent leaned back, set elbows on the chair arms, clasped his hands, and made himself comfortable.

Scully started his denial. "But I'm not—"

"No point," said the agent, flashing his palms, "in any more talk about it. The stage is set. Your actions will determine the fate of your family. Now we can discuss the order I may have for your business."

"How do I—"

Again, the agent cut him off. "It would be unhealthy to doubt my word."

Behind the desk, Scully deflated. Could this be real? Did they know Dwyer was in New York? He'd admitted to nothing, yet he'd been caught in a bind. What could he do?

"The Metropolitan Transportation Authority has a need for a small but steady quantity of punched, shaped, and welded stainless steel parts," the agent said. "Tight specifications. They will be used for door systems that keep failing. We understand you have the equipment to make such parts."

"I...yes," Scully said, finding it difficult to focus on ordinary details.

"Have you ever supplied the MTA?"

Scully shook his head.

"Would you like to? It could be a jump forward for your four sons."

Mention of the boys froze him.

The agent smiled in a way that terrified Scully. "We are past the difficult discussion," he said. "You are experienced, and it is time to shift targets and concentrate on your metal fabrication shop."

Scully tried to. "The business you mentioned—"

"A small reward," the agent said.

"How many pieces?" Scully found himself breathing deeply, hands flat on the desktop, feeling too old for this. "What are the specs?"

The door opened, flooding the space with noise. Tommy leaned into the office. "Sorry to interrupt. Girl now, Dad."

Scully gazed at his son.

"Strapping, handsome young man," the agent said, as if he'd read the Irishman's mind. "You'll leave them quite a business. Some of your machines are state of the art."

What didn't this man know?

"Says she only needs a minute," Tommy added, and Scully saw someone behind the boy.

"Be gracious, let her in," the agent said. "If I leave, I will call later regarding both matters. We can certainly proceed without delay with your submission for the MTA."

Scully nodded to Tommy, though the agent did not move. His son stepped aside and a woman entered. He remembered her from the evening before at Connolly's and tried to keep that off his face. She looked radiant, dark hair brushed shiny, the ends flipped. She wore—a look, a short black coat with large buttons over a dark green sweater, gray slacks, and low black boots.

Bargirl by night, model by day? he wondered, as he caught her eye, praying she wouldn't come out with anything stupid.

"Got time to go over Tuesday's order?" she asked.

He bit back relief and looked toward the agent, who'd glanced up at the girl. He doubted the man missed much, but the girl couldn't be in any agency files. Or could she?

"I can wait," the agent said.

"I dragged the technical expert along with me," she said to Scully. "He'll give what ya need." Then she batted her eyes at the agent. "It's confidential stuff, you understand, so—"

The small man looked at her with delight. "Perhaps we might talk outside while your expert deals with Mr. Scully?"

Scully couldn't warn her. Not warning her, he realized, began the lies.

She weighed his offer and smiled. "Of course." The agent got up, smiling back at her. "Let's be off," she said, and swung the door wider.

Scully watched them move together down the center aisle. Her posture was better than last night, though the sway was the same. They passed the press brake, power roll, other machines. Scully smelled burning metal, saw sparks. Concentrating anywhere but on that scene, he reviewed his accomplishments—the boys worked with aluminum, mild steel, and stainless. They made parts of all kinds, pans, chutes, frames, and ducts.

But what had been so solid minutes before began to shiver and lose its fine edges. His family, the business, each machine he'd scrimped to buy, the work he'd done for the cause, those he'd killed so long before, all of it vanished like an express train through fog. He focused on Dwyer coming the other way, walking the aisle toward him. Dwyer, the agent, and the girl, nodded a brief greeting in passing.

I haven't done anything wrong, Scully heard in his head—but as soon as Dwyer came in and sat down, unless he blurted it out, things could never be the same.

When Dwyer closed the office door, the quiet settled onto Scully's shoulders. He knew he had to provide the bus. "What brings you?" he asked. "We rushed. It'll be ready Saturday morning."

"Aren't you the busy one," Dwyer said, waving a hand at the activity beyond the office.

"Two boys here, two out doing your work."

"And a customer." Dwyer remained standing.

Did he know the agent? Scully wondered why God was giving him no quarter. "Man offers a way into supplying the MTA—maybe a big deal," he said.

"Been drinking this early?" Dwyer asked.

"No. Why?"

"You're flushed."

Scully smiled. "It's the girl. She's a looker. She with you?" He'd batted it back, but he bet Dwyer wouldn't tell him. Watching him consider the question, Scully wondered if Dwyer knew the answer.

"Bought her some clothes." Dwyer leaned against the back of the chair, tilted his head, and offered a faraway look. "Treated her like her parents, the world, should. Real, upbeat, a smart one—hard to find that."

Scully had never seen that look on Dwyer's face. "What you're doing—is it wise?"

"I trust her, Ryan. Can't say that about many."

Dwyer's words made him uncomfortable. "You're here. What is it that ya need?"

The man stood straight and gazed down, all business. "Do the baggage doors open on both sides of the bus?"

Scully nodded. "Thin steel spine in-between, for stability and to help hold up the floor above."

He shook his head. "Need that spine removed, and heavy steel plates fixed to the far left in all three luggage bays."

Scully knew why. "Flat? Standing up?"

"Standing inside the left-side baggage doors. Attached to the frame on the four ends with angle irons, or welds strong enough to push the first blast out the other way."

"Ah.... ." Scully slid his hands onto his lap, lacing fingers. A whine sounded outside; the boys were cutting something.

"You got steel thick enough?"

He focused when Dwyer asked it a second time. "Extra plates the city uses to cover road work. Take the weight of traffic. Got a plasma cutter to make 'em fit right."

"Can the bus take the added weight?"

For a moment, he considered. "It'll slant—but with no luggage and all those tires, it'll be fine."

Again, Dwyer leaned forward onto the back of the chair. "You use ball bearings?"

Scully exhaled, shoulders relaxing, hands flopping apart. He'd been alerted about Dwyer, but not plastique. This had to be very high profile. If the Americans were squeezing him, the threats must be everywhere. "What size, how many?"

"You can leave 'em on the bus for me?"

Scully nodded.

"Pea size, least a thousand." Dwyer smiled. "The fifty includes them, too, right?"

"Sure." Scully recalled the agent's words. "You brought in a pile to cover expenses, that it?"

Dwyer stiffened. "Why'd you ask?"

"It's always tight, running a business. Just the way I think." He imagined the agent in the brown coat handing over a briefcase filled with cash, untraceable, non-taxable.

"Same timing, with the extras?" Dwyer asked.

Scully smiled at the thought of money, and nodded. "The girl looks great, dolled up like that. Could be an actress."

Dwyer laughed. "She let me help choose the clothes. Was like she'd gone to heaven," he said, with the same faraway look as before.

Scully waved toward the door. "I hope she's not giving you up out there. Don't know who he is, he just came in about the order."

"Don't you worry none," Dwyer said. He turned to step away

but looked back. "I'll call around five." He smiled. "Good to check in." When he walked out, he left the office door open.

The moment he'd cleared the aisle, Scully pushed up from behind the desk and followed, moving slow enough not to alarm his sons. He forced himself to wait before stepping out onto the sidewalk. When he looked left, he saw Dwyer and the girl strolling off. She batted at his arm and it appeared they were laughing.

He squinted, scanned the street, and spotted the agent back in the opposite direction, getting into the driver's side of a black, late-model car. Scully stepped behind the doorway before the car pulled past. He saw that someone else sat beside the agent. Once the vehicle rolled by, Scully stuck out his head.

Dwyer and the girl turned right onto a cross street. The black car stopped before it reached that corner and a scruffy man in a beat up leather jacket climbed out of the passenger door. The car pulled away, straight along the street. The scruffy man reached the corner and turned right, trailing after Dwyer.

Scully shivered. Everyone threatened him. Either way, he'd be screwed. His boys came first but, somehow, he'd have to alert Dwyer. After a lifetime, he couldn't sell out. Dwyer would know what to do.

As he gazed down the street, the traffic light turned blood red.

CHAPTER 21
3:14 P.M., Thursday

WHEN the light turned green, Becca made a right and eased into the left lane. "Almost there, sweetie," she said. "It's coming up on the left."

Gary slipped the directions into the door pocket. "I wish I had my cell phone to give you."

"If you did, *you* wouldn't have one," she said.

"We both need them—you more."

"Why?"

He glanced at her. Between thickening clouds, a ray of sunlight slanted through her window. "You'll be alone in the car."

Her glossy hair swayed when she shook her head. "It's a cemetery. The weather's cold and gloomy, and visitors have their own troubles. I'll be invisible. Only the chauffeur, right?"

He recalled looking up in the snow at the terrorist's face, and then finding it on the computer screen. Good reason for her to stay clear. But he'd just upset her—she was already worried about him, and annoyed that she couldn't be by his side.

"What's keeping you in the car is Islamic ritual," he said, "not your husband." She still faced forward, mouth set. "I know. I'll get you your own phone for Christmas. Come with me and we'll get new ones together. You can pick the model, even the color."

"Tell me again why I need one?"

He saw the funeral park sign ahead as she slowed. "So I can call you all the time, whenever we're apart."

"Do I have to treat *you* like a teenager?"

He had a sudden wish that they'd already gotten the phones. "There may be times we *need* to reach one another. It'll be different from when you're at Ridgetop and I'm home."

111

She flipped the turn signal and swung the wheel. "If the man you see *is* the one—what then?"

"I turn away, hide in the crowd, and wait a bit before I stroll back to you. We drive off, and that's it. We bow out."

A metal fence surrounded the park. Visitors entered between ornate pillars supporting an elaborate wrought iron gate. They drove in.

"You keep wanting to 'bow out,' as you put it," she said, turning the car toward the sign reading *OFFICE*.

"Yup."

"The Gary I know would want to pay that guy back for hitting you and shooting at us. You're not backing off because of me, are you?"

He wasn't sure. She pulled up to the curb beside the administration building. "I've already made his life difficult," he said. "Found his car, described the belt, identified him to the feds. They'll be at the funeral in part because of me. Catching terrorists is out of our league—it's their job."

She wouldn't let go. "Maybe I'm just an angry woman. When he slugged you, he made my list."

"Be a good partner and stay in the car, right?" Without her promise, he wouldn't get out of the vehicle. A cloud blocked the sun; it grew darker as he peered at her.

She sighed and nodded.

He opened his door. "Be right back. Don't go away."

Inside, once he'd identified himself, a slope-shouldered man wearing a black suit and a *kufi* on his head, exuding the tranquil aura of funeral executives everywhere, handed over an envelope. It held a marked-up map of the funeral park that led them through a right, a left, and a final right turn.

When he returned to the car, he found Becca in the passenger seat. "What's up?" he said, through the half-open window.

She smiled and he saw mischief in her eyes. "I don't want you to get out of the driving habit."

"You got out."

She chuckled. "That didn't count."

He knew then that she'd been right before. He *would* back off because of her.

Following the directions, Gary pulled up close behind a small, tan SUV because Tony was leaning against it. The man's kufi hid his gray hair, and as he turned toward their car he looked different to Gary, almost like a gentler version of the man who'd slugged him.

The cap reminded him to take his own battered fedora. He raised the windows except for an inch on the driver's side, killed the engine, and grabbed his hat from the back seat. When they both got out, Tony turned toward Becca, waving a finger.

"You must remain in the car."

"Hey," Gary said, "back off. Let her get behind the wheel so she can use the heater."

Tony looked surprised, blinked, and shook his head as if to clear it. "Yes—well, it would be better if she kept the engine off. And not turn on the radio."

Becca squeezed Gary's arm in passing. Dressed for a funeral and parked on a cemetery feeder road, he doubted she'd listen to rock and roll. "If you get cold, use the engine for as long as you need it," he said as she slipped into the driver's seat.

"Of course, of course," Tony added.

Was he serious? The man looked stressed. Gary pushed the hat further down on his head, so it would resist the breeze, and bent to his wife. "See ya—remember to lock up." He saw her trigger the lever and heard the clicks.

"Follow me," Tony said, and stepped off the road to the left. He led the way over a berm and onto a downward slope. After a few paces, their vehicles were out of sight. The air smelled fresh.

Ahead, rows of snow-covered mounds without standing gravestones extended partway up the hill from a road cut through the valley floor. They'd arrived early, but several cars had already been parked on the distant road. Ruddy brown earth exposed a new excavation, and people were clustering near it.

When Tony halted without warning, Gary took two steps before he stopped and turned back uphill. Again, he experienced a flash of recognition.

"You forgot your muffler," the policeman said.

He had; he'd left it home. "I'll keep my hat low." But something nibbled at him, just out of reach.

"Let me prepare you for what you'll experience."

He couldn't help staring at the man.

"We don't use coffins. The boy's body has been washed and wrapped in white cotton. He'll be laid into the ground on his right side, facing what we call Qibla—the direction of Mecca. We'll offer prayers to Allah. Our belief is that the boy is going to—he'll meet—God, and the occasion will be positive for him. No music, flowers, idle talk, or emotional outbursts are permitted at the services."

Looking uphill at the angry face, Gary understood what had been eluding him.

"Do you find our ways odd?" Tony asked.

"It sounds like a thoughtful and caring process."

The policeman gazed at him, glanced upward, and worked his mouth before he could continue. "It's hell on the parents, but we expect about thirty mourners—relatives, friends, and members of the Islamic community. The women are with Leena." He caught Gary's eye. "We have to be our own support group."

He couldn't hold it in. "The man you want me to identify—he's your brother."

Tony stiffened. "You mean my *Islamic* brother."

Gary shook his head and the cop sagged.

"I forgive him for hitting me, but I wish he hadn't shot at my wife, and if he plans to kill people here, you have a problem beyond the *Quran*."

It took Tony a minute to compose himself. "Please, just let me know if—"

"I will." For an instant, Gary thought to look around for Thompson, and reveal to Tony that the feds knew. But he'd leave that choice to them, or Vincent. "Then I want my wife and me to step away from this. You're an officer of American law. I'll leave it to you."

"I—" Tony breathed deeply— "thank you."

"Now, tell me again how you want me to do it."

The man glanced uphill. "He'll come from there. My guess is we'll be chanting when he—"

Gary's stomach seized up. "You gave him the same map you gave *us?*"

Tony nodded.

He could barely get it out. "He knows what Becca looks like."

The policeman pursed his lips and shook his head. "Don't worry; when he gets here he knows to come right down the hill. He won't be looking at cars. The other day your wife was in a hat, facing sideways, and behind a snow-covered car, so he couldn't have seen her clearly."

Didn't the man realize that his brother might have staked out Gary's house, seen the car, been watching when they emerged? How many women had long red hair? He wanted to run back up the hill, get into the passenger seat and drive away. Instead, he forced himself to listen.

"...I'll walk up to greet him. Give me a minute before you look. When I turn back, do nothing if he's not the man, or rub an eye if he is."

"Will the mourners be facing uphill?"

Tony glanced around. "That way," he said, pointing. The hill would be to their right. "I'll watch for him. You'll be beside me and I'll tap you when I leave."

"If he's watching you move, won't he see me?"

"We'll be in a line of mourners, and I'll put a few tall men to our right," said Tony, as if he'd thought of everything.

A half hour later, the mourners had been lined up in three rows, parallel to the open grave. Imam Rashid stood in front, facing the grave, wearing a white *kufi* and long brown coat over his *dishadasha*, and leading the service. Everyone but Thompson, who stood twenty feet away at the low end of the last row, wore a hat. Gary noted the agent had positioned himself between the mourners and their cars.

In minutes, Gary would do the eye thing, one way or the other, and try to make himself invisible in the group. He was wondering whether it would be honorable to alert Thompson—and how he might do it—when Tony's tap startled him. The cop backed out of line and stepped away uphill. Gary didn't move. He tried counting off seconds but wound up listening to the chant.

"*Allaahumma ij'alhu lanaa faratan, wa j'alhu lanaa ajran,*" he heard, and more. He couldn't concentrate. The video in his head showed the car, with Becca, and the hill, with one man descending, another climbing. He couldn't wait—he leaned back and faced uphill, head and shoulders jutting out from the back row.

Tony was moving away at a slow pace. The small man had stopped just below the crest, waiting, scanning the scene, his head revolving like a security camera. Despite the cap, and a pair of glasses the man hadn't worn two nights before, Gary recognized him at once: the chin, the nose, his size, and beneath an unzipped blue ski jacket, a glimpse of the belt dangling down, tip glinting in the sunlight.

The small man froze. His gaze reached Gary like a zap of electricity. Tony's brother whirled and ran back up the hill with surprising speed. The cop stopped and watched him go.

Gary broke away from the ceremony and started up the hill. The man vanished over the top. Gary leaned forward, pumping his arms and legs, running with wild adrenaline, but it took forever before he reached Tony. He flew past and heard the cop begin to follow. He stepped into a depression and his back twisted. Heart pounding, gasping for cold air that seared his throat, he ignored the pain and crested the berm.

Tony's tan SUV was right where it had been—but Becca and the car were gone. He whirled, ready to wave to Thompson, but the agent had also vanished. Chanting voices carried uphill—now they were praying for him.

Panting, Tony stumbled up alongside. Gary watched him rise on tiptoe and scan the area. "Where are they?" the policeman asked, half to himself, and when he got no answer, he turned to Gary. "Did you see—was he the one?"

Gary nodded. "What was your brother driving?"

Tony looked pained. "I don't know." He stared at where the Kemmerman car had been, and his head tilted. "How could he recognize...?" His expression changed. "No, no, it wasn't that—Abdel drove here, so he had to leave in his own vehicle." He looked at Gary in disbelief. "Would she have followed him? Would she do that?"

She'd promised only to stay in the car. His legs gave out, and he sat on a cleared spot at the curb beside where his wife had been. His back screamed, one more alarm in his head.

CHAPTER 22
3:15 P.M., Thursday

LYNN gave Dwyer a hard look and stopped moving after he took her elbow to help her onto the curb. She couldn't know he'd done it so that he could peer at the reflection in the angled window of an Internet café. Their tail showed skill—the man turned sideways at the curb and lifted a hand as if he'd hail a cab.

Dwyer stood at her left, on the gutter side of Broadway, with Times Square two blocks ahead. They'd both buttoned their coats and turned up collars against the deepening cold, but hadn't put on gloves. The roads were peppered with taxis, but because of the hour or the biting weather, few people were out.

Though the man following them had varied his distance, he'd been in Dwyer's sight for more than an hour—on the street, in the department store, even on line behind them when Dwyer bought her a pretzel from a street vendor.

She'd never had one before. She'd loved it, laughing when she pulled off a large twist, offering the piece with delight. She'd insisted he taste it. He'd finished the offering. He would have, for her, whether he liked it or not.

Dwyer couldn't have the man roaming—calling in others, finding a firing position—while they sat in a restaurant. And he wouldn't lead the tail back to the apartment. So he had to act. But Lynn's presence prevented him from turning tables on the man and following him back to his own lair.

He glanced to his right and found her peering at the moving news-in-lights display in the square. Before he could look away, she turned to him with a frown, twirling the Saks Fifth Avenue bag in her right hand.

"I'm not that kind'a girl," she said.

"What kind'a girl is that?" Now and again she'd let him take her hand and even squeeze back. But not for long, as if affection couldn't be trusted.

She started forward as she spoke. "Don't need clothes and things. Don't need shoppin' and strange foods."

He stopped her by taking an arm, turning her back to him. In the window behind her, he saw the tail, a half-block away, step into a storefront. They were alone on the sidewalk. "Don't you believe I know that?" he said. She didn't speak, just glanced down at the hand gripping her arm. He released her.

"Tell me what you got to," she said, petulance in the tone, and didn't move.

He spoke softly. "Lynn, making you smile makes me happy. I take you places because it makes me happy. Holding your hand does, too. Don't you believe me?"

She gazed at him, no flinch in the eyes, staring back while he waited. Then she breathed in through her mouth and nodded.

Her silence prodded him. "When I think you're squeezing me because you mean it—you're your own woman, Lynn, I know that. I'm just—"

"Don't," she said. Her free hand came up, fluttered toward him but stopped short of his chest. "This is too good."

He smiled. "I need a favor."

Her expression changed. "Ha, I knew it was too good."

He looked at her and saw it on her face. She'd been used, paid off with gifts and food, they were having the Big Scene, and now she'd be sent away. Starting from age thirteen, how many times had that happened to her? He knew right then that she could walk off whenever she wanted, but he'd die before he hurt her. How could he say it so she'd understand—so it wouldn't frighten her?

"Fifteen minute favor," he said, "before we get in out of the cold and have some drinks, if you want, and then dinner, if you want, whatever kind of food you want, and maybe tonight you'll sleep tight against me, not 'cause I got you drunk, or fed you, or provided the bed." And be there in the morning, he almost said.

Her eyes grew moist for just the instant before they turned playful. "Any kind of food I want?"

"Any kind you can find, whatever it costs."

She slapped at his hand and the affection burned him. "What's the favor?"

"Listen but don't ask why. We'll make like we're fighting. We'll walk around the corner to the right. You keep on the sidewalk and don't look for me. There's an alley past the restaurant. Stop in front and look into it. Moment a man turns onto the street from where we are now, you walk away fast, like you're angry. Go to the next corner—Avenue of the Americas, goes uptown—take a cab for three blocks, just past the corner of Forty-fourth Street. Got that?"

She nodded.

As he finished telling her where to meet him, she tapped fingers against his chest. "The one in the beat-up leather jacket's the worry, right?"

He couldn't hide his expression.

She saw it and shrugged. "Always watchin'." She slapped at him again. That pulled him back. "You'll come meet me?"

Under it all, he understood that was the real question. Might always be. He'd worried she wouldn't believe the story. She'd figured it out. Glory, what had he found? He caught her eye. "If I don't show in an hour, I'm dead." He saw the surprise. "Would take death for me not to meet you."

She worked her lips and looked away. "We're walkin' on the ice."

"We are."

When she glanced back, he saw deeper into her than she'd ever let him. She nodded, the expression changed, and she yelled out that he was a fool.

119

CHAPTER 23
3:37 P.M., Thursday

BECCA wasn't sure whether the chill or her nightmare had woken her. Cold air was seeping in through the inch-open car window, and she felt frozen in place behind the steering wheel. She stretched her legs as best she could and rotated her feet.

In the dream, her abusive first husband had come hunting for her. Seven years before, she'd fled at night from their Ohio home, taking Melanie, then just thirteen. Until she met Gary, she'd always looked over her shoulder. Being with him had given her the courage to file for divorce. To her surprise and delight, it hadn't been contested. She wished no one ill, but she hoped the man she'd left had found another focus for his attentions. He'd vanished from her dreams. Why had such anxiety returned?

The digital clock said she'd been dozing on and off for almost twenty minutes. Falling asleep in these circumstances embarrassed her. She rolled her shoulders, turned her neck, and glanced in the direction Gary and Tony had taken. The rise to her left blocked any view of the ceremony and isolated her in the car. As Tony had requested, she'd stay inside. Nodding off in the bitter chill might have caused the nightmare.

She should have brought a book along but it had seemed disrespectful. A bit of heat would be good. Thank heaven she'd worn boots, her toes were warm, but her fingers had grown numb. She slipped woolen gloves from her coat pockets and pulled them on.

As she reached for the ignition key, she spotted motion in the rear view mirror. A dark green van eased closer, rolling slowly down the middle of the path. She knew she shouldn't be here—that must have been why Tony had directed them to this isolated spot. She didn't move, hoping the vehicle would keep going. It had dark-tinted windows. Maybe no one in it would notice her. She could hear it crunching gravel. It angled to the left and stopped at the curb some twenty feet behind .

She watched through the side mirror. The driver's door opened and a small man, wearing no coat, stepped out. Holding the door, he stared at both vehicles in front. Clouds had blocked the sun, her head was below the backrest, and she doubted he could see anything in the small side mirror. Still, she held her breath.

When he turned away and peered over the embankment, she saw the pistol in a holster at his back. He reached into the car, drew out a tan jacket and pulled it on. It covered the gun. He closed the van door, strode over the rise, and disappeared.

The whole thing had taken less than a minute. She blinked, trying to retain the memory. In a cap, wearing glasses, the guy might be anyone. But Gary had described a silvery, pointed belt. The image fit. They were there because that man might show up. Now he and his gun had. She shuddered.

Uneasy, she watched the clock blink the seconds. The man with the belt must be pacing down the hill. A minute passed. She forced her eyes closed but they popped open when what she'd seen rolled in her head. Heart pounding, she didn't feel the cold. She glanced at the clock—the digit had changed. Tony would be stepping up to meet the evil man. Now—

Loud panting and rapid, scrabbling footfalls shocked her. That had to be the man returning. Why? This time he might shoot her. She pressed as low as she could get in the seat, limiting her vision to the top half of the side mirror.

The man crested the rise and headed for the van without looking her way. He slipped inside in a flash, the engine roared and the green vehicle accelerated past, spraying gravel. It almost struck the back of the car. She watched the van bump down the path and turn right on a road that led toward the funeral park's exit.

The noise faded. With a whoosh, cold air gusted through the window. No one else appeared. In seconds the man would be gone.

Unsure what to do, she started the car and went after him, though she drove as slowly as any other funeral-goer might. He'd probably be long gone when she reached the street. She could always turn back at the office.

Sight lines were open inside the cemetery. She saw the van reach the internal rotary and head toward the exit. The traffic signal at the street turned red in front of it. The man couldn't jump the light—a stream of vehicles on the outside road had forced him to stop. It must be an omen, she thought, that light and the unexpected traffic. By the time the signal changed she'd almost reached the van, and when it pulled forward and turned right, so did she.

What made sense? she wondered. Gary would be upset with her—but he'd have done the same thing.

She pictured the small man driving his vehicle. She wouldn't get out of the car, wouldn't let him lead her into any deserted places where he could use the gun.

A boxy Nissan cut into the lane in front of her and rode behind the van. She kept her eyes on it. At the second traffic signal, the van pushed through the intersection after the light had changed, drawing honks. Intending to follow, she barely missed rear-ending the Nissan.

Her heart hammered; the light took what seemed hours to change. She eased forward. The Nissan slipped into another lane and turned away. Ahead, large green signs hung above the road, arrows curling in every direction, pointing the way to local highways and the New Jersey Turnpike. The man could have taken any one of them. She must have lost him. She sat back, breathed deeply, and slowed the car.

It stunned her, a block later, when she spotted the van parked along the curb to her right. Did he live there? More likely, he'd waited to see if anyone would come looking. As she approached, she saw the man facing into traffic, watching for her. She had to pass, couldn't stop or turn. She raised her right hand to shield her face and drove by without slowing.

Two could play the same game; first chance, she pulled over. She checked that the car doors were locked, hunched down in the seat and lowered the rear-view mirror, scanning it for the van and for pedestrians who might look like him.

Two minutes later, the van drove past. She averted her face but, when it continued moving, she pulled out and got on its tail. This time, she wanted to leave a few cars between them—Gary had told her about that—but the van slowed, and then slowed further. She memorized the license plate. Finally, right behind it, hardly moving, she grew alarmed.

The man had shot at them yesterday through car windows. Enough. She jerked the wheel, switching lanes abruptly to the van's left, and accelerated past it. The green vehicle didn't follow.

Pulse racing, she headed toward the Turnpike and home. By now Gary must have arranged a lift—Tony could bring him back. She chose the express E-ZPass toll lane and headed northbound, in the right section of the Interstate, with the trucks and slower drivers.

She almost reached for the radio but instead stayed with her thoughts. Maybe it was time for them both to get out of this, though she realized that had been Gary's intention. She'd taken this step alone.

Thickening clouds blocked the sun. She noticed roadside details she hadn't seen on the way to the cemetery. It took almost till Exit 12, weaving among the big rigs and rolling in the center lane at a steady sixty-five, before her pulse slowed.

Cell phones were the way to go. Gary'd been right. She'd program in numbers for him—Melanie, Angela, Megan, the hospital... . A lime green phone she'd seen in an advertisement filled her thoughts. For an instant, she didn't make the connection when the green van loomed to her right. It angled out of lane and slammed into the front passenger side of her car.

She bounced in the seat belt, pain blossoming at her ribs, the wheel bucking out of her gloved hands before she managed to grip it. Screeching, the car headed for the concrete median. She hit the brakes and spun the wheel as an air horn blared, mirrors filling with a giant chrome grille higher than the rear window, air brakes howling, tires screaming.

The eighteen-wheeler walloped the car, spinning it to the left, smashing it against the barrier. Becca's head slammed into the loose visor as air bags exploded. The truck cab chewed at her trunk, crushing it from the rear. The jackknifed trailer reached from the left, pushing her ahead of it, metal shrieking as it tore apart against concrete.

In a flash, it had all stopped. Air bags deflated. In eerie silence, she blinked, found the car crumpled in front of her, the clock dead. Something clanged onto the roadway. Stunned, she sat motionless. White powder covered her blue coat. She heard hissing, smelled burning rubber and gasoline.

She had to get out of the car and away from there.

A spider-web of cracks marred the driver's-side window. She looked out at silvery, corrugated steel—a slab from the side of the trailer blocked the door. Would the passenger side open? She could move her arms and legs, but the seat belt that had saved her was clutching in a death-grip. She hurt where it squeezed.

She pushed and pulled at the locking mechanism, tore off her gloves and tried with both hands to no avail. She couldn't squirm free. She dug fingers beneath the straps but they wouldn't budge. The gasoline odor grew stronger, and she smelled smoke. She'd treated burn victims; the thought panicked her and lent strength. Fiercely, she jammed down on the unlocking device and yanked at the belt buckle.

It wouldn't budge. Smoke blowing in front of the shattered windshield began to turn black, and wisps curled into the car. She closed her eyes.

CHAPTER 24
3:38 P.M., Thursday

WITH Lynn pacing alongside and shouting at him, Dwyer made sure the man had peeked out from the storefront; only then did he retreat around the corner. As they'd planned, the moment they were hidden from the tail, Lynn faced the alley and continued her rant while Dwyer slipped behind a nearby vehicle.

Moments later, through the tinted windows of the SUV screening him, Dwyer watched the scruffy haired man round the corner. Lynn snapped off a final obscenity toward the alley and whirled away. The tail stood quietly, watching the well-dressed young woman flounce down the street, shopping bag in hand, body language reeking of anger.

Dwyer imagined her clearing the corner and laughing—then realized that until he reached her side, she'd only worry. The moment she vanished onto the avenue, the man in the leather jacket stepped up to the alley, craned his neck, and peered in. "Hey, fella, you okay?" the guy called into the darkness.

From behind him, "I wouldn't *mind* shooting, so don't move," said Dwyer, pushing the gun against the man's spine. He'd opened his coat so the weapon wouldn't be visible to passers-by.

The man froze. Below the ragged leather jacket, he wore black jeans and expensive, water resistant walking shoes.

"Into the alley." Dwyer shoved the man's neck. "Last warning. Move." The man stumbled forward and they left the street. Dwyer expected the guy would react. To prevent it, he said, "I take your weapon, wallet, and phone, then I bop you and you wake up to try me tomorrow. If you can find me. Maybe you'll be kind when it's your turn. Worst thing will be replacing all those cards."

While he talked, he pushed the man deeper into the alley. They moved around three small dumpsters filled with black garbage bags; the place smelled fetid. "Hands against the wall now, legs spread wide."

The man assumed the position. First, Dwyer patted him down and found the revolver, a snub nose Smith & Wesson .38 Airweight. Good balance, but a weapon none of the government agencies would issue. It tagged the man as freelance and that presented options. Dwyer held onto that gun and holstered his own.

He examined the cell phone. Nothing unusual. He disconnected the battery, pocketed the pieces. Later, if they hadn't been erased, he'd check for a phone list, calls made and received.

He found the man's wallet and extracted the photo driver's license: *Emile Cartwright*, it read. Dwyer examined it closely. It looked real. The wallet was stuffed with a thick wad of bills. It held a Visa card made out in the same name, and a business card with nothing on it but a phone number. Dwyer knew what that meant. The number would be unlisted and callers would reach an untraceable, computer-voice message machine. It concealed individual identity but screamed Agency.

Pocketing the wallet, he stepped back. He didn't see anyone on the street. "Tell me who and why, Emile."

"You're a mugger—I'm the victim here," Cartwright said. "Take everything, just please don't hurt me."

"A victim who's followed me for more than an hour."

"I'm following you? You're crazy," the scruffy man said. "I've been walking around. I may pop the question tonight, she's a wonderful girl, but there's so much to consider."

"Who and why, Emile?"

"I don't know what you're talking about."

"What if I said tell me or I'll kill you?"

The man twitched but stayed in place, and the threat made a difference. "Please, don't," Cartwright said. "If you'd do that, might not matter if I told you anything."

"Oh, I don't know. You're not my enemy. Someone else is."

The alternative gave the scruffy man pause. "I found you at the metal shop."

"Who gave me up?"

The man shook his head. "I don't know his name—or who he is. Really, I don't."

"The card?"

The tail hesitated before nodding.

"He pointed me out?"

Cartwright took a deep breath. "He's a small man wearing a brown coat—natty dresser. Got my number from a referral. I don't know who he is. He gave me money and told me to call him Professor. That's a bullshit name."

"Coat close with a belt?"

The man nodded. "Yeah. You saw him?"

Two strikes, Dwyer thought. "Was it your job to follow me home and call it in?"

"You got it. Standard surveillance, no surprise there."

"You freelance?"

Cartwright nodded again. "You have no reason to hurt me. This is New York—we'll never cross paths again." He shuddered. "I'll make sure of it."

"Who you think he works for?"

The man shrugged. "CIA maybe. They use the card trick." Cartwright made to lower his arms but Dwyer pressed the gun against him. "I'm just doing a job. He paid for a half-day and then I'm home to pop that question. Gotta tell you, Arlene looks very good to me right now. She's a real blonde."

Dwyer wondered how long Cartwright had kept that lame line in inventory. He kept his voice friendly. "Did you come to the shop with the man in the brown coat?"

Another shake of the head. "He said I had ten minutes to get there. He'd given me the address—we'd prearranged a quick meet, just in case. You and the girl were leaving by the time I reached the place. He pointed you out. Sorry, I know I shouldn't have done it. Not to you."

Cartwright could identify Lynn, Dwyer thought. Strike three. "The agent know me? Were you briefed about me before you locked on?"

Had Scully turned him in? The fat man had appeared flushed when Dwyer walked in on him. Or had the agent caused Scully's upset, and Dwyer's arrival—maybe Lynn's accent—been the brown-coated man's reason for contacting Cartwright? He'd have to ask Lynn if the agent had made a call while they chatted. And he'd have to ask Ryan what was going on.

"The crazy people who hire me always make like they know everything," Cartwright said. "My guess—he hasn't a clue about whatever's going on. I don't, either. He asked me to learn what I could. All I know is you're better at this than I am."

"You must know people who count. You get any word that the heat's on?"

The tail nodded. "A source mentioned they're concerned, but not enough to raise the threat level or bring in extra hands."

"Who do you mean by 'they?'"

Cartwright shrugged. "Homeland Security, FBI, CIA, top local cops, they've all wound up in the same stew. It's hard to know who you're—I mean, I'm—dealing with."

"Why'd you say you shouldn't have followed me?"

"The way you made me and got me in here—it's not new to you."

There'd be nothing more to learn from this guy. "Ready for the bop?"

"Don't suppose I could promise to stay here for an hour—honor among spooks?" Cartwright asked.

"Not a spook," Dwyer said, and shot him with the thirty-eight, once, through the heart.

He expected the gun's strong recoil. The blast wanted to stay in the windowless alley, but a breeze whipped it away before the man could crumple to the ground. Smells and darkness would keep people out of the alley, and the dumpsters would hide the body from the street.

Dwyer wiped Cartwright's pistol clean of prints and wrapped it into sheets of newspaper. No one on the street saw him leave the alley. When he reached the avenue, he tossed the weapon into the trash. The top of the can was open and the wrapped-up revolver, heavier than the fast food clutter around it, sank out of sight.

It would be okay if the police found the weapon. He'd bet it hadn't been registered. It would offer neither prints nor an indication of which way its user might have gone.

He wondered if the agencies had been watching known IRA associates. They'd need a reason to do that. Had they learned of his arrival from other sources? A leak among those that had sent him here? He doubted it. Could it be Siddiq? The man had worked with the IRA before, and many of Dwyer's own people had been against the mission. If the Americans had made Siddiq, were they trying to roll up both ends of the operation? He'd have to warn the little man.

A traffic light stopped him. He glanced at the street sign while yellow taxis and dirt-streaked cars eased through the intersection. The road cleared and he moved forward. Thinking of Lynn, he stepped up his pace. The vision in his mind blotted out the noise of the city.

CHAPTER 25
3:54 P.M., Thursday

BREATHING foul air stung Becca's throat. Banging noises, breaking glass, intruded—the car must be falling apart. When the sounds seemed to be coming from beside her, her eyes flew open and she turned. A gun butt in a large hand was smashing at the remnants of the passenger-side window.

She couldn't see the man—his black coat blocked the opening where the glass had been. He used the weapon to clear fragments from around the edges. The door had a vertical crease that didn't belong—collisions with van, truck, and barrier had folded it inward. It would never open.

She watched the butt chop down along the back of the frame like an axe. Bits of glass splashed onto the passenger seat and splinters bounced off her coat. Smoke poured in through the shattered window, became a choking cloud. The gun moved away and the hand returned—holding a knife. Had she been saved, or had someone come back for the kill?

The arm reached in, a stranger's face followed, but the knifepoint heading toward her, moving with purpose, was all that mattered. Energy drained out, she closed her eyes again. The knife might be kinder than fire. She tensed when it touched her side.

"Help me get you out," the stranger shouted.

She came awake, saw the blade sawing at the seat belt above the broken locking device.

At once she smelled the fire, heard it crackling to her left, behind the metal slab, radiating heat. She gasped, unable to move or speak. When the seatbelt parted, she sagged.

"Move, damn it!" he yelled.

Numb, without thinking, she leaned to the right and reached out

133

with both hands. He did the work, pulling her through the missing window, guiding carefully, arms first, cradling her head, squeezing her torso through the bent frame like toothpaste leaving the tube. Ragged glass clawed at her thick coat. He lifted her legs so they wouldn't be cut. Her head throbbed, neck and ribs hurt as he dragged her over the sill. He held her in his arms, off the ground, as if she were weightless.

They stood in a cloud of choking smoke. If he set her down, would her legs work? It didn't matter; he carried her, folded her into the passenger seat of a gray Ford parked yards in front of the twisted vehicles.

Turning slowly, she glanced back. The jackknifed truck dwarfed the remains of the car. How had she survived? "Truck driver?" she asked, fearing the worst.

"He's out—across the road."

The large man tucked in her arms and legs and slammed the car door. He ran around and slid in behind the wheel. Despite her misgivings, when he insisted, she managed to fasten the seat belt. It ran the opposite way and hurt her shoulder less. She closed her eyes and imagined herself at home—anywhere but here.

When he started the car and eased forward, she had to look back in the side mirror. The trailer was blazing, red and orange flames licking above the vehicles. A wall of cars had stopped behind the accident in every lane but the far right, where hardy souls hugged the shoulder and crawled past. The crash had taken place what seemed seconds before; emergency vehicles hadn't arrived and the stranger accelerated down an empty highway.

She slumped, shrinking from the safety belt, watching the crash dwindling in the outside mirror, thoughts jumbled. The man who'd saved her had arrived so quickly—he might be a Good Samaritan, there by accident, but he had a gun, and a knife.

Had she been saved because he wanted information? The car roared forward, speeding up, going too fast. Had she been kidnapped? Could it happen to her again? Thoughts were blasted away when the rig and her crushed vehicle exploded in a fireball, flashing in the mirror, blinding her as the detonation rocked the car. For an instant she imagined herself back there, breathing liquid fire, tearing apart. Tears started down her cheeks as she gasped for breath.

"You okay?" the man asked. "Need medical attention?"

She straightened and tried to calm but couldn't speak, couldn't stop the tears.

"You're a nurse," he said. "You know about shock. Where you want me to take you?"

How did he know that? Who was he? Squinting, blinking, she peered at him. He looked clean cut, wore a dark tie. She couldn't tell where the gun and knife had gone. He'd slowed the car and slipped among other vehicles fleeing the scene—he was focusing on the road, not on her. She forced the tears to stop.

"Mrs. Kemmerman, make a decision."

He knew her name, too. "Ridgetop Hospital." It came out as a whisper.

"I know where it is."

"Who are you?"

"Jeff Thompson."

He volunteered nothing else, but Gary had spoken about him. "You were at the funeral," she said, gasping at the next thought. "Is my husband okay?"

Thompson breathed in deeply. "He'll be fine. No one else is after him. He ask you to pull this stunt?"

She shook her head.

"Christ, lady, this is no place for you."

She stared at him. "How'd you get to me so fast?"

"Homing device on your car."

"You were following Gary?"

He considered. "Best I could come up with."

She frowned, imagining him behind her while she tailed the green van. Something didn't add up. "I was going home."

"I know. He held back and I let you go. Went with him. I had him." His voice sounded angry. "Never spotted me. Then he targeted you."

"You saw what happened?"

Thompson nodded. "Nothing you could've done." He spoke while facing forward. "He came around traffic, cut across two lanes and slammed you in front of the truck. He made you—wanted you dead real bad. Your husband should've warned you to stay clear."

He had, several times. She felt the tears again. "I'm sorry."

"I called in the van but I'm betting it's off the road and he's switched vehicles." He spoke in a voice staccato with irritation. "There's a service area nearby. He'd steal a car from the employee lot, get off the Turnpike at 14—the damned exit goes everywhere— and switch vehicles again. Prints don't matter, we know who he is. Now he's in the wind."

She didn't understand why tears spilled down her cheeks. "You wanted *him*—you were following *him*—you could have left me and stayed with him."

Thompson shot her a glance, bit his lip, and shook his head.

Before she could thank him, she began to sob.

CHAPTER 26
4:47 P.M., Thursday

LYNN accepted it when Dwyer said he'd slugged the fellow who'd followed them, left him in the alley, and they'd never see him again. Then he asked the question that had been bothering him. "When you were talking with the little guy in the brown coat outside Scully's, did he make a phone call?"

"Yeah, he—" her brows knit— "Should I have told you? Was it my fault that man followed us?" She breathed deeply and shrank in the seat, gazing at the low table in front of them. Their drinks sat on it, liquid dancing from the surrounding hubbub.

"So he did?" Dwyer needed to be certain.

"Asked me to wait a second." Her eyes, round and moist, found his. "It took only that. He turned away, I didn't hear a thing and it was done."

Her left hand lay on her knee, and he stroked the fingers. She looked down at the movement, but he didn't stop. "You did good," he said. "Tail would've happened anyway. Would've been more difficult without you at Scully's. And after."

She didn't brighten.

"This'll be over soon, y'know that."

She shuddered and shifted her hand on top of his. He held her knee, kept still and let her touch him. Something beyond the obvious was troubling her.

"The man in the brown coat," she said, covering his fingers, "he reminded me of guys the foster parents were always introducin' as 'good friends'. Wanted to keep him away from *you*, so I batted my eyes, looked coy—well, you know, I could do that. Even if he'd tried to, he couldn't have... ." Very softly, eyes averted, she murmured, "You were close."

An explosion of warmth spread inside and he had to wait before he could talk. "You never saw him before?"

Lynn had wanted a "girlie" drink, and they sat facing one another in The Whiskey, a third-floor bar at a Manhattan hotel named "W". They were leaning close in the corner of a conversation pit because the noise level fit the trading floor of a commodities exchange.

He found the couches too low and soft, the indirect lighting brighter than a bar's should be. Dinging noises from banks of hidden elevators interrupted the background music, and people streamed in and out like it was a hotel lobby, in part because the gift shop lay at the other end of the long room.

"Never laid eyes on him," she said. Her hand moved away, and he could tell her mood had shifted. She raised the large glass—she'd kept the male bartender describing options until she'd heard one she liked—and beamed at Dwyer. "Never laid eyes on anything like this, either. Three liquors, look at the colors. Tastes like shit, but I love it."

No **way**, he thought, could this girl have any link to that man. Four **middle-aged** women chatted on the adjoining group of couches, paying **them** no attention.

"Should I thank you for bringin' me here?" she asked.

"Manners coming back so late in life?"

She laughed. He could see how her face had relaxed. An innocent lived inside, peeking out with joy and wonder, the veneer layered on by the evil done to her and still pinned in place for protection. What magic had allowed him to break through?

From the left, a serving tray moved toward them. The waitress stepped up behind it and pointed at his drink. "You okay?"

He'd almost finished. They had a little time and good whiskey never affected him. "Hit me again. Greenore Single Grain, double shot, straight up."

"Greenore—never heard of it," Lynn said, when the woman had left.

He bent closer. "I should thank you—it's my favorite, not carried but in expensive places. Small batch, single malt from Cooley's, the only Irish-owned distillery left in Ireland—near Dundalk."

She considered it. "What's it taste like?"

He tilted the glass and stared at the golden liquid. "It's velvety, almost sweet, but a man's drink, with a kick."

"Ooo," she said. "Can I try a sip?"

The delight in her voice forced him to close his eyes. After a deep breath, "We'll get a whole bottle. To take with us when we go."

"Go where?" She fired back without a pause. Every time he spoke of plans. she reared like a wild horse. She'd set her drink down on the low table.

"We'll find a beach after this," he said. "Somewhere warm and slow. You can pick it. Can't wait to see you with tan lines. You'll need bathing suits, sun block—and sunglasses." In sunglasses, he'd bet, she'd look like Audrey Hepburn if her hair were up. "Get you large, dark glasses, like the movie stars."

She looked back at him, and he saw the fear, but with something else mixed in. "Don't talk like that," she said.

He couldn't help himself. "You afraid to trust?"

The waitress brought his drink, giving Lynn time. He asked for the check—he needed to call Scully, and he couldn't do it here. By the time she answered, he was sipping, thoughts elsewhere.

"Sean?" Her voice captured his attention. Head tilted, she stared at him, breathing through her mouth, looking bewildered. "Got good reason to doubt. Always have. But," and she whispered the words, "not your fault."

He wanted to hug her, tell her everything would be okay. Instead, he considered how to put it. "Well, when we're somewhere warm, and we toast to whatever you want with what's left of our bottle, it'll be okay if you still don't trust me."

A series of emotions flashed on her face before she looked back. "My God, you're tryin' to win me."

He didn't know what to say, but then realized words weren't necessary. She was blushing.

"'Lo," Dwyer heard Scully say, the voice sounding as if it'd been relayed from Mars.

"That you, Ryan?" Dwyer stood on the second level, along the balcony railing at F. A. O. Schwarz, holding a disposable cell and watching Lynn slip through the crowds on the floor below. She moved slowly from one display to the next, touching the beautifully presented toys.

When they left the bar, he hadn't told her where they'd be going. At the sight of the glistening store, she'd lit up and slipped her hand into his. She'd pranced beside him on the red carpet, and giggled at the employees dressed as toy soldiers.

He watched her move leisurely along the aisles, eyes everywhere, fingering whatever she could. He wondered if she'd ever been to a toy store before. The better question might be, had she been to one with anyone not exchanging the visit for favors? Half the men who passed her turned to stare, before or after. She radiated a presence quite separate from her looks—he blinked with understanding. For all she'd been through, Lynn Turner had an innocent soul.

"Sean—that you?"

The voice brought him back. Scully sounded surprised. Dwyer hadn't expected that. Scully ought to be waiting for his call, unless the man in the brown coat had made him afraid.

"Yeah."

"Would've got you sooner, but I had no number," Scully said, rushing the words. That meant Dwyer would learn about Brown Coat. But Scully's phone line might be tapped.

"Stop talking," Dwyer said. "Get out of your shop, go to a public phone and call me at—got a pen?"

It took a moment. "Yes."

He gave Scully his phone number, broke the connection and watched Lynn wander until the throwaway cell rang. It had no GPS.

"Now, tell me what's happened."

"It's not my fault," Scully whined.

He saw Lynn lift a stuffed brown teddy bear and hug it. She rocked sideways like a child. He wanted her to have it. "We can't deal with it till you tell me," he said to Scully.

"Well, the man you saw in my shop—the guy in the brown coat who went outside with the girl—said he's with a government agency and they know you're here."

Dwyer glanced around. The crowds were elsewhere on this level, no one within fifteen feet, no one paying attention. "Did he mention my name?"

"No. But now he's seen you."

"Did you tell him anything?"

"Nothing, Sean, swear to God, nothing. He threatened my family. Said if I didn't help, they'd kill my boys. Said if anything happened before I helped or if I told you about it, same thing. Gave me no name." Scully's voice had grown shrill with panic. "I been in deep shit before Sean, but not with the kids. Now you know it all. Who's the leak? What do I do?"

Dwyer watched Lynn run fingers over a display of rag dolls. "You didn't let on to that when we were alone in your shop," he said. "Not a thing to me."

"Was scared, Sean. He was there. Had a gun in the coat and he could've walked in and used it on you. I was scared."

Scully sounded afraid of both of them. "He'll call you?"

"That's what he said."

"Good. Calm down. We get you past this. You tell him you asked around and no one knows anything, so you called Ireland. You heard third-hand that the New York Stock Exchange is a possible target. They didn't know when or how. Someone's come over, probably from the Middle East, 'cause the IRA wants no part of it—but that's all you know. Got it?"

"Tell 'em the real target?"

"I'm looking out for you, Ryan. They won't come at you for getting' it right. You'd better make that call home so they'll know you're not lying."

"The Middle East?"

"Why not," Dwyer said. "The Americans can't know jack shit. Blame it on the Arabs and it'll keep the heat off us."

"The guy sounded sure of himself."

Scully's response pleased him. The old man hadn't sought information. "They all sound that way," Dwyer said. He stepped aside so a mother and daughter could pass in the aisle. They didn't notice him. "Can you move delivery up to tomorrow morning?"

"Means night work, but for you—"

"Take this down—got that pen?"

"Yeah."

He passed along a "212" number.

"What's that?"

"Pay phone outside the Hotel W, near Times Square. Bit uptown from you but be there at six in the morning. Six sharp. Tell me then where and when for the pickup. You think you can get out without being followed?"

"For sure I can. Sean—"

"If you want, Ryan, I'll stay an extra week and protect you myself."

"Oh, good."

"Anything else?"

"What?"

"Got anything else to tell me?"

Dwyer heard Scully's hesitation. "The agent said the contract stuff—the transit business—that's real, separate from the rest."

"Count on it if you want but it's not what I meant."

The pause lengthened until Dwyer knew that Scully must have spotted the tail. "Nothin'," the man said. "Nothin' else."

Dwyer broke the connection. Scully believed his kids were at risk and so he'd be careful. The old man would want to feed both sides to keep anyone from coming after his family. Still, he'd provided Dwyer with a warning, and Scully would surely tell Brown Coat precisely what he'd been instructed.

Once, Dwyer knew, Scully had been tough—you couldn't touch him. But he'd aged and changed. Dwyer glanced down at Lynn, then at the phone in his hand, and considered how he was changing. He dialed another number. Voicemail picked up after a single ring. A computer said, "Yes," and he heard a ding. "Moved up to tomorrow. Let you know more after six in the morning." He didn't need to say, "Be ready."

When he finished, he deleted everything from the phone and used a handkerchief to wipe it clean of prints. He lowered it, made sure no one stood close, then let it fall unnoticed onto the floor beside his leg. He ground it beneath his heel until it crunched, and kicked the pieces beneath a large display.

Scully had said it. Who was the leak? He'd bet it wasn't either of the two men who'd sent him over. The only people he'd contacted in

New York were Siddiq, Lynn, Scully, and Grady Finn. It couldn't be Siddiq—no reason for it, and if Siddiq wanted Dwyer, he wouldn't shop it to a Caucasian.

Dwyer rode the escalator and saw Lynn across the floor, entranced by a large dollhouse with lights inside and lace curtains behind the tiny windows. She stroked its curving roofline. He stopped first where she'd already been, and found the teddy bear. It smiled up as if it knew the secret. You never know with leaks—but not her. He'd bet his life on it. He took the bear with him.

If Scully had been involved in arranging Brown Coat's visit, he wouldn't have said anything about the agent. He wouldn't have the fear. That left Finn. If his old buddy had been squeezed—or just gotten drunk with the wrong person—no telling what he might've given up. Now they couldn't return to the apartment, and he had a job to do before tomorrow morning. He patted the belt around his middle. Lucky he'd carried the cash. He'd learned to move light, like the girl.

He stepped up and found Lynn focused on a cardboard castle populated by armies of tin soldiers, red coats inside, blue out. She ran a finger along the moat. He wouldn't touch her, afraid she'd jump. From beside, he spoke softly. "You ready?"

His being so close surprised her. She pulled back her hand and turned. "Whenever," she said.

He raised the stuffed bear and offered it. She started to reach and then hesitated. Her gaze sought permission, as if it might not be for her. "Saw you hug it," he said. "Want you to have it."

Her face glowed. For the instant, her eyes were moist. Then, "Why?"

"Told you before. Makes me happy to see you smile. The bear doesn't come with strings."

She answered by looking away, pointing toward the marble counters, with chairs, in a corner of the floor. "Can we have ice cream?" she asked. "They serve it right here."

He smiled at the request. Without her, he wouldn't have allowed himself ice cream. Or much else. "Sure."

He held out the bear. She took it with an awkward movement, drew it against her chest and squeezed with both arms, as if it might be ripped away.

"See that fancy hotel out the front window?" he said. She followed his finger and peered toward The Plaza. Flags above the gilded entry flapped in the breeze. "Let's stay there tonight. Eat in the most expensive restaurant you've ever been to. Get a room high up, looking over the lights of the city." The image caught him, the two of them at a window in the dark, two people who didn't belong—except maybe to each other.

"Don't spoil me," she said. She bounced the bear against him, demanding he take it. "You need to pay for this, if you want."

Penance for the thought of a pleasure, he'd bet. She asked for nothing. "Bear's yours. Tell you what. I'll give you cash and let you make our hotel reservation. The way you look, they'll think you're royalty. Ever done that before?"

She might have given the answer he expected, but a cloud crossed her face. "They know what you look like, don't they? And the apartment—they must know about that, too."

She amazed him. He tried not to show it. He led them out of the aisle without pulling at her. "I have a job to do after dinner. It'll take a few hours. You can watch the telly or the view. Bathroom'll be as big as a house—you can soak in the tub till I get back. Oh, you'll look grand in a bubble bath. I'll wash your back if you like. Wish we were there right now."

But nothing could make her smile. "And you'll come back to me unless you're dead, right?" she asked, mimicking what he'd said earlier, on the street.

When he didn't respond, she bit her lip, stepped forward, and pressed against him, hugging him right on the toy store floor, people detouring around them.

He felt her trembling.

CHAPTER 27
4:58 P.M., Thursday

TREMBLING beside Tony in the passenger seat, Gary closed his eyes, squeezed the handgrip—it didn't help, he felt every curve, every bounce, and dread burned his insides. Becca was gone. She'd driven off after the killer. Gary would never again see her alive. No, calm down, he told himself, and worked to imagine this morning's breakfast, everything normal.

He'd almost succeeded when in his mind the shooter's face appeared right in their kitchen. The Arab didn't have a gun; he didn't need one, his laughter acknowledged a mission accomplished and Becca vanished from the table, there one second, gone the next, leaving Gary as alone as he'd been before, after Sarah died. His eyes flew open and his heart tried to escape from his chest.

Tony turned onto his street.

"Don't worry, she'll come home," the cop reassured him as he pulled up in front of the house. He reached for the ignition key but decided to leave the engine running.

Gary couldn't look at the place. When he did, he found the lights out and the driveway empty. He wasn't sure he wanted to go in, but he had to check for messages and make calls.

"Should I come in with you?" Tony murmured.

Gary felt the man's concern, but the engine kept idling and he knew he couldn't trust the killer's brother, didn't want the man in his home. He shook his head and remained motionless in the passenger seat until Tony said, "Abdel would not harm her. She'll come home. He'll call me soon. It'll be all right."

But Gary knew the man named Abdel had tried to kill them the day before, and that Tony had no idea how make any of what he wished for happen. The only strategy the cop had expressed was to

145

wait a few hours, hoping for a successful resolution before triggering a statewide manhunt. Gary understood why. He also understood his best bet was Alegretti.

That energized him. If Thompson had briefed the lieutenant, as Vincent had claimed when he'd visited earlier, then Vincent would know what to do. Gary wished he'd been able to call sooner—but Tony hadn't brought a phone to the funeral.

"If your wife contacts you, please let me know," Tony went on. "I'll reach out for you if I hear anything, anything at all."

Nothing remained to be said. Gary nodded, stepped out of the car and closed the door. Halfway up his walk, hat in his hand, he paused and watched Tony pull away.

Everything normal felt unreal. A cold breeze blew into his collar. His muscles were tightening. The sun had set. Lights were on in houses up and down the street. Cars eased by, delivering commuters from a Thursday at work. Things he'd seen so often, all ordinary, except for now, and he grasped for his keys as he ran up the steps.

After he locked the door behind him, he turned on the front lights for her return, as he had the day before. He hung his coat on the hall tree, next to the ski jacket she hadn't worn to the funeral. He raced upstairs to the office, ignoring his aching back.

There were no messages. He dialed Vincent's home number—he'd enlist Angela to help find the lieutenant if he wasn't there. He tapped fingers on the desktop until the call rang through to voicemail. He tried to keep panic out of his tone, and then called for Alegretti at the station and again had to leave word. Where were they? He recalled that on Thursdays, Vincent and Angela often went with the Carsons to dinner and a movie. A dozen surrounding towns had restaurants and theatres. He'd never track them.

He leaned against the desk. It had grown as dark outside as the night before, when he and Becca had walked home and she'd fallen in the snow and smiled up at him. His insides burned. He wanted to be numb all over. A martini would help. Better, three. Not now.

She had decided to follow the man, but Gary knew whatever happened to her would be *his* fault. Had he been consigned to mourn all those he loved? He busied himself, changed out of the tight suit and into comfortable clothes.

He found the cards he'd been given: Moriarty and Thompson. He dialed the CIA agent. Voicemail picked up before the first ring, and he had to leave word. Despite his anger, he called for Thompson. Again he left a message that he couldn't be sure would reach the man.

Stumbling downstairs, he switched on the living room and kitchen lights. Follow normal routine, he told himself, stay positive. He thought of dinner, and his stomach rebelled. When the phone rang on the kitchen wall, he almost tripped getting to it.

"Becca?"

The pause from the other end deflated him.

"It's Moriarty, Mr. Kemmerman. What's wrong?"

Gary leaned against a wall. The question meant the agent might not know—but there was no point keeping secrets. "She must have driven off after the guy I identified for you. He came to the funeral but when he saw me he ran. I was with the mourners. Becca couldn't join us—she had to stay in the car and she left before I could reach her. Can you put out an alert?" In his gut, he knew it'd be too late.

"When did she begin to follow him?" Moriarty asked.

"Close to four."

"So it's been little more than an hour. I expect he led her on a merry chase, she lost him, and she's on her way home. She'll call you shortly. Or pull into the driveway."

For an instant he listened through the walls, imagining the car easing up beside the house, tires whispering on the asphalt. He heard nothing. "We need to *do* something—*now!*"

"Calm down, Mr. Kemmerman."

"What if it were your wife?"

The line grew silent, and Gary recalled the conversation in Vincent's office. What had happened to Moriarty's wife?

When the agent spoke, Gary picked up the changed tone. "We will get her back safely, Mr. Kemmerman. I assure you."

He didn't believe it and said nothing. How could the agent offer assurances?

"But you will have to help us," Moriarty added.

"Help you? How? Why?"

"Have you pen and paper?"

"Yeah."

"At exactly 10:15 tonight, be on the sidewalk at the entry to Connolly's Pub in Manhattan." He spelled out "Connolly's" as if he were an English teacher. "There is only one pub by that name in the borough. Approach from the west. I will brief you, and things will proceed."

"What 'things'? How will this help my wife?"

"Trust me, Mr. Kemmerman. We know those involved, but I cannot tell you anything further. I have been doing this for a very long time. I will find—and take care of—the man who shot at you and her."

"Bull shit! How will this help me get Becca back?"

After a brief silence, "Have you a better way?" Moriarty asked. "You had best show up."

"What about Thompson?"

"…He's been pulled off the case. It's mine now, and I will not let you down. Be there if you want your wife back."

The line went dead before Gary could respond. Those final words had sounded like a threat. The bright kitchen offered no guidance.

He looked at the phone, hung it up. At least he had something to do. He found the Manhattan phone book listing for Connolly's, wrote it out, stuck it in his shirt pocket. Less than five hours to go. He couldn't wait, couldn't sit, wandered into the dark dining room.

An unwelcome video started in his mind—the first time Becca had been in the house. From almost the exact spot where he stood now, he'd watched her move about, run fingers over the furniture. He'd known she was wondering about his past, and her movements had crackled with unasked questions. Watching her, he'd resolved many of his own uncertainties.

The sound of the doorbell became part of the daydream. At the second ring, he raced to get it. Megan Safrian, a friend and a nurse at Ridgetop, was standing on the stoop. Had she come to see Becca? She couldn't know what had happened. "Megan?"

She saw his face and raised her palms. "Becca's safe."

Her expression of alarm frightened him before he heard the message.

"She's okay, Gary. Calm down. She's at Ridgetop. She sent me to get you."

"She's at the *hospital?*" He leaned heavily against the doorframe. "What's wrong?"

She reached for his shoulder. "She had an accident on the Turnpike. The car protected her. She's *fine*, Gary. Really, she's not injured."

He grasped her wrist. "She isn't hurt?"

"Bruised, a few cuts. Nothing needs setting or stitching. No concussion—we checked." She pried his hand free and took it in both of hers. "It's okay. Calm *down*. She's fine."

"Why didn't someone call me?"

Megan let go of his hand and patted his chest to reassure him—or perhaps herself. He felt the note in his pocket crinkle. Why had Moriarty insisted on a meeting that had nothing to do with Becca?

"She said you had no driver's license, no car, and if she called you'd probably start running to the hospital without a coat," Megan said.

"Tell me on the way." He stepped around toward the car at the curb. "Let's go."

"Gary!" She grabbed his arm.

He turned on the stoop. "What?"

"The coat. Put on a *coat*. I promised. Take your keys and lock the door."

CHAPTER 28
5:22 P.M., Thursday

DWYER's coat lay folded on the plush leather chair beside him. When he refused to leave it at the coat check station, Lynn had kept hers, also. He couldn't leave his; he had his weapon in the pocket. The money belt around his waist was invisible beneath a thick sweater.

First they'd had a drink in the Oak Bar at the Plaza, at a table overlooking Central Park. Out the windows, night had fallen and city lights glimmered. He'd excited her when he told her the opening scenes of the movie *North by Northwest* had been filmed right there, and Cary Grant might have sat at that very table.

Then they'd entered the Oak Room for dinner. Though it had no windows, Lynn had been awestruck by the lofty ceiling and dark, filigreed woodwork rising to a central arch. A candle had been set on the spotless tablecloth, and her ivory skin glowed in its flicker. He thought she'd fit in anywhere.

"What's a shrimp cocktail?" she asked from behind the large menu. "Never had it before."

"An appetizer—served before the meal. Good idea. Try it."

She peeked around the menu. "You like it?"

He nodded. He couldn't wait to see her expression when the dish arrived, when she covered a shrimp with sauce and bit into it. The conversation stopped when his cell phone rang. As he rummaged for it in his coat, he glanced around the room, looking for anyone who might be targeting them. He flipped the cell open, turning back when Lynn spoke.

"Should've shut it, given us peace."

At the sound of Siddiq's voice, he raised a hand to silence her. She tilted her head and peered at him. Soft classical music washed over the restaurant but he no longer heard it. Diners at other tables would be too close.

"Moment," he whispered into it. As he rose, he reached across with his free hand and touched Lynn's shoulder. "Gotta take this. Be right back." She didn't complain. But he paused to brush through her hair with his fingers, making her smile before he left.

He threaded his way out into a corridor and found a deserted, dimly lit spot. "You get the message?"

"Why do we rush?" asked Siddiq.

The little man lived with his survival skills turned up to full gain, Dwyer thought. "Heard an agency got word about us."

"Which?"

"CIA's my guess."

"How did you learn?"

"Man approached my contact—the one providing the bus."

"Did your contact—"

"No. They must be pushing everyone who's ever been connected. Has to be some reason for it. Even if they're guessing, it makes sooner better than later." He heard only silence. "Your package ready?"

"Yes." But Siddiq would not let up. "Describe the agent."

"Small. Looks like a granddad. Brown eyes, glasses. Expensive clothes, good haircut, cares about appearance."

"You saw him?"

Siddiq's tone had moved beyond concern. Dwyer phrased his response carefully. "We walked past one another. Didn't say a word, just nodded. Didn't learn about him till later. At the time, he didn't seem to know me—but he set someone to follow."

"How do you know?"

Dwyer scanned the corridor. "Questioned and eliminated him." The pause lasted so long that he thought Siddiq had hung up. "Won't come back at us," Dwyer said. "But it's a reason to speed things. I'll pass along final plans about six tomorrow morning."

He wanted to return to Lynn, but when Siddiq spoke again, Dwyer knew the Arab had latched onto what he'd heard. "The one who followed you—did *he* work for the CIA?"

"Naah. Freelance. A referral. He'd met the agent once to point me out. Got one of those number-only cards from him, and cash for a half-day's work."

"How do I find your…contact?"

"Now look—"

"I will not approach the man. He will not know I exist. It's the other I want."

A new wrinkle. "Why?"

"How do I find him?"

The following silence made it clear that Siddiq would not answer Dwyer's question. One long night remained. There was no reason to make trouble. Dwyer asked again for assurance that Siddiq would not approach Ryan Scully, and then described the man and where he might be found.

When Dwyer returned to the table, appetizers were waiting. Six large shrimp, with flared pink tails, hung over the lip of the goblet in front of Lynn. She held the small fork like a weapon, eyeing the shrimp as if they might attack her. In the center of the bowl, a mound of red sauce clung to spires of lettuce.

"Y'know," she said, once he'd sat, "I don't need fancy expensive places and—" she waved at her plate with the fork— "these things."

"Bet you'll like 'em."

"I will." She nodded but didn't smile, and the nod turned into a shake. "Not the point." She laid down the fork and leaned forward to emphasize her words. "We could make do with burgers."

He heard the glorious "we."

"Y'see?" she added, brows knit.

"Right, I know that. There'll be plenty of time for that. Find burgers everywhere in the world. But—"

"But what?"

"I wanna see you eat that strange fish with hot sauce." He couldn't help grinning.

Lynn laughed and did not disappoint.

CHAPTER 29
5:25 P.M., Thursday

As Megan pulled away from the curb, Gary twisted around for a glance at his house. The solid building—brick, vinyl siding above, wide chimney, pitched roof, heavy wooden front door—once represented refuge. That had changed after Sarah died.

He recalled sitting quietly in the living room in his robe, feet up on the coffee table, feeling isolated, broken. He'd laughed inside at the room's name as he methodically considered ways to commit suicide. He neither wanted to mess up nor leave a mess that must inconvenience others. An overdose would be best, the pill of the moment, washed down by a pitcher of martinis, no antacids needed.

The car's movement rocked him through space and time. They were heading to Becca and he knew that once again he'd knocked himself off balance. Before he retired, when he practiced crisis consulting, maintaining strict perspective had been a requirement for doing his job. Losing his cool now might get him and Becca killed—yet he'd done just that. If he couldn't deal with his emotions, he'd better keep away from criminals. The feds could reel in Siddiq without his help.

"Are you okay?" Megan asked.

He faced her, but by then she'd turned back to the road. "How'd it happen—the accident?"

She considered before responding. "I'll let her tell you."

"Come on, Megan."

"We're only minutes away."

"You're sure she isn't injured?"

"I told you that twice." Megan shook her head and wouldn't say anything more.

He watched the passing scene. Familiar streets seemed like stage sets. He'd been so focused on loss that everything else had receded.

Megan—usually a speed demon behind the wheel—drove carefully. She must not want to shake me up any more, he thought, and it came to him that Becca was the one who needed comfort, not him. He cloaked his impatience by reviewing what had gone on since Tuesday night. It reminded him of an Indian burn—in whatever direction they turned, the pain and pressure increased.

Minutes later, Megan pulled into the Emergency lot and led him to the hospital. She waved at the admitting nurse, moved past the desk, through the swinging doors and onto the patient floor. He recalled it vaguely from two days before, when he'd arrived in an ambulance, strapped onto a gurney.

To the left, blue privacy curtains, some drawn, divided a row of beds set along the wall. Halfway down the passage, Megan turned, and he saw Becca in a bed, propped by pillows, wearing a blue hospital gown.

She hadn't brushed her tangled hair. She looked ashen. Her mouth opened when she saw him and he rushed over, bending to take her head into his hands, staring into her eyes, seeking something that would tell him that she was okay. Whatever he'd meant to say, nothing would come out. She reached up and they pressed together. Tears wet him—he didn't know whose they were.

"You okay?" he whispered, barely getting it out, stroking her hair, her cheek.

She nodded and they moved apart.

"I'm sorry," she whimpered.

"It's okay. You're back, you're safe, nothing else matters." He found a tissue and dabbed at her tears. "It's okay now." He couldn't let her go; his hand touched her arm, face, shoulder.

She reached for him and they hugged again. "I thought I'd die," she gasped, tears spilling.

He stroked her hair, said "Its okay, okay," over and over, until she calmed.

She took a deep breath and pushed him up. Her tears had stopped when she said, "I followed him."

"I know. You're very brave."

She brightened at the response and went on. "He spotted me. I broke off and headed home." Whatever she recalled caused her to gasp. When she moved her right hand to rub her left shoulder, she winced in pain.

He leaned closer. "You hurting?"

"Just bruised." The hand moved from her shoulder to his cheek.

"You give her something for pain?" he asked Megan.

"I offered. She won't take it—won't take anything."

Becca breathed deeply, fingers at Gary's cheek, eyes on his face as if to memorize it.

"Let's not talk about the accident," he said. The blow-by-blow would come whenever she'd want to discuss it.

Becca shook her head. "Jeff can tell you." She motioned toward Thompson, sitting in a chair at the other side of the bed.

It was the first Gary'd seen him. "What are *you* doing here? Questioning her? I left you a message. You didn't call back."

"When did you call?"

"After five."

"Cell's off in the hospital."

"And you're off this case."

Thompson leaned forward. "I am?"

"Moriarty told me you've been reassigned."

"Gary." He turned back at Becca's soft call. She shook her head again. "Jeff saved my life."

"What?" He stared at Thompson.

"The man with the belt tried to kill me," Becca whispered. "Jeff got me out of the car." He turned back to her. She looked as if she'd have cried if she hadn't been too worn for tears. "It burned up."

He took her right hand in both of his. "All that counts is you're safe, you're back, forget the car, we'll get another. You want a hybrid—let's pick one out together. Whatever color you like."

She nodded and scrunched her mouth, but her eyes were on his chest. "I'm sorry," she repeated. No sniffling this time, though.

"For what?"

She didn't meet his eye, but he saw the determined curl of her lips and knew eye contact was close. "Not letting you get me a cell phone. Going after the man without you."

"He would've been gone if you waited. I—"

"Would've done the same thing," she said, and tapped his arm.

He saw the glint in her eyes. "That's just what I told myself."

The bruises would heal; he knew that what lived inside her was already recovering. He turned to Thompson. "I owe you. What happened?"

When the agent finished, he asked Becca, "Did I get it right?"

"Except my smelling smoke, finding myself trapped and believing—when I saw the knife—that you'd come back to finish me." With all eyes on her, she turned to Gary. "Jeff had the man who hit you in front of him and he broke off the chase to save me. He wouldn't tell you that. So I'm responsible for—"

Thompson waved her off. "My job—my decision."

"I'm grateful," Becca said.

"Me, too," Megan added.

"Shit," Thompson said, looking up at the nurse. "You shouldn't have been here—"

"She's a nurse and my best friend, Jeff," Becca said. "She didn't hear a thing."

Thompson thought about it and turned to Gary. He laced his hammy fingers. "Now, tell me why I'm off the case."

Becca pushed up in the bed, and the movement caught Gary's attention. Color was returning to her face. She wanted to hear what he had to say. Without looking down, she used a corner of the blanket to wipe tear tracks.

"Before Megan came to get me, I phoned for you, Alegretti and Moriarty. He returned it, told me you'd been pulled off the case—that it was his, now. That's all he said about it. Oh, and that he'd find and 'take care of'—his words—the man with the belt."

"Why would he say that?" Becca asked the agent.

Thompson's face twisted in thought, but he didn't look at either of them. In the silence, muted voices floated from down the floor. Megan stepped up beside Gary and reached down to take her pulse.

Becca slapped at the hand. "I'm good," she said without turning from Thompson. When he remained silent, she glanced back to Gary and Megan. "Okay. Out of here, guys. I need to get dressed."

"Is that wise?" Megan asked.

"Just help me, Meg. You know I'm over it."

Megan bent closer to Gary. "Is this going to happen to her again?

Hasn't she been through enough?"

He wasn't sure how to respond, but Becca spoke up as if the question hadn't been asked. "I can't wear the black dress. I just can't put that on again, Meg. Loan me your spare jeans and a sweatshirt. Don't tell me you don't have them here. That'll get me home. I'll drop 'em off later."

Megan frowned and hesitated.

"Come on!" Becca said. "The FBI doesn't need to see a chubby middle-aged woman in her underwear."

Thompson chuckled.

Her liveliness delighted Gary. The case had helped bring her back. Partnership had some benefits.

"Oh, all right," Megan said.

The men rose. Gary bent to kiss Becca. He aimed for her forehead, but she lifted her face. The touch of her lips warmed him. "Well, you're feeling better," he said. She smiled and shooed them away.

Megan drew the curtain. "Shhhh," it called out, following its ellipse. The women vanished behind it.

CHAPTER 30
6:01 P.M., Thursday

"Your CIA buddy lied to me," Gary said. He was leaning against a tan-painted wall in the ER admitting lobby. He and Thompson had faced away from the duty nurse at the other end of the antiseptic-smelling space. "Care to tell me what's going on?"

"No need to go there," the agent muttered.

"Good will doesn't last long around you. No need for you to drive us home, either. We'll call a cab."

Before Thompson could respond, Vincent and Angela stormed in. She rushed up to Gary and grasped both his arms hard enough to hurt. "We got your messages. Is—"

"Becca's fine," he said. "She's getting dressed. Megan's helping. Go on in, Angela." She loosened her grip but still looked unsure, so he added, "She's okay. She'll be happy to see you."

Angela turned to Vincent, though Gary knew she didn't need permission; and he'd have bet by then she knew the rest of it. Vincent nodded, and she moved. Everyone knew the lieutenant. The duty nurse waved her through the swinging door.

"She *really* okay?" Vincent asked, in an impossibly nasal voice. "You sounded desperate."

"You don't sound so good either." Gary glanced toward Thompson. "He saved her."

Vincent asked how, and Thompson told him. The two men displayed none of the hostility toward one another that Gary had expected.

"Listen up," Thompson added, and turned to Gary. "Did Moriarty ask you to do something for him?"

"How'd you know?"

"Had to be a reason he'd return your call. What'd he want?"

161

Gary repeated the conversation. None of it seemed to surprise either man.

"Good," Thompson said. "Connolly's Pub at 10:15 tonight. Let's be there."

"But Becca's safe, and—"

"They may recognize you," Vincent said to Thompson. "I'll cover him."

The agent shook his head. "You sound like shit—and Moriarty would recognize you, too. Stay out of it. Go home, drink hot tea, get to bed early. I'll be with him." He turned to Gary. "Just be yourself—but as if you hadn't found your wife."

Vincent chuckled. "Panicked."

Gary flashed him a look and faced Thompson. "*Why* do I need to go?"

Thompson laced his fingers together. "You said you owed me."

Gary shifted his weight.

Thompson sighed. "All right. Moriarty has hunches. If he believes this will get him closer to—well, the man who tried to kill you and your wife—it's worth our giving him his head."

It would be tough for the man to dodge the question now, Gary thought, and asked, "Why does he want to cut you out?"

Thompson glanced briefly at Vincent and shrugged. "He wants to get the guy alone. If I'm there, Siddiq becomes a capture for others to deal with."

"Has it got anything to do with Moriarty's wife?"

Thompson nodded.

Gary frowned, recalling the glimmer in Becca's eye. "This guy must enjoy killing wives. I'm the lucky one—so far. Let's keep Becca far away from this. What is it Moriarty will want me to do?"

"I can't be sure," Thompson said, "but I think he believes Siddiq, and an ex-IRA killer who's also slipped into New York, must be working together."

"Why me in an Irish bar? Only Siddiq knows me—and I'll bet even Moriarty wouldn't parade me in front of that man. I'd last two seconds." He turned to Vincent. "I gotta let Tony know that Becca's okay. He brought me home from the funeral and acted as if *he* was responsible for her going missing."

"I'll do it."

"Don't dump on him." Gary saw Vincent's cold eyes and added, "He had no idea the man would run or that Becca would follow him. He didn't ask for that brother."

Thompson reacted to that and leaned in closer. "I'm impressed," he said.

Vincent cleared his throat. "I hear you, but it's my job. Let me do it, huh?"

Gary turned back to Thompson and waited.

"We'll both find out what Moriarty wants. I have a name—I'll brief you in the car while we're driving in."

A minute before, Gary hadn't wanted Thompson driving him anywhere. Decisions were being made for him. He considered that and knew he'd do whatever the man who'd saved Becca wanted.

"Need a pistol?" Vincent asked Gary.

Would it come to that? He knew how to shoot but hated the idea.

The men were so focused that they didn't notice Becca and Angela approaching. It startled them when Becca said, "Vincent, you've been volunteered to drive us home."

Thank God, Gary thought, that she hadn't heard the pistol remark. She hated guns even worse than he did. He observed small tears in the fabric of her blue coat. A nick from the gunshot, lacerations from the car window—time for a new coat. Ten months before, Becca had come close to him in that coat, and they'd had a first kiss. Everything moves on.

"They have no car," Angela told her husband. "And what about dinner? They have to eat. We do, too." She turned to Becca. "When we heard Gary's messages, we apologized to Peter and Eileen and ran out of Luka's before they could serve us. After all this, forget cooking. We could stop at the diner." She saw the look on Becca's face and tapped at her arm. "So don't order a whole meal—but something?"

Megan's jeans showed below Becca's coat. She held a shopping bag, probably containing the funeral outfit. Gary saw that her eyes had cleared and she'd brushed her hair.

"Good idea," Becca said. She turned to Gary. "Then I hope we're in for the night."

She was looking out for him, he knew. He wanted to hug her. But he was standing on thin ice. "I have to meet a man in Manhattan later," he said. He couldn't look back at her. Partner or not, he did *not* want her taking any more risks.

"When?" she asked, drawing out the word.

"I'll drive him—and bring him back," Thompson offered. "He'll be home before midnight."

It also told her that the meeting was linked to the case. Gary didn't like the expression on her face.

"It has to do with this...person who keeps trying to kill us, doesn't it?" she asked Thompson.

"I'm pretty sure he won't be there."

Becca grinned at him, and Gary paled. "Jeff, why not join us for dinner? Gary owes you at least a meal for saving me. And you can't go far off if you're doing the driving later."

The agent shrugged. "If it's okay with everyone."

At first, Gary believed that Thompson hadn't sensed Becca's intent. But then the special agent's lips curled.

"Good," Becca said, when no one else spoke up. "Before we hit the diner, Gary and I have a stop to make."

"Where?" asked Vincent.

"The cell phone store on Route 4. It's not really out of the way. We need new ones."

"Why tonight?" Gary asked. "We could check out phones in the morning, before your shift, when we have more time."

She ignored him. "And Jeff shouldn't drive alone. I'll go in his car."

CHAPTER 31
7:51 P.M., Thursday

DWYER and Lynn came up out of the Houston Street subway station and turned toward Greenwich Village. In the dark, with a breeze biting at them, they ignored the occasional passers-by, and sauntered hand in hand as if they didn't feel the chill and hadn't a care in the world. He'd turned right at a corner, left at the next, before she spoke.

"Why do you still do this?"

"I told you they killed my brother."

Headlights flared against her face. "My parents were taken, but I don't go around...killing people."

She beat up only on herself, he knew. "Someone has to hit back— might as well be me."

They walked in silence until she tugged his hand and brought them to a stop beside a shuttered art gallery. "That's past, Sean. We're all burnt out, them and us, from dyin'." When he looked back without an answer, she leaned closer and said softly, "You don't *know* why any more, do you? It's been what you've done, so you just keep doin' it."

Whatever she'd touched inside, he found he couldn't stoke the fire. But he pressed on, as he always had. "Finn's place is just around the corner," he said, aware he couldn't meet her eyes. She let him lead her forward. When they reached the poorly lit street, he stopped and pointed out Finn's brick-clad apartment building.

"Do you *have* to go up?" she asked, yanking her hand away. "We're not going back to his rooms—we're at the hotel and we're leavin' tomorrow morning, you told me. He can't bother us."

"You worried about my safety?"

She looked down the street and nodded.

Dwyer hated to leave in place an agent who might rat out others. He didn't believe Finn would prove dangerous. But he also didn't want to upset Lynn. "Grady and I go back a long way. My meeting him won't cause trouble. I'll be back soon." He took her chin in his hand and smiled as she faced him. "Okay?"

She shook off the hand and nodded uncomfortably.

He glanced around. Streetlights marched down the sidewalks, a few with burnt-out bulbs. Cars were parked everywhere, roofs shiny. In the cold, the few people venturing out scuttled along. Apartment windows glimmered.

Earlier, over dinner, Lynn had demanded that he let her go with him. "I believe you'll come back," she'd said—but she'd been adamant. He'd found himself ready to say yes when, for decades, he'd have said no. At least he'd gotten her to agree to wait downstairs while he visited Finn.

But he hadn't considered where downstairs would be. Looking around, he knew he couldn't leave her on the street. "I'll be safer than you—take this," he said, dropping the gun into her coat pocket. "And this." On a hunch, he reached for the money belt—it took him a few moments to open it—and folded it into her other coat pocket.

"Why? What'll I do with them?" She locked her hands together across her breast, far from the pockets.

"Gun'll just be there for you. A pretty woman out alone at night, you know."

He realized that he'd never needed to worry about such things before.

"Now, come on in here," he said.

Careful not to pull her arm, he led her into a Chinese take-out place, with a half dozen tables, a few doors from Finn's building. He'd given her pocket money that afternoon. While she finally agreed to carry it, she'd refused to spend any. "Order something. You don't need to eat it; it'll buy you table space to wait. Ten, fifteen minutes at most, and I'll be back."

She looked as if she'd never see him again. "I'm not gonna ask if you believe I wanna come back." He squeezed her shoulder, left the small restaurant, and only then realized what she'd feared.

Moments later, he pushed Finn's intercom, announced himself, slipped through the buzzing front door and into the dingy building. Two flights up, surprise pasted on his face, Finn swung the apartment door open. "And how's my buddy?" Dwyer asked, stepping close. They slapped backs and Finn waved him in.

"God knows you're welcome, but it's a bit of a shock seeing you," said the balding, smaller man, pointing to a chair. "You told me to leave you be, not to visit while you're here."

Dwyer noticed that the furniture didn't match and wasn't new. He heard rustling from the bedroom. "Have I come at a bad time?"

"Not at all." Finn smiled, and whispered, "She'll wait."

"Got private things to discuss," Dwyer said. He sat in the chair.

Finn paced across and closed the bedroom door. "We talk low, she can't hear from in there. When's the last we met?"

"Couple years back. Spain, was it?"

Finn nodded but didn't sit. "The apartment I loaned you to your liking? Thought a place like that'd be more comfortable, give a lower profile than a hotel. It's furnished better than this one."

"It's fine. Hey—heat on, Grady?"

Finn appeared confused. "Is it too hot for you in here?"

Dwyer knew the man understood what he'd meant. "Why'd you give me up?"

Finn frowned. "Don't be a fool. Course I didn't."

With his zipped coat, Dwyer would be sweating soon. He rubbed his eyes and leaned back, hands loose on the chair arms. "You know the drill. There are only so many aware I'm here. Do the elimination and you're it."

That agitated Finn. "I'm 'it' for what?" he said, moving around to lean on the back of a tan couch. He kept his voice low. "Why would I tell anyone about you?"

Dwyer shrugged. "I was hoping you'd tell me that."

"I flap off, they'd have to kill me," Finn said.

"Oh, I doubt that."

"You tell 'em I broke trust, you'll get me killed whether or not. It's not right."

He'd thought Finn's slip must've been accidental—a woman, a night too drunk in the bar, the man behaved like that. Dwyer looked at Finn's pained face and knew in this profession, a few words and friendship went all to hell. He wished he hadn't given up the weapon. "I don't expect I'll have to talk to anyone, Grady. Lot of nonsense going on. Tell me what and why—if I know which way to dodge, we get past this."

The revolver must have been in the small table behind the couch. It appeared in Grady's hand. He hadn't been drinking. "I doubt that, buddy. Dumb of you to come if you suspected."

"We go back, Grady. I'm not armed. What's this for?"

"Dumb and dumber." Finn screwed a tubular silencer onto the pistol.

"You don't need that," Dwyer said. "Talk to me."

"Stand up and unzip the jacket. Slowly." Dwyer did. Finn frisked him from behind while pressing the muzzle hard to his spine. Dwyer said silent thanks that Lynn had kept the gun, the money, and hadn't come up.

"Now, sit," Finn said. "Legs out. Fine. I don't have a damn thing to say to you. Don't need to explain myself."

"Too much soft American living?"

"Too much expensive American living." He smirked. "It's called having a life, something you gave up back along the line."

Until I met Lynn, Dwyer thought. "Speaking of giving up, you give up the other apartment to them?"

"Hell, no. Only told 'em you'd come, and who you'd probably meet with."

"Because they threatened you?"

"Naah." Finn shook his head. "The carrot's what counted. They'll give me a small fortune for you." He smiled. "The cash you brought must be in the apartment. That'll be mine, too. I won't tell 'em about it. They won't give a damn—it's you they want."

Dwyer recalled Scully's line about the "pile" he'd brought to cover expenses. The people behind this must be offering everyone money. He had to hand it to the small man in the brown coat—he'd left no stone unturned. "They're deluding you. You believe they'll keep their word?"

"Sure. I'll keep mine, and there may be a next time they need me." The smirk returned. "I have lots of friends." He waved the pistol. "Just hang quiet."

He dialed a cell with one hand. "Got 'em, call back." In less than a minute, the phone vibrated. Finn listened. "Sure thing," he said, then, "Right." Another pause. "You bet. Kind of you."

He hung up and whispered to his captive, "Lucky Sean. I'm to deliver you to them just around the corner. Your blood won't be on my hands or my rug." He spoke loudly. "Stay in there, baby. Got a small job. I'll be back in a half hour. Let's go out, then. Somewhere real fancy."

Whether the invisible woman had heard them or not, she remained silent.

"Never thought it," Dwyer said, as he stepped down the stairs. Finn descended behind him, the gun in his hand in a coat pocket. Finn wouldn't make a mistake. Dwyer didn't mind dying, never had. It would be tough on Katie and his brother's three kids. They'd never know him like he wanted, though what little he had would go to them. But leaving Lynn—that ballooned in his gut, burned hotter than he could've imagined.

"Shit happens," Finn said.

They came outside. Not a person in sight. Dwyer raised his hands, palms forward, a prisoner being marched off. "Lead on."

With his free hand, Finn pointed right. Dwyer turned and the gunman followed. "Down with the hands—cut the shit. We turn right at the corner and wait."

"Geneva Convention rules apply?"

He didn't get an answer. Twenty feet, ten feet, five feet—they were there. Dwyer glanced around. Finn was standing too far back to jump. The gun was out of the pocket and ready; it looked huge with the silencer. The streets were deserted.

"Turn right," Finn said. "On the sidewalk, nice and slow, or I drop you right here. Won't get as much for a body—prefer it the other way."

Dwyer stepped into darkness, imagining the muzzle centered on his back. Finn would lean him onto the wall, arms apart, legs spread, no way to move fast. The ones who'd come get him would want to hear everything he knew. He'd die first, and it wouldn't be pretty.

He tensed and hunched down, ready to jump the man and bat

the gun away. If it had to happen, better it end here. Maybe Finn would slip, or fire wildly—a small chance, but better than none. One, two, and he began to swivel on the concrete, ready to lunge forward, reaching for the weapon.

Two shots blasted at close range. Momentum carried him around, eyes on the gun, ready for it to spurt fire again and finish him.

But it didn't. It wavered, and when he looked up Finn was sagging, mouth open, eyes glazed.

Lynn stood close behind the slumping corpse, holding Dwyer's plastic pistol in two shaking hands.

"What've I done?" she cried out.

They stood at the window, naked and holding each other, twelve stories above the traffic pulsing along Fifth Avenue and across Central Park South. City lights shimmered in the cold.

She'd fastened every bolt she could find on the hall door. Working together, they'd drawn a bubble bath in the large tub, both of them jumpy, talking about anything other than what had happened. They hadn't turned on the lights, except in the bathroom. Its door had been closed, and brightness through the window supplied the room's glow.

Dwyer turned from the city view and gazed at her. She stared out the window, breathing deeply, unaware of his eyes. "Back in the restaurant, when you just had to come along with me, did you know that would happen?"

She rubbed a cheek against his arm, still captured by the lights. "Don't know anything, anymore, 'cept being with you."

"You'll come with me tomorrow. You look good in that outfit. They'll give me a suit. Imagine—a collar and a tie, on this neck."

She didn't react.

"We'll get on a plane, fly away, start a life." Had his brother felt this way when he met Katie? He looked at Lynn, and his chest swelled.

"Sean, get out of this." Her whisper was rough. She turned to him and gazed up, eyes saucers. "Please, I'm beggin' you, get out of it."

"A half a day—then, I promise." It shook him, all that he wanted, all that he'd never known he wanted. His second "I promise," was softer, and she couldn't know the commitment behind the words.

"No," she said, and batted at his arm. "Now, right now—you want, we'll take a cab to the airport. Forget the gun, find us a beach, anywhere you like." Her fingers touched his cheek, and she whispered again, "Right now."

He let out a long breath. "I'm looking for a bubble bath. And you don't have a passport. We'll fix that tomorrow. Make you an official colleen, a tourist going home. When what I have to do is over, we got us a room at the Regency Hotel to shower in, change clothes. Then they'll pick us up, give us our new papers, drive us to the airport."

They were facing each other, and he put his hands on her waist, resting where the hips flared. The touch burned; he wasn't accustomed to the way his stomach tightened, but he had to say it. "I asked them to put your passport in your new name."

Her eyes flooded, chin quivered, he could barely hear the words. "Tonight, Sean, please, tonight."

"You asked to stick close," he said. "You can. I got you a gun. Want you to carry it. Don't want anything happening to you."

Tears were streaming down her cheeks. "Don't need all this."

"What's wrong?"

She could barely speak through the gasps. "Rooms and food, clothes and bubbles." The final words were ripped in agony, "Even teddy bears."

"What do you want?"

She pulled away and ran to the bed, dropping onto her stomach, wailing into the cover.

He'd heard what she moaned before she fled. "Just you."

CHAPTER 32
8:06 P.M., Thursday

SMOLDERING in silence, Gary sat on the edge of the bed as he watched Becca dressing. Normally he'd reach out for a hug. Not now.

She donned each piece of what she called her "secret agent" outfit with pleasure: panties and black slacks, a sports bra with a tight black pull-on above it, thick dark socks, and black running shoes. On the way out of the house she'd add a pea coat and a dark blue knit cap over her pinned-up hair.

Earlier, after the five of them finished dinner, the Alegrettis had dropped Gary off and gone home. For them, dinner had been a celebration of Becca's survival. They'd toasted to her, and Thompson, and Gary. Focused on the upcoming meeting and his certainty that Becca would try to intrude, Gary's joy had been tempered. He'd had nothing stronger than coffee, and while it normally cheered him, tonight he'd become jumpy.

When Thompson, driving Becca, stopped in the driveway to let her out, she'd invited him in. Jeff had to wait somewhere before they drove to the meeting at Connolly's, she'd explained to Gary.

He'd heard the word "they," realized what it meant, and the two of them had quite a row right in front of the agent. He wanted her nowhere near Connolly's. She refused to let him play spy without being close by.

Thompson had brokered a truce. She'd come along but stay in the car. "I'll keep the keys," he'd told them. "She's done quite enough for the day."

Gary'd bet she'd talked the agent into it on the way to or from dinner. Her choice of clothing further upset him. Why did she select that outfit if she planned to remain an observer?

"Grouchy, are we?" Becca peered at him as she pulled a dark

maroon sweater out of her closet cubby.

"Megan and Thompson both said it—you've been through enough today. Stay home. Please."

She stood there, sweater forgotten in her hand. "And you'll go alone."

She hadn't meant it as a question. He nodded anyway.

She shook her head. "You wouldn't get a block before you felt bad." It seemed a throwaway line, but after she started to face away, she turned back. "I don't want you falling apart again."

He threw up his hands. "What does *that* mean?"

She sat beside him on the bed. "I know you want to protect me."

"Right."

"But you'll put yourself in danger."

"Well, yeah, if—"

"You're the man! You're the sleuth—"

"That's not it."

His right hand lay flat on the bed, and she covered it with hers. "I know. You lost your parents when you were a kid, and cancer took Sarah. You're afraid to lose me."

He took the warm hand in his. "I'm afraid for you."

She looked back at him before she spoke. "And for yourself."

Thick armor locked around his gut—she must have heard the clanking—but he tried to speak as if nothing had happened. "Yeah. I don't want to lose you. It's not the first time I've told you that."

"We work best as partners," Becca said. "I'm not giving that up." She looked away and spoke slowly. "If something happens to me… well, Angela gave me the rundown on Gary-the-Hermit—what happened to you after Sarah died." She turned back, eyes swimming. "I don't want that for you again—if anything should happen to me. Promise."

The contact burned and he couldn't hold it. He glanced at the wall in front of him. That promise, he couldn't make. The beveled mirror showed three of her, different angles and sizes. A feeling of dread overwhelmed him. Had it come from the past, or the future? He spoke from far away, and knew she'd pick it up. "Then don't take risks. Stay home."

She sighed, freed her hand, and got up. But then she bent down, and without a word, kissed him on the forehead. By the time the doorbell broke the moment, Becca had pinned her hair.

Gary expected Thompson to be in the living room, where he said he'd be making calls—he wouldn't answer the door. So Gary went to get it, and on the way he didn't spot the agent.

He switched on the outside lights and peered through the front door's stained glass window, sure he'd find Vincent.

But it was the last person he expected: Tony Siddiq. Gary swung the door slightly open to be polite. "Did you get the news that she's back?" he asked, blocking entry.

Tony nodded. He was wearing civilian clothes under an unzipped tan parka.

Open coats must run in the family, Gary thought. "What in hell are you doing here?"

The man shifted his feet, and Gary sensed his discomfort. "I would like to apologize to you and your wife for my part in what happened. I couldn't know—"

"Did your brother ask you to do this? Or maybe the lieutenant?"

"Gary," Becca said from behind him. He turned. "Tony, please come in." She nudged her husband gently but with clear intent, until he backed up.

"I don't want to intrude," the cop said.

Becca spoke forcefully. "Come in." She stepped in front of Gary and waved the man forward. He wiped his shoes carefully on the mat and followed her into the living room while Gary locked the door.

"Let me take your coat," she said.

"I can't stay long." He looked uncomfortable.

"I'm fine, Tony," Becca said. "I'm back and unharmed. You and Gary have to talk. Give me the damn coat."

She'd never raised her voice, but her words had startled both men. Tony offered up the parka. She carried it to the hall tree in the vestibule rather than folding it over the couch, a measure of her seriousness about them talking. It piqued Gary's curiosity.

"Would you like a hot drink?" he asked the man.

When Tony hesitated, Gary answered the question. "He wanted

coffee this morning, Becca. Would you please make it for both of us?" He looked at Tony. "You don't have to drink it. I want you to know you're welcome. I'm pissed, but not with you."

"If I could have prevented it—"

Gary saw how the man shrank. "Here, sit on the couch."

Becca headed into the kitchen.

"You know what your brother is, don't you?" Gary said, still standing.

Tony ran a hand through his thinning hair. "What he has become. Once—he wasn't like that."

"He's tried to kill us three times. He's getting better at it. I doubt we have any luck left."

Tony closed his eyes, and his question emerged. "I don't know what to do. What would you do?"

Gary heard the unspoken "if you were me" and said, "Why don't you ask Rashid?"

The cop shook his head.

"The lieutenant dump on you?" Gary asked.

Tony looked back at him, eyes veiled. "Your friend is a good man."

Gary thought it through. "You have a decision to make. I'd bet the lieutenant'll help you whatever you decide."

Tony nodded.

"Was the question serious?"

Again Tony nodded, holding eye contact.

"I never had a brother."

The man waited.

"You could do nothing, turn him in, or handle it yourself— convince him to leave, or... ." He couldn't say it. "You're not your brother's keeper."

"But I am." Tony looked pained. "I took an oath to become a citizen, and then a police officer." The only sounds were coming from the kitchen. "I came to ask your forgiveness—and your thoughts."

"You have my forgiveness. I'm not sure what I'd do if he were my brother. I couldn't do *nothing*, not if it would allow him to murder others. I'd feel—I'd be—responsible for their deaths if I didn't try to stop him."

Tony slumped, but when he glanced up, his eyes were clear. "Thank you."

Becca entered, bearing two mugs. "You take it with a little milk, if I remember," she said to Tony, holding out his coffee.

He smiled at her but didn't reach for it. "Would it be acceptable if we had coffee another time? I have things to do."

"Of course," she said.

He got up, they exchanged pleasantries as they moved toward the door and Gary handed him his coat. The man trudged off with a certain purpose in his step. When Gary returned to the living room, Thompson was standing beside Becca, holding the mug meant for the cop.

She handed Gary his coffee.

"You'll do just fine tonight," the special agent said.

"You think what Tony and I discussed will make a difference?"

"I'll get my tea," Becca said, and left.

"You gave him an agenda. He made up his mind. Yeah, you made a difference."

Gary circled the mug with his hands, letting it warm him. "I'm still pissed at you."

Becca returned, and Thompson glanced her way. "Great outfit," he said.

Gary saw the agent's lips curl, and knew the remark had been payback for his comment. Before he could respond, Thompson turned to him and laughed. "Come off it—you couldn't have told her 'no' even if she hadn't enlisted me."

CHAPTER 33
9:47 P.M., Thursday

FROM the passenger seat beside Thompson, Gary gazed out at the lights, buildings, cars, people—but found it difficult to pay attention. The special agent headed deep into Manhattan, toward Connolly's Pub. The Ford jounced into potholes and swerved around double-parked vehicles, but neither that, nor the thought of the unwanted meeting, was fueling Gary's distress.

"If you go into Connolly's, how can you be sure Becca will *stay* in the car?" he asked Thompson.

"Cut it out," she called out from the back seat.

"What if Moriarty spots her?" he asked, leaning closer to the agent as if the answer might cut her out of the action. "You said the guy with the belt won't be there, but what if he is?" Thompson didn't reply. Gary understood the silence as an effort to stay out of the family quarrel. The car bumped over something, and he leaned back. "We don't want her to get out, but she's a sitting duck in the car."

Becca's hand settled on his shoulder. "A duck, huh? What if you're hanging out in a bar with terrorists because a rogue CIA agent sent you, and one of them kills you, and I'm sitting here like a good girl? You want me to demand that *you* not go in?" Immediately, and much more softly, she added, "You think life will be any different for me without you than for you without me?"

The jolt from a pothole stung Gary's back. He used the pain to mask his reaction, and laid a hand over hers. "I'll get it done as quick as I can. You'll stay in the car till I get back?"

"Where else would I go?"

The words echoed what he'd offered her the day before, when he intended just the opposite. He turned to Thompson. "What do you want me to do?"

The agent kept his eyes on the road. "Play along with Moriarty. He doesn't want you or your wife harmed. He wants to get to Siddiq—who for sure won't be in an Irish bar. My guess, my partner will ask you to meet with one of the Irish regulars, a man named Ryan Scully. He's short, older and going to fat, has a mane of gray hair and a fleshy nose that makes him look like the drinker he is—easy to spot. I'd bet Moriarty is squeezing both you *and* Scully. It's okay if you express your anger about him to Scully. Go ahead, tell the Irishman you just want out."

"Won't that piss him off?"

"It doesn't matter. An honest reaction will help sell Moriarty's message—whatever it is. If we're following his hunch, we might as well nudge it along."

"You're keeping your CIA partner in the dark, aren't you?" Gary asked. "You don't want me to talk about Siddiq's attempt on Becca, or our discussions—right?"

The edge returned to Thompson's voice. "You're too smart for that. Push into this, and maybe then you won't be safe. Your job is in, out, and done. Your wife's job is to wait in the car. If I get involved, then you use your new phone to call a cab and go home. Alegretti can watch over you until this clears up. Understood?"

Gary waited but heard nothing from Becca. "Guns, cars," he said. "What's the gentleman with the silver belt got left to target us with, plastic explosives?" He didn't expect an answer.

Thompson eased the car past the entry to a parking garage and pulled up to the curb at a bus stop. "We're here. The pub's around the corner to the right, down the block and across the street. It's got a sign out front." The agent spoke while facing the windshield, peering out as if he could see the place.

"If you need to, tell Moriarty you left your car in this garage. Once he briefs you and leaves—or goes inside—we'll turn the corner and park where we can watch the pub entrance. After a bit, I'll follow you in. It won't matter if Moriarty sees me."

Gary hesitated.

"You want the speech about good versus evil?" Thompson asked, facing him. "May not be stirring the way I tell it, but it's true."

From the back seat, Becca chimed in. "He doesn't need it."

"Right on time," Moriarty said, intercepting Gary after he'd turned the corner, a quarter block from the old-style swinging wooden sign that marked Connolly's. Gary thought that the small CIA man might have been teleported to the spot where he abruptly appeared.

"You know where my wife is?" The nastiness in his voice must be a reflection of Moriarty's lies and his concern at Becca's closeness. His gut told him nothing good could come from it. The breeze whipped at his hands. It was a long day.

"The man to whom I will introduce you has associates who do know where she is," Moriarty said.

"How in hell does that help me—or her?"

Moriarty gripped Gary's left arm, more for contact than restraint. "Listen closely, Mr. Kemmerman. The man you'll meet inside is named Ryan Scully." He released the arm, pulled a photo from a coat pocket, and displayed it. "This is what he looks like. I've told him that you would be here to speak with him on my behalf—"

"You're in contact with terrorists?"

Moriarty looked at Gary as if he were a fool. "Scully is not a player, simply an American citizen of Irish extraction, a family man, who may provide goods and services to old friends."

Who happen to be terrorists, Gary thought. "My wife is missing. I don't give a damn for your plans. Just get her back and let us out of this."

"Time is short, Mr. Kemmerman. Listen, please. Tell him to contact Dwyer. D-w-y-e-r. Do you have that?"

Gary nodded. "About what?"

"Listen closely. He's to tell Dwyer that the man his associate clubbed, and then shot at—that being you—has gone to the authorities. Federal agents now know the shooter is Abdel Siddiq." He spelled that name, too, and had Gary pronounce it. "That is all I ask you to do, and it is all the truth."

The agent hadn't mentioned the attempted murder on the Turnpike. He must not know about it. "You don't need me to tell him that—do it yourself."

Moriarty offered his cat-and-mouse smile. "Scully will likely ask, 'Who is the man who went to the authorities?' When you tell him it is you, he will then be able to describe you quite well. My guess is he'll make a phone call, either right after he leaves you, or at the first contact time."

"He'll know I'm in there for no good reason."

"Tell him I threatened you. He'll understand that. In fact, he may be friendly after that."

"Where will you be? If I'm sticking a wrench in their spokes, I guess you'll follow Scully when he leaves?"

Again, the playful look. "Do you like good Irish ale?"

He didn't react.

"If so, order one. Try what's he's having, though they are all excellent. When Scully leaves, wait ten minutes at the table. Check your watch to be sure. Then—only then—you can walk out, get your car, and go home, with our thanks."

He recalled why he was supposed to be here. "Not without my wife. I won't even go in if this is all you got to offer."

Moriarty laced fingers like a basket, thumbs pointing out. "She will be returned to your home before morning."

"Bullshit!"

"I promise you." He lowered his voice. "Besides, have you a better option? Knowing the situation, do you believe the local police, or even the FBI, have a prayer of finding her alive? I will slide her out without breaking doors down or exchanging gunfire. That would not be healthy for her, and perhaps not for you."

For a moment, Gary forced himself to remember that Becca was safe in the car. "Do you have a gun?" he asked.

"Of course."

"Why are you doing this?"

"It is my job."

"It's not the analyst role you mentioned this morning."

Moriarty pursed his lips. "How would you feel, Mr. Kemmerman, if the man you identified should murder your wife, and do it in a manner designed to give you nightmares for the rest of your life?"

CHAPTER 34
10:13 P.M., Thursday

CONNOLLY's smelled of beer and burgers, and featured dark wooden walls, dim lighting, crowds, and noise. Three-deep, jostling people lined the bar. It seemed everyone spoke and no one listened. It amazed Gary that so many young people were out drinking on a Thursday night. His first adventure was squeezing past them along the narrowed aisle. As he moved, he was looking carefully at the booths to his right, hoping Ryan Scully would be sitting at a table rather than buried among the revelers

The din faded somewhat in the back room, once he'd passed the bar. Booths lined both walls. He moved slowly, scanning faces, wondering if he'd have to pry his way back through the crowd to no avail, and then be asked to repeat the same nonsense the following night. But as he approached the rear of the pub, he recognized the man. Scully was on the last bench along the wall to his left, facing him, alone in a booth, looking exactly like the photo.

As upset as the heavy fellow appeared, when they made eye contact the older man's mouth tightened and he paled. A crumpled gray coat lay on the bench to his right, and he wore a hunter green cable-knit sweater that had several small tears.

Gary slid onto the bench at the other side of the lacquered wooden table. "You Ryan Scully?"

The old man looked up with a sad smile. "Was my picture as beautiful as yours?"

Gary nodded. Scully lifted his stein. "Could use another. Want one?" He snorted. "May be the best thing happens here."

"Sure."

"Got a preference?"

Gary shrugged. "Whatever you're having."

"Ah, you've been told about that, too." He nodded toward the aisle and a waitress appeared at once. Scully didn't say a word; he ordered with two fingers and sat back against the bench.

"I might as well get right to it—no point in killing the evening for us both," Gary said. "He asked me to deliver a message."

The Irishman looked away and rubbed his chin as if something had alarmed him. "By 'he,' do you mean the man by the back of the bar?" Scully nodded toward a spot down the aisle.

Gary swiveled, shifted when his back complained, leaned into the aisle around the seatback—and saw Moriarty. The small man stood facing them. Shadows obscured his face, but Gary imagined the cat-and-mouse smile. He turned back to Scully and nodded. "The little bastard in the brown coat."

The Irishman breathed deeply. His left eye twitched. "What ya got?"

"You're to tell a man named Dwyer—want me to spell it? The agent did. Like a fucking English teacher."

Scully blew air through his mouth and shook his head.

"Anyway, you're to tell him that the man Dwyer's associate hit and shot at has identified that associate—one Abdel Siddiq—to the authorities. The feds know who he is, and that he's here." Gary saw the man's eyes cloud over and guessed from this point he'd get only lies.

"Name's new to me," Scully said. "Why'd the fool in the brown coat—" he leaned to his left, peered behind Gary, and shook his head again— "damn, he's gone. Why'd he not deliver the news himself?"

"I think the fuckers specialize in head games."

That made Scully smile. He turned it on the waitress as she slapped steins down in front of them, but he didn't speak until she'd marched off. "Oh, but you don't know the half of it." He brought himself up short. "Or do ya?"

"I don't know a damn thing," Gary said. "I'm retired, living with my wife in Jersey—happened to be in the wrong place at the wrong time and the guy they tell me is Siddiq slugged me. He'd run over a boy in Tuesday's storm but it was an accident. He couldn't have avoided it, but then he slugs me anyway. I didn't know it meant anything until he shot at me next day—and my wife, I might add. Your brown-coated friend asked me to come because Siddiq will recognize your description of me and know the news is true."

The Irishman took a swallow, set down the glass and carefully wiped his mouth with a napkin. "So he's using you as some kind of bait?"

"Not anymore. You tell Dwyer and Mr. Brown Coat'll let me off the hook."

Scully thought about that. "You know the guy's name?"

"I asked him," Gary said. "He laughed, told me they don't give out names. He offered me an alias, which I'm happy to pass along. It's Moriarty." The anger he felt was real. "That name's a master criminal in the Sherlock Holmes' stories. Scully, what's this about? You know?"

"What's your name?"

Gary had to chuckle. "The little guy knows, and that's one too many."

Scully's eyes glinted. He raised the glass and took three swallows, lowering the level. Gary noticed the bloodshot eyes and wondered how many the Irishman had already downed. "You looking to make a night of it?" Scully asked, after he'd wiped his mouth.

"Hell no. My car's in a garage around the block—sooner I'm home, the better. The wife's getting nervous."

"She know about this?"

"You keep secrets from *your* wife?"

Scully grinned and nodded. "You interested in how I'll get word to this make-believe Dwyer?"

"I don't give a shit if there isn't a Dwyer—I just want out."

The Irishman nodded again, reached into a pocket and tossed a few bills onto the table. "Garages cost plenty. I got the tab. Been fun, but mind if I say goodnight?" He rose and pulled on the dirty gray coat. Then he gripped the table for support and leaned back toward Gary. "Got any last words?"

Gary raised the stein. "May we never meet again."

Wondering whether he'd have to add Scully to the list of those after him, he didn't turn to watch the Irishman push off down the aisle. Moriarty, and maybe Thompson, had seen him do his job.

He flipped the new phone open and glanced at the time: 10:26. In ten minutes, he'd squirm past the crowd, locate the car, and he and Becca would be on their way. If Thompson needed to stay and play spy, they'd take his suggestion and call a cab. Whatever the fare.

He imagined Becca in the stilled car, in her secret agent outfit, peering toward the pub entrance, longing to get involved. The ten minutes began to feel like forever.

Scully didn't look back, his turmoil churning anger and fright together. He couldn't reach Dwyer until morning, on that damn pay phone outside the hotel. When they did speak, what in hell could he tell him? That the man in the brown coat had forced another man to deliver a message—this is the message, this is what the deliveryman looked like, and make of it what you will?

"What's this about?" the messenger had asked. Scully understood only part of it. The Arab name came as a shock. No wonder the feds were all over it. Maybe this *would* be his last job; maybe he'd really retire, put out the word that he'd closed down. As he moved forward, it seemed everyone in the bar was watching him.

He shouldered open the door and stepped outside. Mired in concern, he didn't feel the chill. Home was to the left. Stumbling, he swung around to the right, toward the garage and the bus. He'd best be sure his part of it wouldn't cause problems.

A step later, he felt the pistol against his head. Afraid to turn, he froze. "Move," he heard. The voice belonged to the man in the brown coat.

"What now?" Scully cried, flinching from the gun. "Got the message. You saw." He barely could get the words out. "We speak again, I'll tell him, I promise, whatever you want."

The agent's free hand pushed at Scully's back, forcing him into the service alley between the pub and an apartment building. In the darkness, the gun pressed against his neck. He wound up back behind a row of garbage cans.

"What's the target?" Moriarty murmured.

"What do you mean?"

"Not a sound," the small man hissed. The muzzle pressed against Scully's mouth. "Not a breath."

They stood frozen, with Scully trying so hard not to breathe that he finally had to gasp. He did it through clenched teeth. The air smelled fetid; his wife would smell it on his coat and complain, believing he'd fallen down drunk in the gutter. He couldn't see the street, but the gunman could. Warm coat and all, Scully began to shiver.

The agent moved first, pressing the muzzle tighter against Scully's teeth as he spoke. "Tell me where, or you won't deliver any message." The gun moved back so he could speak.

Scully recalled Dwyer's insistence that he reveal the real target. He hated to do it, but that's what he'd been instructed. He sagged against the brick wall. "Stock Exchange."

"Which?"

"New York. The big one."

"When?"

"You can shoot me now, but I don't know how or when." He imagined his sons being told he'd been found shot dead in the stinking alleyway beside Connolly's. They hated his drinking and his bar friends. They'd be convinced he'd staggered out drunk and been robbed.

To try to please, he fed the man the rest of what Dwyer had said. "You threatened me, and the locals don't know a thing, so I called Ireland. A contact from way back said the Exchange might be it, and that's all I know." The edge of a brick stabbed at him, and he shifted uncomfortably.

"Close your eyes," the agent said.

He did, expecting to die. His heart pounded out of his chest. Would it be the heart or head? Did it matter? He imagined his wife laughing. What would the boys do? Could they run the business without him? Seconds passed, he heard his ragged breathing, and wondered how long it would take the man to fire. He peeked—and found himself alone, glued to the wall, face twisted as if the muzzle was still there.

It took a minute before he could move. Wary, he peered out of the alley. The bastard had left. He'd gotten what he wanted and gone to report it. No one was walking on the street. Scully stepped out stiffly, feigning calmness. On shaky legs, he continued in the direction he'd been going.

Six blocks away, Tommy should be in the garage with the bus. Scully'd confirm that the work would be done before morning, and then get home and try to sleep. He'd better not take pills tonight, not with all the alcohol. If he were lucky, he'd get four hours before he'd have to leave. Halfway to the corner, he recalled what he needed to do. The man in brown might be following.

Swiveling as rapidly as he could, he scanned the street for figures he expected would duck into shadows. Once, he'd been good at this. Another sign that it was time to hang it up.

The only people in sight were far down the street and moving away. The woman waved her arms at her companion, and they turned the corner without looking back. Struggling to stand still, Scully peered around. He sensed motion in a Ford parked up the block, across the street. Just then a delivery van eased by. Unsteady, he wavered and had to blink his eyes from the headlights. He saw nothing, now. Must have been the truck throwing shadows.

Besides, he had no weapon, and with the ale in him, it wouldn't be sensible to fight. He glanced around again and found the street deserted. The only thing in motion was the whistling wind. *I'm too old for this*, he thought. He slapped at his coat to check that he hadn't lost the garage door remote. After a final peek toward the Ford, he turned his back on ghosts and headed for the bus.

CHAPTER 35
10:29 P.M., Thursday

ALONE in the Ford, hunched in the back seat, Becca kept a close eye on the pub. Thompson had left the car minutes before, taken the keys, and told her to hunker out of sight and keep the doors locked. But curiosity forced her to peek. Every time a vehicle drove past, headlights flared, ghostly shadows floated through the car, and she ducked away from prying eyes.

Earlier, when Thompson returned and moved the car around the corner, he'd told her that Gary and Moriarty were in Connolly's. Before the agent slipped away again, he'd said he'd be back soon, and admonished her to stay put. She'd seen him take up a position across from the pub. She couldn't find him now. No telling what had gone on during the time she spent below window level.

She watched a small man emerge from Connolly's. His movements were precise—it didn't seem like he'd been drinking. The stranger didn't mean anything to her until she saw his grandfatherly looking face and short, brown coat. He fit the description of the CIA agent Gary had told her about. The man turned right, striding rapidly, staring straight ahead as he passed her by across the street.

Seconds after the little man resolutely turned right again and rounded the corner, Thompson emerged from some hidey-hole, glanced both ways like a trapped rat, and quickly entered the pub.

It's like a silent movie, she thought, the characters so different looking, one moving with purpose, the other skulking about. It surprised her when the man in the brown coat returned even more rapidly than he'd departed. The timing couldn't be accidental. Had he been aware of Thompson? She wondered if he'd only pretended to leave in order to fool the FBI man. But why would the CIA agent

189

avoid his partner?

The small man glanced about, and she froze as he squeezed between cars, stepping into the road as if he'd come right at her. She couldn't slide down—the motion would give her away. But he had his eyes on the pub entrance and moved past without noticing her. He bent behind a parked car directly in front of Connolly's. She saw him pull out a pistol, though he hid it with a coat cuff.

If he were to look over his left shoulder, he might see her. Gun in hand, that couldn't be good. She wouldn't duck below the window, but she sat very still.

Several beats later—she imagined the director counting off seconds on his fingers—an older man, rotund, with a mane of gray hair and a fleshy nose, wearing a gray coat, pushed out through the pub door. He looked like the person—Ryan Scully, if she remembered correctly—Thompson had described to Gary.

Almost immediately, the guy with the gun slipped from behind the car and locked onto him. In a ballet aided by the weapon, both men vanished into the alley beside Connolly's.

Five, four, three, two, one, counted the director in Becca's head, and Thompson emerged from the pub. The special agent glanced both ways and peered at the car where she was sitting—she imagined, confirming her presence. Normally, she would have waved. But nothing was normal with guns out and people watching. With a sense of relief, she watched Thompson move off without acknowledging her.

He strode toward the alley, paused, and peered in. She knew two men were standing there in the dark, but he must not have seen them. He hesitated and continued forward. She wanted to open the door and call out to him—but she might get him shot, and she knew Gary wouldn't want her to give her position away. How many other characters might be waiting in the wings?

Thompson stopped at the corner and turned in a slow circle, peering in all directions. Then, with determination, he about-faced, headed back past the alley, the Ford, and the pub, and kept going down the block in the other direction. He strode out of sight.

She turned back to the alley and prepared for gunshots. If the powers allowed it, she'd be a witness, identifying the CIA agent. But then the man in the brown coat stuck his head out of the alley and scanned in both directions. Finding no one, he strode off to his right, in the opposite direction from Thompson. He must have put away the gun. Again he turned the corner, in even greater haste than last time. He vanished, she imagined for good.

Where was the man he'd pinned with the gun? Should she look in the alley for a body? She shuddered. She hadn't heard a shot. She'd give it a few minutes. Besides, the man with the gun had returned once before—she didn't want *him* catching her.

Gary should be out of the pub by now. Were others inside holding him back? Maybe she'd better join him in there and tell him what had happened on the street. They could check the alley together. If Thompson returned to an empty car, he'd probably look for them in Connolly's. The countdown in her head resumed: five, four—

It startled her when the old man in the gray coat stumbled out of the alley, almost weaving. Had he been injured? No, he straightened and looked around. Good, she thought, no dead body. Then the Irishman gazed directly at her.

A passing car allowed her to press back against the seat. The gray-haired man still scanned the street. Unless the fellow was waiting for someone to meet him, he was behaving just like the others. Finally, he wobbled off in the same direction the CIA agent had taken, though he didn't turn the corner. His movements suggested that he might be under the influence.

She squeezed her eyes shut and edited the action she'd been watching. The CIA agent had sent Gary to meet Scully, and then drawn a gun on the old man *after* they must have met. Odd. Thompson had emerged right behind the Irishman, as if he'd wanted to follow him, but before he could, the CIA man had pulled Scully off the street. The old man must be at the center of the action. He hadn't shown that he was carrying a gun.

She blinked and found him walking unsteadily down the street. Despite his awkward gait, he moved as if he had somewhere important to be. He was getting away.

She knew what Gary would do. He wouldn't hesitate. *If I'm really a partner, I shouldn't, either*, she thought. *If nobody notices me, it won't be dangerous.*

The men were concerned because of her gender—so unfair. She had ID, money, the all-important new cell phone, and—she chuckled—she was wearing her secret agent outfit. When she needed to, she'd call Gary. It wouldn't be like last time. Tony's evil brother was not here to try again.

When Gary returned to an empty car, he'd be upset. Thompson would be, too. But she'd call. Maybe, because she'd been in the right place and done something about it, she'd uncover information that would help them break the case.

Decided, she turned off the phone so it couldn't ring and give her away. Once more the director in her head counted down and, quietly, she opened the street-side door, pleased that the inside light didn't flare on. She pushed down the lock and closed the car. The small noise it made vanished in the breeze. In the distance, the Irishman continued along the other side of the street without taking notice.

Using parked cars as shields, she bent low and ran through the shadows to follow wherever he would lead.

CHAPTER 36
10:33 P.M., Thursday

WATCHING from deep shadows around the corner from Connolly's, Moriarty was surprised to find a woman in black following Scully. She lunged from car to car, nothing smooth about it, all eagerness, no craft. He focused and recognized Becca Kemmerman—and that upset him. She had to have come with her husband. Why would the man toy with him, pretend his wife was missing, and still show up knowing she was safe?

Thompson must be behind it. The car the woman had come out of might be Thompson's. Could the agent be hiding from him, waiting to follow?

He peered up and down the street. Scully staggered along as if he were still in shock, apparently unconcerned about a tail. Even an amateur could stay with the old fool. Moriarty didn't believe for a minute that Scully's revelation—the New York Stock Exchange—would be the real target. The man, knocked off balance, might be heading toward his secret.

Moriarty would follow, catch the woman, send her back, and shadow the Irishman with or without Thompson prowling behind. He started forward—but stopped when a sharp blade pricked at the right side of his neck, over the carotid artery. He froze, startled that the person behind him had been able to sneak up so silently. The touch held firm. He'd die if he moved, a twist of the blade all it would take.

"You can have my money—I won't resist or look at you," he said without moving.

"Go left," he heard, and a tremor ran through him.

He moved without feeling as the knife guided him around the corner, back into the alley where moments before he'd held Scully.

193

By the time a hand on his shoulder stopped him, in gloom behind the garbage cans, he knew what he'd have to try, so without turning he spoke.

"You have a lovely family here. They are pious—and American citizens. They own a home and are active in their community. They have given you three nephews and a niece. The oldest boy is on his high school soccer team. They call him, I believe, 'Lightning.'"

"You *killed* my family," Abdel Siddiq said.

Moriarty had always meant to tell the man the truth. Just not this way. "No, I did not." The knife slicked at his neck. He felt blood, knew it was a flesh wound, ignored the sting. "I will tell you the truth, and you will decide." The flat of the blade tapped and he went on.

"We mounted an operation in Beirut to take you. Kill if we had to, but we'd try to capture you first. My instructions—and I passed them along to the Lebanese most carefully—were to wait until you came out of the house. But you know their security forces, or at least the way they were back then. They brought heavy weapons. They were afraid of you. As jumpy as they were, it might have been movement at a window, or noise from a passing car, that triggered them. They opened up. You know the rest. You were not there."

"Who was the Lebanese officer in charge?"

"A Colonel Rafiq. I understand he has since been dealt with, perhaps for another of his many indiscretions."

"Convenient. I cannot check."

"You know I have never killed innocents or children. But Rafiq may have been a wise man. That day he laughed at my concern, said the killings would become my fault no matter, no one would believe otherwise. He protected his own family that way." Moriarty tried to keep his tone the same, but couldn't. "And cost me Helene."

"*That* was not random," Siddiq rasped.

"I know. My wife was visiting her parents in a small town south of Chicago. She had no connection to my work. You tracked her down and cut her throat." The memory seemed a million years old. He'd been alone for so long.

"I did as you had."

Moriarty shook his head, ignoring the blade. "I never harmed your family."

"You would do the same."

Moriarty considered. "I believe I'd have come after you but not your wife and children." A bone-weary sensation came over him. He thought of poor Mrs. Kemmerman, no one left to tell her to go home. If Siddiq spotted her husband coming out of Connolly's, she'd be a widow—if she lived through it.

"What I did hurt you *worse*," Siddiq said, after a short silence. "Now I finish things."

"That's our problem." Moriarty felt light, already gone from this dirty alley. "We have to give up so many normal things to keep believing what we do is right."

"I am part of a great—"

"Have you seen your brother's children?" Moriarty had heard Siddiq's rant before from Muslims, Jews, Serbs, Basques, Irishmen, even those who raged to no God or nation at all.

There was a moment's silence. "Why do you ask?"

He didn't care how he phrased it. "If you've lost interest, then the attack in Beirut killed part of you, too. Visit them. Allow yourself to know them. Family gives life meaning."

Siddiq slashed his throat.

CHAPTER 37
10:36 P.M., Thursday

ONCE the pub door swung shut behind him, Gary glanced up and down the street. No Moriarty. No Scully. Gone forever, he hoped. He lifted his head and took a deep breath. The chill brought relief after the crowded pub, where it seemed every gulp of air had passed over food and been filtered by other lungs. The sky between buildings showed no sign of snow. Getting home would be a snap. Thoughts of Becca and home warmed him. They'd have the Safrians over, in part as a thank-you for Megan's kindness.

He looked for Thompson's Ford and found it across the street, near the corner he said they'd turn. He started for it, wondering if Becca would comment about beer smell on his breath, cigarette smoke in his hair. Smoking wasn't allowed in there, but... . The ale had given him an appetite, though he knew better than to eat so late. This cold snap called for a stew. He'd ask Becca. She made it so well.

With one foot off the curb, he stopped before he realized the Ford was empty. He squinted. Perhaps she'd hunched down below the windows. Or had she—they—left the car?

Told you so. He glanced both ways, ran across the road onto the other sidewalk, up to the car, and leaned down to look in. No people. No keys. No sign of trouble.

He pressed his forehead against a side window, checking the back seat for anything Becca might have left as a message, but found nothing. Neither she nor Thompson had been in Connolly's when he'd left. The car doors were locked. If she'd been forced out, wouldn't the locks be open? Had some plan she'd made with Thompson caused her to wear that silly outfit? Had the special agent asked for her help?

Why hadn't she alerted him on the new phones? He smiled, dug into a pocket for the cell, glanced up—and through the car windows he saw a man emerge from the alley across the street. A small man, with an open coat. Gary didn't need to spot the silver belt to recognize him.

Adrenaline kicked in. This guy had tried to kill Becca twice and damn near succeeded. Had he found her? Gary pressed against the car, heart hammering. The man had a gun, ran fast, and had him marked for death.

Was Becca lying dead in the alley?

He watched Siddiq glance around, perhaps looking for him. The man scanned in all directions before turning right and moving off. He reached the corner, turned right again, and disappeared without a backward glance.

It would be safer to wait a few minutes, but Gary couldn't. Bent forward he rushed across the street and into the alley, stepping into a darkness that forced him to stop because it blinded him. He blinked.

Soft sounds came from further back. His eyes were adjusting to the dimness as he moved slowly between the walls, stepping carefully, until yards ahead something at ground level stared back. He froze. The pinpoints vanished as the small creature scuttled off. He moved in that direction.

Moriarty gazed up with eyes that would never close. The agent's throat had been hacked open. A pool of blood oozed along the ground inches from Gary's shoe.

His stomach churned—ale reached his throat and he stepped back, swallowing, peering about. The alley contained the body, four garbage cans, and nothing else. Shaking, he pulled off the lids, one by one, checking carefully, mindless of the smells. Amidst the horror, relief washed over him. Becca wasn't there.

Where could she be? If she needed to hide, shouting for her, phoning her would be a bad move. Only one player might lead him to her, the son of a bitch who kept appearing, every time with another assault. Siddiq had known to come here—so he must know Scully, Dwyer, and whatever Thompson was searching for.

No one could help Moriarty. If Becca were safe with Thompson, great, but if not, Siddiq might lead Gary to her. He couldn't risk being delayed by reporting the crime. Maybe he could help finish what Moriarty had started.

Before he slipped from the alley, he turned off the cell. Quickly and carefully, he caught up to Abdel Siddiq. Once the man reached his destination, Gary would call Thompson and Becca.

Siddiq strode along openly, although from time to time he did turn as if he might've passed his destination. From a distance, keeping across the street from the man, Gary evaded the random checks.

Forcing himself to contain his anxiety, he followed.

CHAPTER 38
10:41 P.M., Thursday

THE streets were coming up empty for Thompson. He'd given Scully all of a ninety-second head start when the Irishman stumbled out of Connolly's, worried and wobbly. But when Thompson emerged into the cold, the street had been deserted. How in hell had the old sot vanished so fast?

There would have been no point in checking behind every car, in every alley and recessed doorway. Instead, after a quick look around, he'd pursued the Irishman on foot in the direction of his home. Several blocks later, when it became clear that Scully had not headed that way, Thompson started back to the Ford.

Scully's wife had him on a curfew—the Irishman had to be home in seventy-five minutes. Thompson would be waiting. Meantime, Gary could give him Moriarty's message and Scully's response. By now, the Kemmermans would be together in his car, chafing at the wait.

When he reached the Ford and found it empty, it didn't disturb him. He'd kept the car keys, so the Kemmermans must have sought refuge from the cold in Connolly's. They'd be hoisting a few and waiting for him, relieved their involvement had ended. He didn't blame them.

Thompson pushed through the pub door into bedlam. Patrons stood three-deep at the bar, and he had to lean inches from the closest bartender, and then flash ID, to get her attention.

She hadn't seen the Kemmermans as best he could describe them. But she did help by blowing her whistle. That quieted the crowd long enough for her to ask for them by name. She got no response— and you would have had to be dead not to hear the shriek on that reed-thin woman.

They must have taken his advice, called a cab and gone home. Thompson got into the Ford, started it, and turned on the heat. He dialed for Moriarty, left word, and then pulled away from the curb.

CHAPTER 39
11:04 P.M., Thursday

HEART pounding from excitement, Becca ducked behind a car at the curb on Forty-fourth Street, east of Broadway, when the old man stopped in front of a closed parking garage—its sign had been turned off and both metal gates were down.

She'd gotten closer to him as he slowed and she knelt only two cars away. The Irishman glanced around, pulled something black out of a coat pocket and turned in her direction. She kept still in the semi-darkness, peering through car windows, hoping it wasn't a gun. Even that didn't frighten her—she was helping, and it felt good.

At once, she heard an electronic whir. The metal garage door closest to her clanked as it rose off the ground. A buzzer sounded from inside. The man pocketed the remote and, hands on hips, watched the slowly rising barrier.

She used the diversion to slip alongside the next vehicle, almost behind him now, so she could see in. The door thumped at the ceiling; motor and buzzer cycled off. Inside, the cavernous space resembled a darkened theater—except for light glimmering from around a bend in back, to the left.

"That you, Dad?"

She barely heard the voice—the speaker had yelled from deep in the garage. She couldn't see him. The Irishman waddled inside, moving toward the streak of light, then stopped. Leaning close to the ground, Becca stepped around the car and darted quietly up beside the doorway to peer in. A second man appeared from the left and joined the old guy near the back wall. Their lowered voices echoed, but from outside she couldn't make out the words.

When they turned away from the entry and moved further back toward the light, she padded into the garage, slipping into darkness between a vehicle and the wall, squeezing onto her knees in the tight space, listening intently. The floor felt cold and rough against her hands. She smelled urine. Loud clanking above startled her; she froze and then jerked when the buzzer sounded. Pushing up from her knees, she bashed her right shoulder into the wall and bounced against the car. Behind her, the door began to descend.

The Irishman must have used the remote. She had to get out. In the movies, heroes dropped, rolled, slipped beneath descending barriers by millimeters. She tried to turn in the tight space—and the door slapped down, leaving her in darkness. The buzzer stilled and in the silence her excitement curdled into fright. What had she done?

"Came to check it out," she heard, from the old guy. With the door shut, sound carried.

"Down here, Dad," the younger man said.

She blinked, facing them. They might have seen her, but she was standing in darkness and they'd turned toward the light. As they moved down the ramp, she took a deep breath, hunched lower, and slunk forward from vehicle to vehicle, using them as cover until she reached the last in line.

She risked peering through the van's windows and looked around. Bisecting the wall across from her, a heavy concrete barrier blocked a murky up ramp. The men were descending the second ramp along that wall, set at the very back of the garage. The wall to her right, at the rear of the space, held two doors and a closed pedestrian elevator. The only light floated up from the space at the foot of the ramp.

If fate had brought her here, she might as well discover what she could—and that must be in the space below. Swallowing her anxiety, she slipped from the car past the doors to the start of the ramp, flattening against the rough concrete wall.

"Oh, Tommy, beautiful job, beautiful job," said the older voice, from out of sight, the echo more pronounced.

The ramp had a four-foot-high sidewall. She bent low and sidled down like a crab until she could stand behind a round concrete column at the bottom.

"Got the steel plates in?" the Irishman asked.

"Only had two. Put 'em in the back two bays, driver's side like you said. Hope that'll do."

Becca snuck a glance around the column. The Irishman leaned forward and peered into one of the open bays, while the son he'd called Tommy—a strapping young man—stood watching him. The older man shrugged, straightened, and nodded. "It's this or nothing."

"We can cut the price."

"No need. They'll pay." The man she'd followed reached out, patted the side of the bus and shook his head. "Poor bus," he said. "Poor beautiful bus."

She wondered why he'd used those words.

"You sober, Dad?" Tommy asked.

The kid must not know, either, she thought.

The old man chuckled. "Had only ale, not to worry."

"How many?"

"Two, my boy, no more. I know you're looking out for me. Point is, I gotta pee."

"Bathroom's up the ramp." Without a delay, footsteps echoed off the walls.

Mouth open, pulse racing, Becca froze against the column.

"Hate to walk uphill," the old man said, not far from the other side of the pillar. The footfalls stopped. "Got an elevator down here, right? Yeah, we do, I checked this morning to make sure it worked. Brain doesn't do so good when I gotta pee this bad."

The boy laughed, wall angles fracturing the sound. "It's the ale, Dad, not the bladder. Elevator's back the other way. Follow me."

The sounds receded. Soon, she heard the whine of an elevator. She listened while its door opened. The old man began to speak, but the closing door cut off the words. A motor revved and the elevator cab started upward.

She realized that if she stayed put, they might see her when they came out on the floor above, so she stepped around the column and into the space they'd vacated.

A vault-like room spread out before her. They must have been welding—she smelled it. Lights shone on a modern touring coach with dark-tinted windows. It sported the blue-and-white Academy Bus logos. It had one front and two rear axles. Tools, small equipment, and cut pieces of flat metal were scattered beside it. Except for the welding torch and helmet, she couldn't tell what they'd been used for. The three baggage compartments along the side of the bus were hooked open. Its front door also stood open.

The elevator noise ended, and faint voices flowed down the ramp. Listening for their return, she crept toward the bus. Were they just doing a repair job? Maybe not, judging from the father's words.

From above, something slammed. The old man must have gone into the bathroom.

She moved behind the bus and memorized the Maryland license. Alongside, she bent down and peered into each baggage compartment, just as the old man had done. The rear two luggage bays had the opposite sides sealed off by what looked like steel plates. Maybe the vehicle pulled into places where it could only unload from the right side—but even so, sealing the bays that way made no sense to her. Rounding the vehicle, she read the sign above the front windshield: *CHARTER*.

She glanced around the depressing space and gingerly climbed the steps into the bus. Half-expecting a third person to be pointing a gun, she raised her face above the stairwell barrier. It was empty. Inside, stale air smelled of disinfectant and burnt metal. Further back, away from the glow filtering through the open doors, tinted windows left the interior dark, gloomy.

She stepped in and found well-maintained black leather seats. There were fourteen rows on one side, with a small storage area in back, and the driver's side had twelve rows, ending at a lavatory. Both sides had overhead storage compartments running the length of the bus, much like on an airplane.

She moved back along the aisle, searching for a clue that would tell her why the CIA, FBI, and Gary, were interested in the older man and his poor, beautiful bus. She reached up, about to explore a few of the overhead compartments, when from outside something smacked against the side of the vehicle. Instead of jumping, she dropped low into the aisle.

"Good job, my boy," said the Irishman. His voice floated through the door. She hadn't realized how much time had passed. She'd heard no elevator sounds. Maybe they'd walked.

"Those plates won't move," the young man said. "Don't know

why they want them, but like you said, if people are willing to pay for such crazy things, we'll provide 'em." She heard a heavy thump. It sounded like they'd dropped a baggage bay door. She squatted lower so they couldn't spot her.

The old man chortled. "Indeed we will! Pay's good, too. Warm enough in here for ya? At least the toilet flushes."

"Phones are dead, but everything else works."

A second door dropped. "Let's sit and talk for a bit," the old man said. "Tell me what's up with your brother."

Becca realized they might want to sit in the bus. As the final bay door slammed, she raced for the lavatory. *Please be open!* She pushed the lever and, when the door swung toward her, stepped into the small space and locked herself in. Maybe they didn't have a key. She thought to put her ear to the door but found she was shaking, and leaned instead onto the metal sink.

Surrounded by solid walls, she couldn't hear them talking. But if she stepped out she might walk right into them. She tried to slow her heart, breathe quietly, and she waited.

She didn't hear when Tommy said, "No, Dad, I'm not going to Connolly's." She did hear when something hissed. A softer thump followed.

It had all happened so fast: car to street to garage to bus. She believed she'd discovered something important, though she didn't know how it fit. Gary would know what to do but she couldn't call him now. The Irishman and his son might hear.

After awhile, very faintly, she heard what sounded like the buzzer from the garage's street door. She dared to crack open the lavatory. Around her, the bus, and the garage, were as dark as an empty coal mine.

Time to get out. Using seat tops as guides, she moved forward in the aisle and found the bus door had been closed. She fumbled for the handle, and pushed. The mechanism wouldn't budge. She braced, heaved at the door with her feet. They'd locked it.

She dropped into a seat and considered her situation. No telling how many of them would come back, or how soon. Pushing out an emergency window and jumping to the ground would gain her little if they'd locked the garage door. The loose window frame would signal her presence and undo her hiding place.

She took the cell from a pocket, flipped it open, and turned it on. The glowing image of a tropical island reassured her. The one thing she and Gary had done was to program in each other's cell numbers. Maybe tomorrow she'd have time to scan the instruction manual. Using the backlit keypad, she dialed in the dark.

Nothing happened, except several seconds later the light went out. She closed and opened the phone to turn the screen back on and found she had no signal. Underground, surrounded by concrete walls inlaid with steel…she wouldn't let it upset her. After the last two days, several hours in the dark would be a snap.

Gary would be worried. He'd forgiven her for losing the car—he'd understand again, she hoped.

She counted on the garage opening for business in the morning. There'd be workers, customers, and other vehicles. They'd unlock the bus—it must be scheduled to go somewhere. In the hubbub, she'd walk out. The phone would work on the street, and she'd call Gary. By now, he'd probably organized the CIA, FBI, and police in a citywide woman hunt. Her pulse quickened when she realized it didn't matter who or how many were searching—no one would find her.

She got up from the seat and moved along the aisle to the back of the bus. Better she be in the last row, in case the driver came aboard while she napped. There would be time to sleep, if she could—it might be six or seven hours until the lights went on. At least she had a sink with water, paper cups, and a toilet.

Gary wouldn't be the only one upset. What would Thompson believe when he found her missing from the car? How many times could the man save her?

CHAPTER 40
11:42 P.M., Thursday

THOMPSON had been waiting in the Ford near Scully's building for almost an hour before the side mirror revealed the Irishman waddling into sight, shoulders slumped, head down.

The agent squinted at the street behind him, checked in all the mirrors for Moriarty or the Kemmermans, but found no one. Where the hell were they? Why hadn't Moriarty called back?

The Irishman almost had his key in the front door of the building when Thompson jammed the gun against his spine.

Scully trembled and dropped the key ring.

"A word, Mr. Scully." It came out like a growl.

The old man turned slowly, shaking, palms open, and his eyes widened. "Who the hell are *you?*"

The man must have expected Moriarty. Scully kept his hands in the air while Thompson frisked him: a wallet, handkerchief, garage door opener.

"Take my money," the Irishman pleaded. "Got no credit cards."

Thompson motioned with the automatic. "Pick up the keys."

Reluctantly, the old man bent to claim them. "This way." Scully moved like he faced execution. The agent led him to the Ford. Once Scully climbed in, the gun motioning the way, Thompson shut the passenger door and moved around to the driver's side, watching the empty street and the Irishman in the car.

"Where's the man you met at Connolly's?" he asked, as he slid behind the wheel.

Scully rubbed his left hand with his right and gazed at the floor, avoiding the weapon. "Which one?"

Thompson tapped his ribs with the muzzle. "The man who delivered the message."

Scully's mouth sagged. "I've no idea. None at all. I left first. He was still at the table. Lives in Jersey. Wouldn't tell me his name."

"What happened right after you left? Where'd you go?"

"Who are you?" Scully asked again. Thompson held up his ID. Scully examined it, closed his eyes, and slumped in the seat. "Everyone in the world's after me. Tell me what *you* want."

"What happened after you left the pub?"

"Don't you guys work together?" the old man asked.

Thompson got it. "Tell me anyway."

"Your other agent—man in the brown coat, he never showed a badge or gave a name—dragged me into the alley." Scully tightened his lips. Thompson waved the pistol. "Said he'd hurt my boys, so I told him the New York Stock Exchange was the target. I don't know shit about it, just called Ireland because of the threat and that's what they told me. I don't know if it's truth. That's all of it."

"*Is* it the target?"

Scully fidgeted. "Man in Ireland believes it."

Thompson leaned forward, placed the muzzle between Scully's eyes, and pushed just hard enough. "When and how?"

"You all ask the same questions." The Irishman closed his eyes before he went on. "I can only tell you what I told him. He was touchin' the gun to my neck, and I just knew he'd fire."

Thompson waited.

"I don't have *answers*." The eyes stayed closed and the words came faster, with a heavier accent, and a layer of panic. "No idea. Had to get *something* from Ireland to keep your man off my back, but they won't talk to me—been years since I was in it. You back out, they don't trust you anymore."

When it was clear he'd finished, Thompson sat back and asked, "What was Kemmerman's message?"

Scully's eyes widened. "You don't know that *either*? Christ Almighty!" He shifted in the seat, peered across the car, and didn't say anything until his eyes locked with Thompson's. "He told me I was to tell a man named O'Brien that he'd identified a guy named Siddiq. Only, as common a name as it may be, I don't know an O'Brien. Don't even know what a Siddiq is."

"That all of it?" Thompson saw a small smile.

"I guess he thought, if I was active, I might pass it on. I don't know who I'd tell it to. Like I said, it's been awhile. Being a special agent, you know that."

Moriarty must have been trying to stir things up, Thompson thought. "You haven't seen the messenger or his wife since you left the pub?"

Scully looked down at his hands and shook his head. "I wouldn't know what she *looked* like. He said she was home."

"Where'd you go after the other agent finished with you?"

"Beer with my son Tommy."

"Bullshit. He lives in Brooklyn." There was the smile again, contained, but telling a story.

"But he sometimes works in midtown, got a second job here," Scully said, the panic gone from his tone. "We went local. Want the name and what I ordered? Only had one. Nursed it. The boy's watchin' out for me. Fact is, he reports anything else to the wife, I got a good chance of being out on the street. You keep me here much longer, you better come in and explain." He grunted. "She won't like it, but you'll get me off the hook for bein' late."

All that nonsense must be to mask something, Thompson believed. "Where's Tommy work?"

"Bunch of midtown garages. Does good in my shop, but he's great at fixing all kinds of cars. Works too much—needs to spend time with the wife"

Why, then, had Scully delayed the boy with beer? Thompson wondered. He picked up Scully's narrowed brows, the shift in tone, avoidance of the question.

"If we find you're involved in—"

"You don't need to say it—your other man warned me." Scully smiled. "Small guy's scarier than you." Then he laughed. "So's the wife."

CHAPTER 41
Friday, December 14
4:18 A.M.

"NEIGHBORHOOD's still scary—gritty, bums, flop-houses pushed out this way. Called 'Hudson Yards'. Suits us fine," the counterman told Gary. "We never close. Customers know we're here all hours, what with Port Authority, the Post Office Building, and Javits Center. Good, blue-collar folks." He nodded at Gary. "Most don't keep your hours, though."

The coffee shop, with a plate-glass front window bearing the name and dotted with photos, menus, and news clippings, had proven a godsend to Gary. He'd found warmth, coffee, Danish, and chatter to keep him hidden and alert. The window decorations obstructed the view from outside but allowed him to see out—and if Siddiq chose to patronize the shop, Gary would vanish into the small bathroom and lock the door.

Earlier, he'd asked the lone employee if he could hang out and buy coffee while he waited for a friend who'd probably make it by sunup. The man had been happy for company beside the all-news radio that blared from behind the counter. That's how Gary had heard reports about the unidentified body found beside Connolly's. It'd been called a murder. The newscaster had said the poor man hadn't been identified.

If that was still the case when this business ended, he'd offer the police what he knew. The cops would love it. They'd lock him up first, then check.

He pointed to his cup. He could use a third refill, even though the shock of the ugly murder had set him on edge. His throat felt raw. When the employee turned to reach for the pot, Gary peered out the window at the bright front lights of the dingy apartment building almost directly across the street. They'd illuminate Siddiq. For the past hours, few others had come or gone.

Refill in hand, Gary moved to a side table and sat facing the building. Tailing Siddiq had proven unexpectedly easy. After the small man strode away from Connolly's, he'd gone several blocks, moving with determination, turning to check the street behind him, then entered a cab in front of the 70 Park Avenue Hotel at Thirty-eighth. Gary had grabbed the next cab in line. For the promise of an extra twenty, his driver had slipped in behind Siddiq.

When the lead cab pulled over, Gary had asked his driver to push past it down the street before stopping. Through the rear window, in the dark, he'd watched his quarry enter the building. Fifteen minutes later, blowing on his hands and stamping his feet to keep warm in the chill breeze whipping off the river a few blocks away, Gary'd spoken with a young couple coming out of the building. The front entrance, he'd learned, was the only one in use except when the fire alarm went off.

When Siddiq emerged, he'd follow the man, and then he'd call for Thompson. If he couldn't reach him, he'd call the FBI's New York number. Siddiq had just killed a federal agent, and who knew what else he had in mind?

But where was Becca? Why hadn't she called?

The evening before, there hadn't been time to fully charge the new phones. His battery was nearly drained from trying both her cell and their home phone—of course he'd left the charger at home. She should have gotten there hours earlier, and checked for messages.

CHAPTER 42
5:49 A.M., Friday

"THE man looks worried, like he's carryin' a load heavier even than the bag," Lynn whispered to Dwyer. He knew she didn't have to lower her voice.

They were standing off the street in the recessed entry of a shop that wouldn't open for hours, watching Scully slowly approach on foot. The old man's blue jacket looked like oil had stained it, and his baggy gray trousers must have given up their crease years before. Scully had no idea they were waiting.

Dwyer had been certain that the man would walk to the pay phone. Scully hated to pay for cabs and didn't like the subway. Dwyer studied the Irishman's heavy gait. Lynn had hit it. He *did* look worried, clutching the handles of a stuffed brown-paper shopping bag. What was in it?

"That groceries, or a bomb?" she asked.

"You can shoot him before he sets it off. I brought a pistol for you."

She bumped against his side. "Kiddin', right?"

About the extra pistol in his pocket, he hadn't been. He wanted her to have it. It would give her a chance if anything should go wrong. But he'd wait for a better time before insisting.

She looked upset. She'd slept poorly even after he coaxed her into the bubble bath and they'd made love. Watching her toss in bed, he'd realized that perhaps for the first time since she was thirteen, she had something to lose. He'd heard the whine of tires, a few rowdy voices floating up from the street far below, and beside him, Lynn's soft breathing had grown precious. He'd reached out to stroke her hair, trying to soothe, careful not to wake her.

Since they checked out of the hotel, she'd barely been able to bite back what he understood was a premonition. He chalked it up to nerves. He'd promised several times to be careful, and agreed she could stay as close as she wanted if she followed his instructions. "I'll stick like glue," she'd said.

By mid-day, they'd be together in a limousine on the way to the airport. But he couldn't let himself think about that—too much to do before then. He glanced at her; he'd be the one sticking like glue.

"Ready?" he asked, and when she nodded, the two of them emerged and angled out to flank the Irishman. In a plastic bag, Lynn was carrying a black cover for Siddiq to use for the short time he'd hide on the bus. Dwyer believed the Arab had become so crazed about being spotted that he would not even go into stores.

Their sudden presence startled Scully, and he slowed. "Keep up with us," Dwyer said. "What's in the bag?"

Huffing, the old man matched their pace. "Have a look," he said, and offered it up. As Dwyer took it, Scully frowned. "You gave me a start with that short dark hair. Reminds me of someone better forgotten."

Earlier, in the hotel room, Lynn had helped Dwyer cut and dye his hair.

"No talking now," he said to Scully. He gave the bag a shake and doubted that it contained a weapon or explosives. Maybe a tracking device? He'd check when they were off the street. He kept it.

Scully nodded to Lynn. "Ma'am."

"Down into the subway," Dwyer said. The three of them clattered down the grimy flight of steps, Scully beside the girl, Dwyer behind. He guided them along a corridor under the street, and when they'd turned a corner, he pulled them off the walk and into the cave-like entry of another closed store. Cell phones and cameras filled windows behind thick steel grills, and an empty cardboard container, torn apart, lay propped against a back corner of the entryway. The damp heightened the smell of urine.

"What'd you bring us?" Dwyer asked, raising the bag, though his eyes never left the passageway.

"Bus diver's uniform," Scully said. "Got you a cap, too. Make you look official behind the wheel."

Dwyer hadn't expected it. He nodded at the old man.

"Told you we think of everything," Scully went on, though his tone betrayed a certain anxiety.

As they waited, Dwyer rummaged through the bag. He fingered the brim of a cap; everything else felt like fabric, buttons. All the while he took the measure of passers-by, who came in waves driven by traffic lights above and train arrivals below. A train rumbled in the caverns, metal shrieking.

Once he believed they hadn't been followed, Dwyer led Lynn and Scully back onto the street through a different entrance, down the block and around a corner from where they'd descended. He took Lynn's arm and guided them into the Internet Café they'd passed the day before, which served breakfast from six o'clock.

"What's this?" asked Scully, confused at the destination.

"A treat for us," Dwyer said. When no one was there to seat them, he led them toward a corner table in back, almost invisible from the street, from which he could scan the approaches. "Lynn needs to eat. Eggs, bacon, hot muffins—we like 'em. Thought you could do with a meal, too. My treat."

"Yeah," said Scully, acting edgy, standing as if he might not sit.

Lynn slipped into the chair beside Dwyer, but he had to wave at Scully before the old man would join them. "Not your last meal," Dwyer said. "Does your pained look mean there's trouble with the bus?"

Scully almost choked. He coughed into his hand to clear his throat, and then glanced toward Lynn, who was watching with interest.

"You can speak in front of her," Dwyer said, and waited quietly through Scully's frown.

The old man shook his head. "Bus is ready. It's not that." He glanced toward Lynn. "You sure?"

"Tell me," Dwyer grumbled.

Scully gripped the table, his voice at a whisper, and the words ran into one another. "Last night the agent I told you about put a gun to my head outside Connolly's. He wanted to know where, when, and how. Like he knew something."

Dwyer leaned forward onto his forearms, listening, watching the old man's face.

"I told him—" Scully glanced at Lynn again— "what you told me to. Only that." His next shake of the head focused Dwyer. "Few hours later, front of my place, no less, another of the bastards does the same, sticks a gun into my back, asks the questions all over again like he has no idea about the other one."

Deep in thought, Dwyer held up his left hand. When he lowered it, he asked, "Describe him."

"His badge said FBI. Jeffers Thompson. Big man, gray eyes, hair sandy and short. Hard face, rough voice. He and the first one *have* to be working together, but it didn't sound like it."

"You tell him, too?"

Scully blinked like a trapped rat. "Only what you said I should." He dropped his eyes. "Got me off the hook."

"He ask anything else?"

"When, how—I don't know that. Told him he could shoot me, but I don't know."

"He'd shoot you?" Lynn whispered, and dropped her eyes when they both looked at her.

"Think he might've?" Dwyer asked.

Scully considered. "No. He was pissed, for sure, but no. First guy, the small one you saw? He would've."

Why had they let Scully go? Dwyer wondered. Maybe they thought he'd be easy to track. "This morning, you get out of the house without being seen?"

The old man glanced at the girl again before speaking. "I got a basement passage—old stuff, entry's concealed—connects with buildings behind mine. Comes out on a different street." He looked down at his hands. "Saved a few of us, years back. A different time."

Dwyer recalled the streets, buildings they'd passed on the way over; for a moment, he imagined snipers in every window, silent black helicopters hovering. He knew there were talented people risking their lives on the other side. "How'd the FBI man end it?"

"Told me to get the hell out of his car and watch my ass while I still had one."

Funny line, Dwyer thought, but he saw that the old man found no humor in it. "You wearing the same clothes as last night?"

Dwyer recognized the old Scully in the return glance. "Changed everything. Washed my hair, too."

"Coat?"

The old man nodded. "Course. Wore the gray yesterday."

"Both of them coming at you like that, must have shaken you."

Scully started to answer, paused, and expelled a breath. "I'd like to say it's the old days, but yeah."

If the Americans were on to the plan, Dwyer knew, the three of them wouldn't be eating breakfast. But what Finn had leaked shouldn't have brought in the CIA. Something else was out there, maybe from Siddiq's end. Moving up the timing could still make it work.

"We can load the bus and drive it?" he whispered, and then held up a hand to stop the conversation as a waiter came close. They nodded for coffee, and the guy whipped out a pad for the rest.

Dwyer watched Lynn while she ordered. Worry kept her subdued. He wished it were already hours from now.

"Bus is ready," the old man whispered. Scully's words brought Dwyer back, and he turned to the man. The waiter had moved off. "Did all you asked, 'cept we got plates in only the back two bays."

It would do. "We can load?"

Scully nodded.

"Is it far?"

"Four blocks, in a closed up garage. That's part of what I gotta pay for. Thought you'd appreciate the location."

Dwyer leaned forward, asked him for the address, memorized it. "Is the place open?"

"I got a remote for the front door—keys for the bus, too."

Dwyer nodded, held up a finger for them to wait, and left to find the pay phone he'd spotted in the café. He used the more secure landline to call. It surprised him when the Arab answered on the first ring. They arranged to meet at the garage at seven. Siddiq said the material would also be delivered and the driver alerted. All the boy would need was a time to appear on the designated corner.

The job done, Dwyer ambled back to the table. Coffee had arrived. Scully sipped his, but the cup sat untouched before Lynn, and she watched him approach with her mouth set in a pout. "Time for a good breakfast," Dwyer said, as he sat, inhaling the aroma.

"He's lookin' at me like that," Lynn said, eyes reaching.

Scully lowered his face in embarrassment.

Dwyer laughed. "Probably can't get what you showed him out of his mind."

Lynn flushed but refused to look away. "That's not funny! You know I wouldn't ever again—"

"I *do* know." He didn't have to say it loudly.

She blushed furiously and bit her lip.

He turned to Scully. "After we eat, you'll come help us with the bus. Have to get us into the garage, anyway." Dwyer didn't mention money, one reason he knew Scully would want to be there.

The old man nodded and sipped coffee without looking up, the troubled expression back on his face.

CHAPTER 43
6:20 A.M., Friday

GARY was sitting at his table, coat unzipped in the overheated coffee shop, nursing his fourth cup. Others had begun arriving at a few minutes of six—he wondered if shift changes could be the cause. The early risers wore gray, blue, and brown uniforms, grunted familiar greetings to one another, and looked half-asleep. There were a few hard-looking women among them. Three people were standing at the takeout counter, and at six of the eight tables slumping customers in thick, unopened coats were leaning over steaming coffee as if the smell would enable a first sip.

Earlier, to stay alert, Gary had monitored the activities of the man who'd kept him company, and two others, in white aprons and baseball caps, who appeared behind the long counter. Through the swinging door they'd carried in trays filled with cream cheese, bags of bagels, loaves of bread. Gary thought he saw shiny metal containers of tuna and egg salad.

The countermen were slicing tomatoes, lettuce, and onions with such abandon that Gary wondered how they kept fingers whole. Toasters hummed. The shop was filled with different aromas. Eggs, bacon, and hash browns sizzled on the grill; pots of freshly brewed coffee, brown and orange-lidded, sat in a line on warmers.

But his focus was on the brightly-lit building entrance across the street, and after so long it didn't seem real when a small man stepped out. Gary dropped the half-eaten Danish and leaned over the table, barely getting the cup down without spilling, peering through the window between the posters, blinking to make sure. It was Siddiq.

The killer put an arm to his face, appearing to wipe his mouth, and looked around. It took all the discipline Gary had to keep still when the man glanced at the coffee shop window. Then Siddiq turned east, toward Ninth Avenue, a computer bag hanging over his right shoulder and an attaché case in his left hand. He had his right arm over the bag—no one would pull it away.

Gary dropped a bill on the table, thanked the counterman, and got up. He had to squeeze past a postal worker stumbling in. Outside, dark and cold hit him and he zipped his coat. The morning air smelled fresh, though his nose was stuffed. An hour before dawn, the sky between buildings had turned an icy blue, and shadows clung to the streets.

A quarter-block ahead across the road, Siddiq was striding along like any other executive on the way to another Friday at the office. TGIF, Gary mused, imagining his jumping Siddiq and finding soiled clothes in one bag, a laptop and paperwork in the other. He'd be the one dragged off to lockup.

Even at that hour, vehicles filled the road. Gary kept to his side of the street, rushing to keep up with the fast-pacing killer. When the traffic light at the avenue turned red, Siddiq started to cross anyway, but had to pull back when aggressive drivers almost ran him down. Gary knew what would come next and slipped into a building entry as the man turned.

The closer they got to midtown, the more people were on the streets and the easier it became not to be noticed. Glowing signs and building lights brightened the cityscape. Twice, Gary had to detour onto exposed walkways in the road because construction blocked the sidewalk, but he wasn't spotted.

They reached Times Square. While Siddiq waited for the traffic light at Broadway, crushed among a throng of commuters, Gary read yesterday's sports scores on the moving news sign. Doing it felt odd; nothing else was normal. As soon as the light changed, he double-timed at the edge of the crowd to stay close.

He tried to use the cell—it lit up, but he couldn't get a call through. The battery icon was blinking. He slid it into a pocket.

The forced march warmed him. He'd just unzipped his jacket part way when, half a block ahead, across the street, Siddiq stopped and nodded to two men and a young woman who were waiting on the sidewalk. At first, Gary was too far off to be sure who they were. The four of them stepped out of the pedestrian flow beside the metal doors of a garage. There was no signage announcing the facility, no lights anywhere in the building. It seemed dead, shutdown.

Gary slipped behind several slow moving sailors, French, he guessed, in dark hats with a white stripe and red pompon. The three men across the street peered around, but none spotted him.

Only Siddiq and Scully could identify Gary—the woman, and a large man with sunglasses and short, dark hair, were strangers.

Scully pulled something black out of a pocket and aimed it at the closed garage door. With a clatter and a bell from inside, the steel door rose. Gary ducked into a bagel shop, using its doorframe as a shield when the others checked around one last time before filing into the dark garage.

Once they turned, Gary scurried from the shop, checked that he had space between oncoming cars, ignored his stiff back, and sprinted across the street toward the opening, taking an angle to the right. In a moment, from inside, they couldn't see him.

He wondered what was in the large, heavy bags that Siddiq was carrying. Whatever was going on must be developing in the garage. Earlier, just inside the entry along the right wall, he'd seen a line of vehicles that might offer cover. Traffic flowed past on the street, but neither the drivers, nor those in the garage, made any effort to attract customers into the poorly lit facility.

Hugging the wall close to the opening, he tensed at sudden clanking above him. A buzzer sounded and the heavy door began to descend. With no time to think he bent low and slipped into the garage between the first car and the wall. The door whined, slapped down, and left him in near darkness.

From her seat on the bus, Becca heard faint noises as the garage door opened and then closed. She thought there were whispers coming from the upper level, but inside the buttoned-up vehicle she couldn't be sure or tell who they might belong to. She cringed when ceiling lights flared on, but for a while nothing else happened. She peered through the tinted windows. No one. The elevator remained silent.

After a night folded into the double seat, she yawned and stretched, loosening her back, arms, and legs. The chill air in the bus smelled stale. If the garage was beginning to stir, others would come, and she'd be able to get off, and out. Gary would know what to do about what she'd heard and seen. She smiled, closing her eyes, imagining breakfast.

Air hissed—the bus doors sprang open. Shocked, she scooted back into the lavatory. As quietly as she could, she locked the door and pressed her ear against it. Footsteps thumped up the steps.

"Lynn, toss the black cover right there on the second seat," said a man. His accent was similar to Scully's. "That way, he can't be seen from the front, and he gets off quick."

"The row's got a tool box on the floor between seats," said a young woman. Her accent was thicker than the man's.

"Will it prevent him from hiding there?"

"Naah," she said. "Looks like a large lunch box."

"Leave it. It'll give him something to sit on."

"Bag with the uniform, too?" she asked.

"Toss it on the driver's seat."

"There you go," the woman said, and then, "Don't want the gun."

Becca's eyes widened.

"Do it for me," the man said. "I'll know you're protected. Wanted to hand it to you while we're alone."

"Sean—"

"I know, I know. Last time. This morning's the end. But for now, you keep the pistol where you can get to it. Look, it protects the both of us."

"Don't you trust 'em?"

"Not the Arab. Maybe he'll leave *me* alone, but not you."

"Why are we here at all?" Becca heard the plea in her voice. "It isn't worth risking—"

The words ended as if he'd covered her mouth. Moments passed, and Becca heard softer sounds, before the woman said, "Okay if we do a lot of that?"

"Starting later today."

She chuckled. "Good lookin' bus. They keep it clean. Can I use the loo?"

"Why not?"

Becca backed up in the lavatory and stood grasping the cold metal sink. For moments, she heard nothing. Then the knob to her hideout jiggled. The door rocked in its frame as the woman outside pushed and grunted. The knob turned, just a little. "Won't open," the woman called out.

"Probably stuck. Want me to come get it?"

Becca worried that her heartbeat was loud enough for them to hear.

"Sure, why not."

Trembling, hearing his footfalls approach, Becca glanced around for a weapon.

"Y'know, there's a regular bathroom upstairs," he said, from the other side of the door.

"Well, okay, I can wait. You been in it?"

"No. Maybe this will do better." The knob moved again. Becca closed her eyes.

"No reason to beat up on the poor door," Lynn said. "Won't be fancy upstairs, but I've done the hole-in-the-ground thing."

The man laughed.

Two sets of footsteps left the bus, and Becca breathed. She'd have to wait for other people, ones without guns and Irish accents, before she emerged.

CHAPTER 44
7:05 A.M., Friday

THE NYPD captain, rows of medals on his well-pressed uniform and braid on the brim of his cap, peered down the street. "Integrity Protecting the Works of Man," he said, blowing air through his mouth, shaking his head, flipping a hand reddened from the cold at the carved marble frieze atop six massive columns fronting 18 Broad Street, the New York Stock Exchange's main building.

"What?" Thompson asked, following the man's eyes. They were standing at the corner of Broad and Wall Streets, with Exchange Place crossing beyond the 18 Broad building and, to their right along Wall, the entrance to the exchange's main trading floor.

"Delta barriers, retractable bollards, thousands of security cameras including license plate readers...every vehicle stopped and checked by explosives-sniffing dogs...my guys in vests, toting machine guns—don't think it's what the people who made that sculpture meant when they carved it.

"We're treating it as a practice run," he went on. "A test, so we can try out our high-tech goodies. Telling the golden-crumb crowd to pretend they're at an airport and we're making them safer. Hell, they're getting hit from all directions—with everything going electronic, half the people who used to work here are gone." He turned back. "And I think you're nuts."

Thompson said nothing.

A group of cops had gathered fifty feet away down Broad, where an officer was distributing a flyer. The captain waved, and they spread out. Thompson had seen men armed with heavy weapons, located like chess pieces on balconies and at facing windows up and down the street. At least one of the official vehicles sported armor and gun slits.

"Thompson, is it?"

The captain's words brought him back, and he nodded.

"Well, Special Agent Thompson, the crazies set off a bomb in 1920, in front of 23 Wall—blew a hundred pounds of dynamite, even knew about shrapnel. But these days, nothing short of another airplane will get them near the exchange. They don't go after hardened targets anyway—you heard bullshit, probably a diversion."

The man had a slight Irish accent. Thompson wondered whether, somewhere, the captain and Scully were related, whether all of them, all sides, were related. "We don't want this to just push them a few blocks away—another financial exchange, a shopping street, glass walled office tower," he said. "Anything we can do about that?"

The captain pressed his lips together. "I'm told destroying the big exchange would have 'catastrophic, cascading impact,' so we *have* to force them off somewhere else. If there's a nut with a bomb, the color code of the day doesn't mean a damn thing. If the crazy is ready to end it and the explosive works, we can't stop 'em. I'm told we win if we move them around the corner, even if the death toll's higher. And with this neck of the woods changing over to apartment buildings and luxury stores, it probably would be."

They had decided not to close the exchange. Shutting it would be a gain for the terrorists—and for how long might it need to be closed? If America responded that way to threats, what next?

The captain went on, "You want my view? ...Well, I better keep my mouth shut. These days, speaking reality and naming our enemy is a hate crime." He peered at Thompson. "I asked questions and got shut down. You're doing this on a hunch, aren't you?"

Thompson met the officer's gaze. "Maybe one day over a drink. Bet we'd have plenty to tell each other."

The captain's eyes crinkled, and he nodded.

"Your guys have the photos?" Thompson had been authorized to provide images of the only two players they knew, Siddiq and Scully. Their faces had been copied for the officers on duty and posted more widely.

The officer nodded again, thoughts elsewhere. "Foolish for them to attack here." He chuckled. "They'll own the place soon enough."

Thompson shook the Captain's outstretched hand and backed

away. Barely after seven, and it looked like food lines in the old Soviet Union, columns of people in coats, breath steaming in the cold, doing the one-step before checkpoints near massive, institutional buildings.

When he arrived, he'd pulled in at the edge of a bus stop before the barriers, lowered his visor and attached the FBI card.

Where the hell were the Kemmermans? They'd never called, and their home phone went to message. Would Gary have taken his wife to a hotel to get away from this? He might, but she wouldn't go willingly. Moriarty hadn't checked in either. Thompson had a bad feeling about that. Even Scully had dropped out of sight. In hindsight, the Irishman had to know more than he'd let on.

Thompson had paid an early morning visit to Scully's home but missed the old man. The wife had said he'd left at five in the morning—he never got up that early—and hurried out of the house with only orange juice for breakfast. At Thompson's urging, she'd called the business, but no one had answered. The boys wouldn't open till eight, she'd said, and Scully didn't like traveling on the subway, so he wouldn't be visiting them. She'd smiled when she said their wives wouldn't like it, either.

To her obvious chagrin, he'd left without telling her where he was going. Wherever he'd headed in such secrecy could be key to the situation. Scully's son Tommy had to be awake. He turned away from the noise, pulled out his phone and punched in a number.

"'Lo," a sleepy-sounding woman answered.

"Tommy there?"

"Minute." He waited.

"Yeah?"

"Tommy?"

"Ya got 'em."

"I need the address where you met your dad last night. He wants me to make a small delivery."

The hesitation was obvious. "Ask him for it."

Although the boy wouldn't know what might be going down—Scully had always kept his sons out of these dealings—Thompson had guessed that Tommy would resist.

"Yesterday, I did," the agent said, with a chuckle. "Well, you know. He said he couldn't remember. Laughed about the joys of finding his own home. He'll find it again, he said, when he looks for it, but he couldn't give me an address."

The young man also chuckled. "That's dad. Try him at home."

"I did. Your mom is pissed. She said he left early and didn't say where. Maybe he's waiting for me."

Tommy offered up the address. It might be long shot, visiting that place, but Scully had flinched when he mentioned it—and Thompson had no other leads. He pocketed the phone, turned back and found the captain striding toward him. Men in snappy uniforms always seemed to be marching when they moved.

"Hey," the officer called, and waved, so Thompson waited. "Look, we got brass in that big white trailer." He head-motioned down the block. "They'd like you to review how we're organized. Mayor's big on cooperation." The captain almost sneered. "Says he'll get the FBI across in a positive light."

Thompson read the signals. "Only if you're cool with it. Little I can add to what we've discussed. Otherwise, I have a conflict. You can give my regrets."

The officer held in what he'd been about to say and gazed at Thompson for a long moment. He smiled and nodded. "Come on along."

"If we can keep it brief."

CHAPTER 45
7:11 A.M., Friday

"DID you bring a black cover as I asked?" Crouched behind a damaged gray van, peering through tinted windows, Gary saw that the nasty voice belonged to Abdel Siddiq, the man who'd slugged him three days before. The Arab, Scully, and the other couple were standing together in the back. Dim lights had come on above them, in an office at the rear, and on a ramp across from him leading down. The brightest glow seemed to filter up from a lower level, out of his view.

"Yeah, and we'll just put it on the bus for you," said the larger man, in an accent that sounded like Scully's. Siddiq, fiercely holding on to both bags, nodded. The large man and the young woman moved down the ramp, out of sight.

Siddiq and Scully entered the office but left the door ajar. Lowered, partly closed blinds covered the windows on the room's wall and door. Several of the slats had been broken. One of the men turned on a lamp; light angled downward through the blinds, flared through the cracks, and made patches on the floor.

Hoping to learn something, Gary slipped from behind the van, flattening against the back wall, moving closer to the door. He heard Scully describe how he'd gotten a bus, but when the Irishman began to address what he'd done to it, Siddiq barked, "Be quiet!"

Gary glanced down the ramp but couldn't see anything. He held his position, had to swallow to keep from coughing. A bus. It must be on the lit-up level below. But it wouldn't be safe to sneak down now. Deep in thought, he forgot where he stood.

The young woman's laughter tinkled on the ramp. Startled, Gary raced back to the van, squeezing behind it just in time. He knelt beside a wheel, heart thumping as footfalls paused yards from his position. The girl whispered something, and then the couple must have gone into the office—rattling blinds and a slam announced the door had been closed.

Almost at once, what sounded like angry conversation started inside, though Gary couldn't make out the words. He peeked around the front of the van. The office windowsills were four feet above the floor. With lights on inside, he knew it would be difficult for them to see into the darker garage—if they were paying attention.

Crouching on tiptoes, he retraced his steps and carefully peered through the lowest bent slat. The angle offered a chest-to-head view. As he watched, Siddiq opened one of the bags and laid something onto the desk. Gary couldn't see it—but whatever it was, it riveted the others' attention.

The garage had been locked up and dark before the five of them entered, so he doubted that anyone would be in the space below. The people in the office were focused on the desk. He'd have enough time. On all fours, he slunk beneath the windows, past the office, and down the ramp, trying to keep beneath the top of the concrete wall, though the slope forced him to straighten a bit.

When he reached the bottom, he rose up behind a round column at the foot of the incline. He peeked around it. A luxury touring bus, as shiny as if it had just been waxed, rested close to a side wall of the bunker-like lower level. He crouched again, listened closely, peered in all directions, and then raced across the floor, lunging between the bus and the wall.

When no one took notice, he circled the vehicle. It had a Maryland license—he memorized it—but otherwise nothing seemed out of the ordinary. The sign above the front windows read *CHARTER*. He unfastened and peered into one of the baggage bays. It was empty.

He closed it as carefully as he could but it still clanged softly; he thought he saw motion in the bus and flattened against its side. After silent moments he breathed again. Tiptoeing up into the bus, he found no one there, and nothing inside seemed out of the ordinary.

Was the vehicle meant to carry terrorists? Did Siddiq's bags contain powerful explosives? He was considering that when through the open door he heard voices, footfalls descending the ramp. He started for the door—but if he stepped out, they'd see him. The bus offered the only place to hide.

Heart pounding, he glanced around, found a black blanket had been tossed across the second-row seats on the passenger side. It would have to do.

The voices had reached the bottom of the ramp. Through a window, he saw the four of them turn toward the bus. Siddiq was still carrying both bags. They'd be on him in seconds—he had no time.

He dropped to the floor between the rows of seats, pulling at the blanket, then bit back a cry when his shin pounded against what turned out to be a metal toolbox lying on the deck. He shifted to press his back against the outside wall and sat on the box, shoulders squeezed between the seats, knees bent. He tucked the blanket over and around him and leaned forward, trying to minimize his bulk, listening as they approached.

CHAPTER 46
7:21 A.M., Friday

"Why are there only two metal plates?" The angry words were coming through the open bus door, and Gary recognized Siddiq's voice, recalled the face on the street, on Thompson's computer, in the cemetery.

"Did the best we could," said Scully. "The plates are hard to come by, and heavy."

One by one, Gary heard them lift, and latch, all three baggage-bay doors. He tried to relax his muscles. A cramp might be the end of him.

"You have the ball bearings?" the killer asked.

"We do, we do," Scully said. "Over there."

Gary imagined Siddiq checking. "We'll put it all in those two. Dwyer, use these in the middle bay. Peel off—you know how. Attach the blocks to the metal plate and press ball bearings into it. I'll do the rear one." Gary felt movement below the floor. The bus rocked.

"I can help," Scully said.

"Soon." Siddiq's voice was muffled. "Wait there."

Gary heard them clambering about beneath him. His nose leaked, and he sniffed as softly as he could.

"What's this stuff?" the woman asked.

Siddiq replied from inside the bay, "That will be Scully's job."

The wait seemed forever. Gary raised each foot in turn, wriggling ankles and toes, and bent his lower back forward. Below him, he heard thumping. It sounded like marbles had dropped, and one of them cursed. More thumping. Time passed and again the bus rocked; the men must be emerging.

Siddiq spoke from outside. "You—climb in and press these blue pills into the explosive so they stick. Half in each bay, and spread

235

them around."

"Can I help?" asked the woman.

"Lynn, why not wait in the bus?" said the man Siddiq had called 'Dwyer.'

"Maybe later." She didn't sound pleased.

"What are these things?" Scully asked.

"We'll be in there with you soon," Dwyer said, probably to the woman. "I gotta put on the driver's outfit."

"Super Warfarin," Siddiq answered.

"And what might that be?" asked Scully.

"No more questions. Do it."

"Course. Of course." Scully sounded frightened. Again, Gary imagined the Arab's face. He heard movement below, then slapping noises.

"In another form," Siddiq said softly, "the pills are a blood thinner known as Coumadin. The blast may force the compound into wounds. It's been done...before. There will be no first aid to counter the effects—at least, not in time."

Scully switched bays and thumped some more. Finally, Gary heard him step back outside.

The banging had come from under the floor Becca was standing on. She had no idea what the noise meant, but it finally stopped. The faint voices filtered in from outside the bus. The lavatory door hinged to the rear. Very quietly, she cracked it open and peered out. She was alone in the vehicle. She held the door so it couldn't swing on its own and leaned across the aisle to peek through a window. To minimize her silhouette, she crouched.

She saw the Irishman she'd followed, and the man with the belt. Two strangers were standing with them beside the bus—a large man with short dark hair, and a woman with long, dark hair. The woman was facing away, toward the large man. He and Siddiq had their eyes on Scully. The Irishman wiped his hands on his coat and looked uncomfortable.

"Don't mean to raise this, Dwyer," he said, the words carrying to Becca through the open door, "but if you've got the fee, it would be good. I've done what you asked, now I'd like to go help my sons. I'll

236

give you the bus keys and let you out. Then I'll close it down, head to the shop, and forget this ever happened. Tommy can stop by later for the tools."

Siddiq bent to look into the middle luggage bay, and stepped past Scully as if he needed to check the one in back. Scully ignored him, waiting for an answer from Dwyer. Becca saw Siddiq slip off his scarf.

"Sure," Dwyer said. He turned back to the woman. "Lynn, go wait for me inside. Go on, *now*."

Lynn glanced around, and Becca saw she was quite pretty. "If I must," she said, without enthusiasm.

Dwyer nodded and motioned toward the bus door.

The woman turned away from the men and started forward.

Becca knew she had to hide, and quickly—but she hesitated, caught by the scene. When Siddiq swung the scarf over Scully's neck, it came as a total surprise to her and to the old man. The killer's hands yanked the ends, drawing the fabric into a noose. Scully's mouth sagged; hands flew up, picking at the scarf; legs stomping about as if throwing his bulk would break the chokehold.

Shaken, Becca fled back into the bathroom. As she quietly flipped the lock, she heard the woman climbing the steps. Even through the closed door, gurgling, strangling noises reached her. She gripped the sink.

The sounds stopped.

Gary heard Lynn climbing the steps. Without saying a word, she sat heavily onto the row of seats directly in front. He closed his eyes, aware of his unreasonable prayer: that the murder taking place out her window would prove diverting.

"Put him into a bay," Siddiq said.

"Keys and the garage door control first." That from Dwyer.

"Ah—"

"Got 'em. Help me." Another thump.

"He'll add to the blast," Siddiq said. "The girl, too."

Gary didn't hear a question mark. She had to have heard. She didn't move or make a sound.

"You'd need to take me first," said Dwyer. "Wouldn't be a wise choice. And she's an expert—got an automatic, she'd kill you quicker than me. You won't surprise her now."

"You are sure about her?" Siddiq asked.

"I'd bet my life on it."

"You have."

"Wouldn't be the first time."

In the silence, Gary imaged them glaring.

"Let me check both bays," he heard Siddiq say, "and attach blasting caps."

Siddiq hadn't agreed to let Lynn live; he'd sidestepped. With the girl sitting so close, Gary breathed silently through his mouth—his nose was stuffed—and considered his position.

Someone else climbed into the bus, and he held his breath.

"Let's go in back," Dwyer said to Lynn. As she got up, the pressure lessened on Gary's right shoulder. Paper crinkled from across the bus.

"He'd kill me," she said with surprise as she moved. "Why?"

They moved back in the aisle. Outside, Siddiq slammed a bay door.

"He'd kill his own mother."

Gary heard one of them drop into a seat further back in the bus. One sitting, one standing, both armed, and the killer outside. He listened while he flexed his fingers and moved his feet. At least, he thought, Becca isn't here.

CHAPTER 47
8:14 A.M., Friday

Dwyer stood in the aisle with Lynn in the seat beside him. He faced forward, watching in case Siddiq made a move.

"Did y'have to kill the old man?" she asked, and he heard the alarm in her tone. "He was harmless."

"Wasn't because he looked at you," Dwyer said, as he pulled his arms into the bus driver's jacket.

Her left hand reached up and touched his chest. "Last time," she whispered, gazing at him.

He felt the fingers and glanced down. "Things work out; last time."

"You promise? I'm pleadin' here."

The tears streaking her cheeks surprised him. He knelt in the aisle and took her hand. "I promise. Told you that last night. Listen. I moved us back here so we could talk. Siddiq needs me to drive. When his own driver boards, he won't need us anymore. I want you to sit halfway along the bus, low in an aisle seat, with the pistol in your hand—"

"But Sean—"

"I got another gun. Want you low so people don't see, so no one outside can target you, but I want you watching, and ready."

Lynn nodded.

"Siddiq'll come on board and crawl under that blanket up front. I'll drive till we're heading north on the Avenue of the Americas and pull into the bus stop, southeast corner at Forty-eighth Street." He heard the Arab close the final bay door. "His guy'll get on, he'll get off, and once I know the boy can drive the bus, we'll get off. Let's be watchful. We don't want surprises."

"You are there?" Siddiq called, from just outside the stairwell.

Dwyer rose and spoke to her in a whisper. "Middle of the bus, stay low, gun out, be ready."

He moved forward in the aisle.

Gary heard Dwyer's whisper, and a moment later Siddiq climbed into the bus.

"What's that?" he heard Dwyer ask, from almost directly above him. Had they seen the mound he had to be making under the blanket? Any moment now, two men with guns would yank off the cover and find him curled so tightly he could barely move.

He dug fingers into his thighs and held his breath.

"A garage door opener," Siddiq said. "When this white button is pressed, it will detonate both blasting caps."

Gary imagined the Arab holding the small box up for inspection.

"I will place it on this tray so the driver can reach it," the killer said.

"Is he ready?" Dwyer asked.

"I will call now. Then we can move."

Moments later, Siddiq said, "This space blocks the phone."

"I'll drive us up the ramp. If you can't call from behind the door, we'll open it. Gotta leave through it, anyway."

"Fine."

The seat in front pressed back against Gary when the Arab dropped into it.

The bus rumbled to life. Dwyer had to back it up to turn in the tight space. When it headed up the ramp, the angle pressed Gary against the second row of seats. The vehicle turned right and stopped, idling. He heard the bus doors hiss open, and Siddiq move down the steps to make his call.

Gary visualized the setting: steel doors, vehicles lined up to their left. What would happen when the killer returned to claim the flimsy cover he was hiding under? He took a deep breath, but before he could move, Siddiq climbed the steps.

"We are ready."

"No one's gonna see you through these windows," Dwyer said, "but if you still feel you need to hide, now's the time to get under the cover."

With a whoosh, the bus doors closed.

CHAPTER 48
9:42 A.M., Friday

SIDDIQ's footfalls stopped directly in front of Gary. Heavy breathing sounded close. Fingers touched the blanket.

Gary tensed—and heard a loud metallic rapping. From outside, someone had begun hammering on the metal gate in front of the bus. The fingers left the blanket as the pounding continued, metal on metal.

"What in hell's that?" asked Dwyer.

"We have company." Siddiq sounded as if he'd moved forward. "Open up. I will wait outside the bus. You raise the garage door and find out who it is. If you can handle it, proceed on without me. You know where to go. If necessary, I will shoot so you can drive."

"Make shooting a last resort," Dwyer said. "Too many people around, and a police precinct's a few blocks away. They'll close down the streets and we won't reach your driver."

The pounding stopped.

"Then *you* will drive and push the button. The mission must not fail." Siddiq might have seen something on Dwyer's face, because he added, "Traffic moves slowly. I will follow on foot. If Allah wills it, *I* will come back on board."

The hammering on the door resumed. Noise from the idling engine had taken away the killers' chance to wait it out.

The bus door opened with a whoosh, and Siddiq thumped down the steps. The air smelled of exhaust. Seconds later, Gary heard clanking and buzzing as the garage gate rose. The bus moved forward, slowly, then stopped. Sunlight poured in. The vehicle must be partly out onto the sidewalk. He heard the driver's window slide open.

"Whatever the FBI wants, I'll do—please, put the gun away." Dwyer said it without a trace of Irish accent.

"Who are you?" came Thompson's gruff voice from outside.

"Craig Vinaterri," Dwyer said. "Want to see my CDL?"

"Yeah."

There was a long pause. "Why a Jersey commercial driver's license with a Maryland bus?" Thompson asked.

"I live in East Rutherford and know the area." Dwyer sounded like millions of others from New Jersey. "Academy brings in tours from all over. Guys like me do the New York experience."

"What's in there?"

"An empty garage, perfect for making repairs."

"What broke?"

Dwyer laughed. "Something about a shock. I haven't a clue. Call Academy."

"I will. Where are you going?"

"To pick up forty-six happy vacationers from Pikesville, just northwest of Baltimore, and take them to the Vanderbilt Mansion first, then lunch, and on to the Roosevelt Homestead. It's cold, but clear—they'll love the Hudson views."

"Pickup from where?"

"Christ, officer. The Milford Plaza. Two-seventy West Forty-fifth Street, just east of Eighth, okay? Those people and their luggage should be waiting for me in the lobby about now. Not good if I'm late. Bad for tips."

It sounded to Gary like Thompson was alone. That made it difficult. He wiped his nose with his sleeve.

"How do you get to those mansions?" the agent asked.

"Think I'll get lost? Jeez. Take the Deegan straight up to the Thruway, then off at Exit 17 to I-84 east to Route 9 north. The targets are all of two miles apart. The restaurant's further, in Hyde Park. We don't want to be late there, it gets crowded. Rangers give the tours at both places, and Fala's ex-home closes at five. You wanna come along?"

"Fala?"

"Jeez—FDR's famous dog," Dwyer said. "Didn't they teach you about the speech in school? It's part of our history."

Gary waited through another pause while the engine continued to rumble.

"What's in the luggage bays?" Thompson asked.

"Empty space waiting for their bags. At least at the hotel they'll help me load up. It's a bear, doing it alone."

"Show me."

"You want a look, here I come."

Dwyer descended the steps. Gary had started to rise when he realized that the woman was sitting there, gun in hand. If she yelled or fired…. He forced his muscles to relax, and listened. He heard a bay door bang open, the forward one, closest to him.

"Satisfied?" Dwyer asked from outside. "I'll do all three if you want. You'll find the same. Then I'll pull the bus forward and you can try the other side. Come on back and take a look."

Gary tensed. Dwyer sounded convincing, but if Thompson said yes, they'd have to kill him. Dwyer must have asked him to move back into the garage so the shooting wouldn't happen on the street. He imagined Siddiq would use a silencer. It came to him that disrupting the bombing counted more than Thompson's life, more than anyone's life.

"Are there storage compartments inside?" the agent asked.

"Sure—small ones. Over the seats. Doors close like on airplanes. This bus has it all."

"Let's take a look."

Gary heard the bay compartment close. "Follow me," Dwyer said.

Footsteps came up the steps.

"Who's she?" Thompson asked, from above Gary.

"Our tour director. She's studying her notes—you can't tell the mansions apart without a scorecard, and there are dozens of points of interest on the way up." Dwyer's voice got louder. "Wave to the man, Lorraine."

Gary heard three ceiling compartment doors open and close.

"Wanna check the bathroom?" Dwyer asked. "It's at the back of the bus. I cleaned it out last night so it smells fresh. The long-haul drivers hate doing it, and I get more work from the line if they like me. Tourists tip better if the bathroom's clean." He laughed. "It's something all the old people talk about, and they appreciate it, even if they wait for the rest stops."

"Sorry I bothered you," Thompson said. "Go pick up your tourists." His footfalls moved forward.

"What's the reason for all this—I mean, what are you questioning me about?" Dwyer asked.

Thompson started down the steps. "Just a routine check around the neighborhood."

How like him, Gary thought.

"Do me a favor?" Dwyer asked.

From outside, Thompson said, "What?"

"Once the bus is clear, toggle the switch marked 'door,' just inside on the garage wall to the right. I promised I'd close up the place behind me—they left tools on the lower level. Guess I can trust the FBI not to take anything. Company'd probably blame me. You drop the door, I won't have to block the street."

Gary didn't hear an answer. He imagined Siddiq had slipped out onto the sidewalk. As Dwyer drove past, he'd smile at the killer. Siddiq would stride off and get lost in the crowd, keeping the bus in sight. Gary would have only Dwyer and the woman to deal with. Would she shoot? If he attacked her man, she certainly would.

The bus moved forward.

"Are you and the boy ready?" Siddiq whispered into the small phone. There were people close by, but the noise level was high and only his assistant would hear him. Everyone was rushing, and Siddiq moved along with them, blending in.

He'd watched the bus creep around a corner in heavy traffic, and then he'd headed the other way, down Broadway, toward where he'd parked his car days before. He'd drive into Jersey through the Holland Tunnel, before they'd have time to close it.

"We're waiting where you told me he's to get on," Carlos Arrington said.

Siddiq had briefed the agent earlier, but he hadn't known the girl would be aboard—and armed. The driver had been instructed to trigger the bomb immediately; on that corner, the blast would be devastating, and it would kill the boy, Dwyer, and Arrington. But protecting the girl would make Dwyer wary—he might prevent the blast until they were both away.

"There's a change in plans," Siddiq said.

"What's that?"

He pictured the curly haired man standing on the bustling corner, down the street from Radio City Music Hall. "A woman is on the bus with Dwyer. Both have guns. Don't let them get off."

"Her, too?"

"Kill them both. On the bus is best." Siddiq listened closely, waited the pause before Arrington replied.

"Will there be time for me—"

"People will be milling about. You know how to slip away. Is this clear?"

"Yes," from Arrington.

Hearing it, Siddiq ended the call and pocketed the phone. A block later, after changing pace, with different people around him, he allowed himself to smile.

CHAPTER 49
10:18 A.M., Friday

GARY chafed as the bus jerked to a halt; another traffic light must have stopped them. Being blinded was the worst. Beneath the cover, he listened closely for the engine revving, but again unexpected motion rocked him back on the toolbox. Dwyer had made several turns and stops since they left the garage, and Gary hadn't heard a word from him or the girl.

Thompson had taken his best shot; there'd be no cavalry to the rescue. Gary's heart had slowed, though, and an odd calm suffused him. He'd identified the toolbox and surprise as his only weapons.

He'd have a better chance after Dwyer and the girl left, when he and the bomber were alone. But his back was tightening, his legs close to cramping. Once again he flexed his feet and bent his back.

The bus stopped. Doors open. Someone bounded up the steps.

"Can you drive this, son?" asked Dwyer, back in accent.

"Where's the trigger?" a young man asked.

Dwyer chuckled. "Here's the box. Battery's in the tray. Don't touch it—don't try to clip it on till Lynn and I leave, or you won't complete your mission. You understand?" The boy said nothing. Gary imagined Dwyer holding the pistol. "Show me you can drive it," Dwyer added.

Gary heard shuffling; they must be changing positions.

"Just a few feet now. Show me."

The bus jerked forward, and for a moment kept rolling despite Dwyer's orders to stop.

"Now you're blocking the street. Wait here the moment. Leave the doors. I'll get the woman, we're off, and you do what you must."

"Can I get up now?" Lynn asked from back in the bus.

"Stay put. I'll check around and come get you." Dwyer's footfalls moved past in the aisle.

Now—Gary slid off the cover and blinked, rising, ignoring his stiffness.

"On to our beach," Dwyer said, from several rows back, moving away, blocking the girl's view.

Gary turned and saw that the boy—he couldn't be more than seventeen—had grasped both pieces and was pulling the battery connectors free so he could use them. Gary lifted the tool case as quietly as he could and was sliding out into the aisle when his cell phone rang.

The sound died as if it had killed the battery, but it had trilled like a fire alarm and he stood exposed in the aisle, both hands on the box. The boy looked up at him.

"Christ," yelled Dwyer, spinning back and raising his automatic.

A door banged open at the back of the bus. "No!" screamed the figure that lurched from the bathroom. "*No!*" Gary saw her throw something white at Dwyer and charge down the aisle, pointing a black object.

Dwyer spun to meet the new threat as Becca came at him, phone in hand.

Gary coiled to heave the metal box at the big man, rush forward and save her, but—he winced at the hand he'd been dealt and bit his lip, turning to where the suicide bomber was working frantically to snap leads onto the nine-volt battery. Horns blared behind them, innocent people, cars with gasoline tanks.

Enraged, Gary swung the heavy metal box in a furious arc. The boy hesitated just long enough. The box caught him square in the face, crushed it, slammed him back against the window. His head hit safety glass with a sickening thud.

The battery and remote had dropped onto the tray and Gary released the toolbox to grasp them, flipping a few of the tiny controller switches as he whirled and saw Becca leaping between rows of seats.

Dwyer's weapon went off so loudly Gary thought the bomb had exploded. Blood sprayed before she dropped out of view. *Blam!* The second bullet ripped through seat tops. Her legs hung into the aisle, motionless.

Dwyer spun back, gun hand revolving toward Gary, when a round came in through a window, showering glass, tearing away the top of Dwyer's head, pushing the big man sideways. He died before he could look surprised, leaning against a seatback for a long moment before sagging.

"No, God *no, nooo!*" Lynn wailed.

Feet pounded up the steps. "What the fuck!" barked a stranger.

Gary tossed the battery back into the bus as he whirled to face Arrington—an angry man with curly hair and bushy brows, wearing a dark green jacket and holding a pistol.

The man scowled when he saw the injured driver. "Son of a bitch!" He raised the weapon.

Gary stared into the muzzle.

A shot blasted and a woman screamed, "*Damn you!*"

He saw the stain spreading on the green coat; the gun wavered and, *Blam!* a second slug spun the man around and through the open doorway.

Gary started toward Becca.

"Sean, oh Sean, oh God," Lynn Turner sobbed. Her small fists beat at his body as if she'd bring him back. The gun she'd used lay in the aisle.

"Police!" shouted a rough voice. "Drop the weapons! Everyone down!"

Gary ignored it, squeezed past, and ran to his wife.

EPILOGUE
8:03 P.M., Friday

"WHAT'S wrong?" Becca whispered. Her voice woke Gary. He'd pulled a chair up beside her hospital bed hours before and finally dozed off. He blinked, saw that her head still lay on the pillow but her eyes were on him. The doctor had shaved her hair, treated the injuries, wrapped her head in a bandage. Gary had been told that the dressing looked more serious than the wound.

He leaned toward her. "How are you?" It came out as a croak, and he had to clear his throat.

"What's that?" she asked. She raised her left hand slowly to point at the blue surgical mask tied over his face.

"I caught Vincent's cold."

She frowned and tried to turn her head, slowly, first to the left, toward the ceiling, and then back against the pillow. When she succeeded, the worry left her face, and she pushed up on her right elbow, facing him. "Just a stiff neck," she said, noting his concern. She rubbed at it with her left hand as she rotated her head, then said, "I'm alive."

He couldn't answer, wiped his eyes with a sleeve.

She reached out and touched him. "They let you in the hospital with a cold?"

He regained composure, blinking before he could focus on her. "Special circumstances—but once a nurse, always a nurse, that it? Want the sicko to leave?"

She answered with her eyes.

"You must've been exhausted," he said. "You've been out for hours."

"I can't believe I spent last night locked on a bus in the dark." He waited while she sighed. "I was afraid to sleep. They might've come

251

back anytime."

She pointed to a cup on the stand. He handed over the water and helped her sip. "When they finally did show up," she went on, "I hid in the bathroom and locked the door. I didn't know you were there."

"They wouldn't let me stay while they treated your wound," he said. "But Vinnie got to you—he told me you left Thompson's car to follow Scully."

She hung her head.

"You are the bravest woman I have ever met."

She smiled at the sheet. "When I'm not being stupid." She glanced up. "But you know—"

"I'd have done it, too."

When they stopped laughing, they gazed at one another, and he wanted so badly to hug her.

"Before I conked out," she said, "Vincent told me about *your* night and morning. You got less sleep than I did."

He reached out to knead her shoulder. She glanced at his hand; he knew why, and smiled. "I washed my hands with the antibacterial goo—don't want you to catch the cold. You'll be home tomorrow. Angela says hi. She promised to cook for us for a month."

Out of the blue, eyes on him, she whispered, "I saw you turn away. You *let* that man shoot me."

He had to clear his throat. "Call it partnership dues. When you dove away from the gun, you whacked your head against the side of the bus. Doctor told me that once he saw what little the slug had done, he worried more about the bump."

She stared at his chest. He recalled when she'd done that before. "Not what I meant," she said. There was a silence. She lifted his hand from her shoulder and took it in hers, though her eyes stayed down. "You made a decision on that bus, didn't you?"

He couldn't speak, waited till she looked up, and forced a nod. "Melanie told me not to worry, hard heads run in the family."

Becca made a face and studied him for a moment before she gave it up and brightened. "Is she here?"

"Of course. How could I not tell her? She's grabbing a bite with Vinnie, though I warned her about the cold. They'll be back any minute. I don't think she's happy about your becoming my sleuthing partner. *You* told her about it, so *you* deal with it."

"That's not her decision, but I guess she has a right. Thanks for the warning." She reached up and touched the bandage. "I must look beautiful."

"She saw you while you were asleep. And if you knew how beautiful you look to me—" He had to bite his cheek.

"How many people did you save?" she asked, eyes brimming.

"I don't know, but we both did it. If you hadn't been there, he'd have—"

She touched his arm. "I forgive you. Tell me I look beautiful tomorrow, after you bring me home and I get settled."

"But I have a cold."

"I'll take my chances. Meantime, is there anything I *don't* know about?"

He grinned. "Well, Thompson and Vincent gave me slightly different stories."

"I'm all ears."

"You and I, we're the only ones to come out of it clean."

"That poor girl. She wanted him to walk away from it. She pleaded with him."

"She also shot two men, and she knew about the bombing."

"Hey, Becca, you're awake," Vincent called from the doorway.

She spotted him. "Another blue mask."

"We didn't have them when we got here. They heard us hacking—took some clout to get us in." He stopped beside Gary, gripped a shoulder in greeting, and spoke to Becca. "Melanie's in the bathroom. She'd have waited if she'd known you were up. I got her to eat, a little, anyway—she's worried about you. How you doing?"

"I'm fine. But maybe it's not over. What about the man with the belt, the worst of the lot? No one's mentioned him. Did he slip away?"

Gary reached into a pocket. "Just between us, partner," he said to her, "here's Vincent's addition." He handed her his driver's license.

"How'd you get it back?"

"The man tried to visit his family," Vincent said. "Gave them no warning, but the feds had it covered. They won't say whether they got him alive, and, *big* surprise, Thompson didn't even mention it to Gary."

Becca turned to him. He claimed a hand. "Our guess—the CIA is torturing the bastard in Syria."

"Normally, I'd mind," Becca said.

"Tony, his wife, and the three of us know, and that's it," Vincent added. "They want to keep it under wraps."

"...Vincent?"

He shrugged. "Okay. Angela knows, too."

Gary slipped the license back into his wallet.

"How's Tony taking it—I mean, knowing his brother is...?" she asked.

"You can guess," Vincent said. "We're staying close, his wife is great—he'll be okay."

Gary stroked Becca's hand to get her attention. "You know about the CIA agent?"

"Vincent explained. So many deaths."

"Hey," Vincent said, raising a hand, "your good buddy Thompson told me you'll both be receiving some sort of commendation from the FBI. But they don't want it public—might cause panic." He snorted. "I think you saved his ass. He got *to* the bus, but the both of you were *on* it."

"Small payback for saving Becca," Gary said.

At that, she turned to him. "I feel different, now. You'd be okay without me—in case—wouldn't you?"

He may have squeezed her hand too hard. She didn't seem to mind.

THE END

ALSO BY E. J. RAND

SAY GOODBYE, the first novel in the Reluctant Sleuth series starts out:

~PROLOGUE~
TUESDAY, FEBRUARY 17
7:35 A.M.

IF NORMAN LYONS had known he was going to die that morning, he would have worn different clothes. After tossing all night, he rose early and switched off the alarm before it sounded. Anxiety numbed him while he dressed for work in the bedroom closet, with the door closed so he wouldn't wake Hannah. He doubted his socks matched.

It took clearing off the walk and digging out his car, working up a sweat in the falling snow, to calm down. Then, there he was, snuggled in the warmth of his little Toyota, heart racing and fear pounding at his head.

The forecast called for seven inches. Snow blew right back onto the plowed highway, and the surface was treacherous. Fat flakes slapped his windshield, limiting visibility even with headlights. His glasses remained wet. He drove carefully in the right lane while he fretted about his discovery.

The car rocked as his driver-side wheels thump-thumped into a pothole hidden beneath the snow. He tensed, but the tires held, and he thanked Hannah for pressuring him to buy new ones. The jolts shocked him out of his distress. He needed to calm down. More auditors get fired than murdered, and no one would shoot him in the office. If he had to, he could find another job.

Novel two in the series is PERFECT COVER:

PROLOGUE

WHY was Janelle screaming?

Despite the shrieks, Rosa curled up and would have slipped away, but she felt her head being lifted and something soft pushed beneath it.

"Wake up!" She'd heard the deep voice before but couldn't place it. Her head throbbed. She squeezed her closed eyes, concentrating. She and Angie were at Ridgetop Hospital, cleaning Five Medford, everyone asleep but them and the nurses. Why was she lying on something hard and cold? She was freezing. She heard Janelle whimpering. What was going on?

Gray and black squares rippled like waves when she blinked. She smelled disinfectant. The dented metal cabinet below the slop sink split into two, then merged. Had she been drinking? No, with effort she remembered—she'd come in to get rags. What was she doing on the floor? Her left arm was pinned; she shifted to free it and groaned from waves of pain in her head.

"Doctor's on the way, you'll be fine." Rosa recognized Nurse Safrian's voice. "Lie still—talk to me."

Why would she say that?

Rosa turned her head and flinched. Lieutenant Reed was in her face, staring. She felt fingers squeezing her right wrist. The nurse was taking her pulse. The security man bent closer. She wanted him gone, the nurse gone, wanted to be back cleaning without anyone's attention.

"*Madre de dios!*" Janelle wailed, "*Aiee!*"

Startled, Rosa glanced up. Her head spun, eyes closed, and then she saw Janelle staring, mouth open, eyes wide.

Heart pounding in her throat, Rosa fought dizziness and glanced down. When she saw the blood, she began to scream.

Coming soon from Deadly Ink

DARK SEA
— E. J. Rand

PROLOGUE

Wani Hartono recalled a scene from a movie—the killer feeding his victim, piece by piece, into a wood chipper. The crew had watched it months before, in the passenger lounge, between cruises.

He was concentrating, leaning over the sorting table and pressing the edge of the plastic sheet tight against the side of the eighteen-inch waste disposal intake. Then he lifted the final piece off the plastic. It was a man's arm, severed at the elbow, and he checked to be sure no rings remained on the hand.

Metal might jam the machine. Large bones could also pose a problem, but he'd operated the system for eight months and knew what it could do. He braced as the ship heeled to starboard—the sea was up—before sliding the arm into the loading chamber, elbow down, fingers reaching as if to escape.

For the next fifteen minutes the galley would be deserted. He and Irwan handled garbage detail, working different shifts on the 300-passenger vessel. If things ran smoothly, no one checked what they processed.

He locked the safety lid and switched on the machine. Seawater flooded in and he could hear the dull rumble as it began to chew the waste.

Curling the plastic so it would trap remaining blood, he stepped back to undress. He lay onto the sheet the white coat, trousers, and latex gloves he'd been wearing. On top of that, he set the five-pound dumbbell he'd taken from the fitness room—had to hold it steady through another roll of the ship—then he folded the bundle, fastening it with fishing line. After four years at sea, he knew knots. If the blood attracted deep-water predators, they'd mangle everything.

The sound of the machine changed and he tripped the lever that flushed it with fresh water. The waste had been expelled below the surface of the Caribbean.

He redressed. With the bundle under an arm, he locked up. He'd gone to sea for better pay. After tonight, he could go home.

Minutes later, on a lower deck throbbing from the propeller, he tossed the bundle over the stern. Its splash vanished in churning wake.

Annette Faurote

Tessy

Harry

Printed in the United States
218732BV00003B/1/P